# *If I Die Before I Sleep*

# *If I Die Before I Sleep*

*ERICK BLORE*

If I Die Before I Sleep
Erick Blore

© 2023 by Erick Blore

ISBN 978-0-9834906-0-9

Published by Eclectry Books
Updated 5/4/24

Cover photo edited from photo by cottonbro studio: https://www.pexels.com/photo/photo-of-a-woman-sitting-beside-statue-3778550/

*"To sleep, perchance to dream."*
*~William Shakespeare*

For more books by Erick Blore

# ❋ CONTENTS ❋

# ❄ Chapter 1 ❄

## NOVEMBER 2010:
## GOOD NEWS, BAD NEWS

Sara bounced her leg on a red plastic chair near a green plastic plant in the florescent lit corner of a white room. Next to her a young man slouched, stroking Sara's tangled strawberry blonde hair. From the seventh floor was a spectacular view of the George Washington Bridge spanning the Hudson River, but Sara's eyes were filled with visions of the future.

She had turned eighteen at the beginning of September. Her birthday was the first time she and Kyle had slept together. During the past week Sara learned that she was two months pregnant when she came with her parents to the medical center to talk her primary physician Dr. Anderson about her ongoing struggle to sleep. She had informed the doctor that she had not menstruated, and he had a nurse test her to confirm the 'good news'.

And Sara needed good news. Her frame had grown thin, her hair had lost its luster, and her bright hazel eyes were puffy and dim. Although the room was warm, goose bumps speckled her forearms. After a shiver, she pulled down the rolled up sleeves of her pink cardigan.

"Is this going to take all day?" said the slouching young man as he checked the time on his cell phone. "I was supposed to meet up with the band. We were —"

"Hello Sara." Doctor Anderson entered the room. After his first sip of coffee, he added with a jovial smile, "Long time no see. Sorry to keep you waiting."

"Yeah, I've been spending a lot of time here lately it seems. Didn't think I'd be back 'til the delivery."

"And who is this gentleman with you today?"

"This is my friend, Kyle—he's the father, and yeah, I guess a 'gentleman'. My folks are on vacation so they couldn't be here. Back on Tuesday, I think."

Dr. Anderson extended his hand. "Nice to meet you, Kyle."

Kyle's handshake was limp. He hastily brushed aside his dyed bangs and fixed his posture. "Thanks. You too."

"Sara," Dr. Anderson said and turned to grab a folder, "I was hoping your parents would be here today. You said they'll be back on Tuesday? Did you tell them about your appointment today?"

"It may have slipped my mind," Sara said with a wink to Kyle, "but, it's no big deal."

"Well, and I'm happy to say that so far everything looks good. I don't handle maternity, so I'll be referring you to one of our other doctors. They'll bring you through our program."

"I still can't believe I'm going to be a mom," Sara exclaimed. "It's so cool! Oh, and don't worry, we'll get the insurance thing with my parents straightened out."

Dr. Anderson smile. "The insurance is not really an issue. The main issue is your health and the results of these tests that I came back from the specialist. The doctor informed Sara of the disease 's name. Reluctant to begin with the symptoms, he explained a bit about its history. "It's a very rare condition..."

Sara took Kyle's hand. "Well, how long will it take before I can get back to normal? This isn't going to hurt the baby, is it? It's driving me crazy. But, we caught it in time, right? I mean, I'm not going to have to give more blood, am I? (I hate that.)"

Kyle rolled his eyes. "It's only blood."

"I would say that you're in the earlier stages," Dr. Anderson continued, "and there are certainly some treatments to ease the discomfort, but a cure? Unfortunately, despite all the research, there isn't one."

Kyle found the topic of disease much more interesting than babies, so clearing his throat, he asked, "So it just goes away on its own then? I mean, you said it only lasts like seven to eighteen months. I mean, it's just a little insomnia, right? What did you call it again?"

Dr. Anderson's heart sank. "It's called 'Fatal... Familial... Insomnia.'"

Kyle smiled nervously. "So are you saying Sara's going to die from this? Is that what you're saying?"

Dr. Anderson placed the chart on a table and took a seat in front of Sara. "Sara, I'm sorry. I don't know how to tell you this, but you need to know for your own sake and for your family. This is going to require a lot of faith and determination, but you need to be strong for that little baby of yours."

Sara nodded; it was easier than asking him to continue.

"I'm afraid you only have about a year to live, and even less than that before the effects of this disease begin to manifest itself in ways that you may not want to know about, but as your doctor, I need to inform you. We will do all we can to save the baby, but yes, there is a possibility this will affect the pregnancy."

Sara's leg stopped bouncing. She leaned over in the chair and laid her ghostly head in her hands.

"This can't be happening," she said, "not now." She then followed her tears to the floor, dropping to her knees in front of the doctor––the red plastic chair falling with her. Her face remained in her hands as she wept and wailed in his lap. After a minute, a nurse ran into the room to find out what all the screaming was about and to assist the doctor.

# ❄ Chapter 2 ❄

## APRIL 1786: Vienna

It was late in the month of April 1786 when an unseasonable snow storm whipped through the air like the Great Freeze of 1709. The refitted oil lamps along the street flickered but scarcely punctured the evening's bleak doldrums. Pedestrians kept their cherry ears beneath the collars of their long black coats and tried not to slip and fall upon the steaming piles of frosted horse dung. There would be no greeting of neighbors this evening, for pleasantries were replaced with a cold determination to thaw one's bones with hearth and tea.

The piercing chill and the crunching of snow beneath Eduard Strobl's feet was unnerving as he plodded through the dark and blanketed streets of Vienna. But, it was anger that most quickened his pace. He had suspected his accounting partner of skimming from business profits, and after staying late that day to double check the rolls, he decided to confront the man the next morning. Now three streets away from home, Eduard rehearsed what he would say the next day.

"Ludwig, I've gone through the books once and again. Look at these discrepancies—all on days I was out of the office. Explain that!"

"Exactly! Now, if you would please remove your things. As your friend, I'll save you the embarrassment of calling the—"

"Yes I would—!"

"No sir, I cannot abide a thief. The lining of your pockets has put a hole in my own... The filling of your purse has emptied my own—no... the lining of your—"

A sudden gust blew, and Eduard scrambled to retrieve his hat as it rolled in the snow. After backtracking half a block, he grasped the "darn thing" and placed it snuggly upon his balding head. But just then, another interruption stalled his pace. He heard a scream and then...

"Get back here!"

A hospital orderly chased a hysterical patient running from the Fool's Tower toward the road in his undergarments. This giant of a man apparently had fled from the hospital on his way back to his room from dinner and was making a loud fuss about a chair. Before the orderly could tackle him, however, the patient dropped as though dead. The orderly kicked him, but he put up no fight.

"Get up, you imbecile!"

The patient's eyes were open, but unresponsive. Another man as tall and imposing as the tower itself came out of the building. With his long leather boots and wiry legs, he nudged the man over onto his back and slapped his scruffy cheeks. The spectacle fascinated Eduard, but he also felt compelled to defend the man, who for all his size seemed powerless to stand, never mind fight.

"Enough!" Eduard yelled through the fence bordering the road.

The man on the ground became aware and looked over at Eduard. Their eyes engaged, but the nervous patient quickly looked away and began to struggle until he was limp again.

6

The orderly dragged the man back to the cylindrical brick building while the doctor stared Eduard down. The wiry man then returned into the daunting structure that was built only two years prior. Eduard admired the architecture, but conceded to his daughters that it was a bit creepy, especially having it so near their home. This little episode did little to change his assessment of the place.

Regarding this tower, it was part of the Allgemeines Krankenhaus, the largest and most advanced medical facility in the world, first built in 1697 under Emperor Leopold I for the treatment of veterans. In 1784, under Emperor Joseph II, the Narrenturm, or 'Fool's Tower,' as it was called, was designed by the popular architect Isadore Carnevale as an auxiliary. It sat on the edge of the hospital, and was employed for the treatment of the insane. It housed about one hundred and forty men and women, chained to the walls for proper rehabilitation. Eduard passed it at least twice a day, going to and from work, but on this particular day its passage was becoming an unwelcome obstacle, stealing both his hat and his concentration and then...

"Get out of here, ya whiskered devil!"

Eduard's first step sent a hissing cat scurrying through the snow. The hospital was overrun with these disease-ridden felines—catching rats that took shelter in the warm walls, seeking morsels from charitable patients. There must have been hundreds of them walking about the facility or hiding in abandoned basement cells. Some said they were the souls of patients who had passed. The doctors had tried to rid them through traps, and rocks, but in the end, cordial cohabitation was the only option.

Without further interruption, and after three more cumbersome snow covered roads, Eduard arrived home. It was a welcoming red house about ten minutes walk from his favorite place to fish on the Danube River, and twenty from work. The two stories were narrow, but enough space for his wife and daughters. The snow pile near the threshold was smoothed flat by the opening of the door, and the warmth inside pulled him in and smothered his chilled face. Eduard's wife, Nadine, heard the familiar stomping of boots on the floor and came out of the kitchen to help with his coat.

"My dear," she said, "I believe you could use some tea."

With one last stomp and a quick kiss, Eduard said, "Spiced wine, please. The tea is keeping me up at night."

"There is a bit left." Nadine walked back to the kitchen. "I'll warm you a glass while you settle."

Hot wine sounded good. In fact, it sounded, "Perfect," Eduard called out, "and is dinner prepared?"

Nadine finished pouring the wine with the hum of a folk song. She loved to sing, loved to pretend she was an opera star, or a gypsy; from the time she got up in the morning until evening retirement she had a tune in her mind and on her lips. "Fifteen more minutes," she said as she returned into the living room. "I hope you'll not disapprove of Wienerschnitzel again."

Eduard removed his boots by the fireplace, and slumped into the warm seat nearby. He returned to contemplating his talk with Ludwig until Nadine placed the wine gently on the table beside him.

"Dear..." Nadine waited for her husband, "Dear, your wine, it's ready."

"Oh, forgive me." Eduard reached for the glass. "I was just thinking."

Nadine kissed his forehead.

Eduard sighed and turned his eyes back to the fireplace, but saw only the knotty door to his office. And there was Ludwig inside, likely doing the underhanded. "I need advice," he said while Nadine stirred the coals.

"What's wrong?"

"I suspect Ludwig's been stealing from the business."

Nadine moved in between him and the fire, kneeling down to meet his eyes. With one hand on his knee and the other brushing the hair back behind his ear she continued, "Ludwig wouldn't do such a thing. He's a mouse, and honest as the sun. Are you certain?"

"Certain as Saint Peter's confession." Eduard reached for his wine but knocked it to the ground. Normally he would have laughed it off and cleaned it himself, but instead he just looked at it... and looked.

"Allow me." Nadine walked back to the kitchen for a towel. As she returned and wiped up the spill she counseled, "Since you asked for my advice, I would double check the books. If something is wrong, let him explain. It could be a misunderstanding."

Eduard's mind flickered and fled with the logs on the fire, at once attached and then detached. His trance was then interrupted by a stampede down the stairs, followed by the appearance of wooden figures to his left and right.

"Hello sir," the marionette with a mustache said, "So good to see you today. Lovely weather, no?"

Eduard held out his hand to greet him. "Why, hello there." On the other side of his chair he was greeted again.

"Daddy," said the wooden woman in a white dress, "the teacher told me today that I'm reading better than all the other girls in class."

"Well dear, that's great to hear, but you do know that paper is made from old wooden dolls, don't you?"

"Oh daddy, that's not nice." Anna appeared in front of her father to reprimand him. "Now you've scared Little Miss Vivian, and she'll never read again."

Eduard pulled Anna, his twelve year old, closer. He motioned for her to let him hold the puppet, to which she reluctantly complied. After placing the doll upon his knees he said, "Now Miss Vivian, surely I was bluffing. Reading is very important, and they don't make books out of puppets, okay? You and your friends have not a thing to fear." He then gave the puppet a hug and returned it.

"What about me?" said the mustached puppet with an eight-year-old girl's voice.

Eduard relieved his concern also. "You as well, Mr.... whatever your name is. You've not a thing to fret about... well, unless this cold keeps up and we need firewood. You know how toasty your mother likes to keep this house. Between the oven and the hearth, I'm surprised these very chairs haven't been subjected to the flames."

His children screamed and ran back upstairs to protect their dolls.

Eduard left his thoughts with the fire and went to the kitchen to assist, but it was nearly done. As he watched Nadine navigate along the clean tiled floor through the hanging herbs, glazed pots, meats, and cheese, he sighed. The aroma of her cooking filled his nose pleasantly.

"All the children in the city love the dolls and marionettes you make." Eduard looked on as Nadine mixed spices into a bowl. "Diederich down at the store must love you for it. Surely you should receive more than forty percent of the profits from that miser."

"Diederich is fine. I'm just glad mother's craft has finally paid off. I understand now why she took to it. It can get so dreadful around the house when the children are gone. A little extra income never hurt either."

Eduard continued to stare while Nadine snapped a sprig of herb hanging from a shelf. "You're perfect."

"Dear me." Nadine swatted away the exaggeration.

"No, really. My rare snowflake of silver, my diamond descending from the heavens."

"Mr. Strobl. You do go on." Nadine continued to mix dried herbs into the clay bowl. "You know, I still recall the first time you called me that. It was our first winter together, and you said that although all snowflakes are unique, I was the most fair, that the beauty of others would melt away, but mine would shine forever."

Eduard laughed. "I was quite the sweet talker then."

Nadine stopped, looked over her shoulder and chided, "So, it was a lie?"

"Oh, it'll always be true." With his arms extended and his voice regal Eduard proclaimed, "You are my *regis* and I your *rex*, You are the jewel in my crown, my—"

"Alright your majesty, you'll spin your queen dizzy."

"My apologies, Madame." Eduard remained chivalrous.

"Well, don't be too penitent. It's been a while since I've seen you like this; I confess I miss it dearly."

"I suppose I've been a bit gloomy."

11

"It's this weather." Nadine gave Eduard a pat on the back and continued mixing. "Can you throw another log in the oven? And are the children ready to eat?"

"They just returned upstairs." Eduard came closer to kiss her neck. "Shall I retrieve them?"

"Thanks, and tell them to wash and—Eduard!"

Nadine dangled and clung to the mixing bowl as Eduard grabbed her up in his arms. He swung her back and forth so that her legs swept the air, and sang an improvised tune.

"Alright, alright! Please, your bell doesn't wish to further ring; put me down and retrieve the children. Look, I've spilled. No need for all of this if you're just in a passion."

Eduard placed her feet on the ground again. After putting another log in the brick oven, he headed up the stairwell, pausing on the first step and bouncing on his toes. The old stairs were creaky and cracked, but Eduard had worked on weekends to install the new steps upon which he now walked with pride—every noiseless step a testimony to his skill as an amateur craftsman and proud carpenter's son.

"What's that you say?" Eduard yelled back to the kitchen.

Nadine appeared around the corner with a wheel of cheese. "What's that, dear?"

"Did you just call me?"

"No, you just called me."

"I meant before that."

"Didn't say a word; just slicing some cheese."

"Curious."

At the top of the steps was a small pine planked hallway. The first room on the left was the master bedroom. Eduard walked in and blew out a candle that Nadine had left burning on her bureau then continued down the hall to the first door on his right which was Julia's room. The children were sitting on the floor playing with their dolls.

"It's time for dinner now—no Julia don't complain. If you—because your mother said so—Shhh, listen: If you'd fancy your friends to accompany then you need to help set the table."

The children ran down the stairs and into the kitchen to grab forks, knives, and two extra plates from the cupboard for their "guests".

"Daddy said it's alright," Anna politely informed her mother.

"Well, just don't dirty them. You can put make-believe food on, and that'll do... No, your father didn't say you could have desert first... Is that so? Shall I ask him when he comes down? And, Julia, for the last time, wash those hands!... The bowl is over there... Then poor it out and retrieve clean water."

The Strobls were a typical Viennese family. Eduard worked long hours while Nadine raised the children and made dolls for extra income. They ate together, prayed together, and together enjoyed the benefits and opportunities of the bustling city.

"Excuse me! Did your father sit yet?"

"Sorry, mother." Anna stood back up with the others at the table.

"*Guten appetit*," Nadine said.

Eduard took his seat, followed by the rest of the family, and said grace:

13

"Bless us, O Lord, and these thy gifts which we are about to receive from thy bounty through Christ our Lord. Amen."

"Amen."

During dinner Eduard asked his children about school and the friends they had been making since it opened. Education had not been easy to come by in Eduard's childhood, so he wanted his children to appreciate the opportunity they had been given since Vienna embraced the 'rational' life under Joseph II. The Emperor, being influenced by the works of Voltaire and the example of Frederick II of Prussia, had had many religious fraternities dissolved in order to increase funding for these new schools. He also did away with other wasteful practices, such as parades, pilgrimages, unnecessary holidays, and was even working to abolish the death penalty. All of this, along with a reformed legal system, medical advances, and an influx of high-culture made Vienna a beacon of the new 'Enlightenment'. Through all of this, the Emperor was supported by the ever-growing brotherhoods of the Freemasons and Illuminati.

"Well, your teacher is right about the Turks," Eduard instructed Anna.

"But I thought we didn't like them."

"Well, we've certainly had our fair share of problems with them. In fact, it was not very long ago that that zealous defender of the faith, Vlad III Dracula, and his mighty Dragon Fellowship had to battle them with the spear." Eduard turned to his youngest daughter Julia and pretended to jab her. "But, we owe our kaffeehäus to them." Eduard tipped his cup of coffee to Nadine. "So it's

14

important to look at people for their good qualities too, and not assume they are any worse than you and I."

"Wise advice," Nadine said, "especially if you're friends with that person and have worked together for a long time."

Eduard stopped chewing and caught Nadine's eye as well as her hint.

As midnight approached, Eduard lay in bed. In his thick, long underwear and night cap, he stared at the candle on his night stand. As was typical, Nadine was fast asleep while he was deep in thought with a Bible on his chest.

"Naked came I out of my mother's womb," Eduard read to himself, "and naked shall I return thither: the Lord gave and the Lord hath taken away; blessed be the name of the Lord." Part of him enjoyed the questions that the quiet night stirred in him, but as the night grew quieter, the greater part of him despised the endless musings, tunes, and visions in his head. Somehow or other it always lead to prayer, which he suspected was God's way of afflicting him into Jobian submission.

"Dear God, please notify the devil I'm still faithful," Eduard said, "so he can flee and give me some rest. No use tormenting me further; I'm not going to 'curse you and die.'

# ❄ Chapter 3 ❄

## HORRIFIC BEAUTY

After being helped up off of the floor, Sara lied down on the paper covered bed. The nurse who had helped Kyle and Dr. Anderson returned again with a cup of water for Sara to alleviate the sob induced coughing.

A voice suddenly sounded from a speaker in the ceiling. Another nurse paged Dr. Anderson for assistance.

After calling back on the phone near the door, Dr. Anderson walked back over to the bedside. "Listen, I want to give you and Kyle some time, so I'm going to step out for a moment, but Linda here will be close by if you need anything. We have much more to talk about, but it can wait for now if you'd like. Maybe when your parents are back we can all get together to discuss it more."

"Thank you, Doctor Anderson," Kyle said, now trying to muster the strength to comfort his friend alone.

The doctor, along with the nurse, stepped out of the room, leaving the door open a crack.

Sara took another sip of water and lied back down on the bed. "Why is this happening? Maybe it's a mistake."

"Sara," Kyle said from the bedside, "stay positive. We never know when our time is up—heck, the world could end tomorrow, or we could get hit by a car on our way home."

"Oh Kyle, I love you. I feel like I could just cry forever. I wish I could wake up and shake this off like a nightmare. God, I'm only eighteen; this stuff is supposed to happen to old people. I'll never get to raise children, or go for a Sunday drive with my folks, never even see Niagara Falls. We'll never grow old and sit in rocking chairs on the porch like we joked. It doesn't even seem real. Remember that time..."

Kyle was only half listening to Sara's reminiscing, for he was still hung up on her declaration of love. It came so easily to her. It was not as though she had never said it before, but he never took it very seriously. He wanted to return the gesture for her sake, and felt no harm in saying it now.

"Sara," he interrupted, "I, um... love you too. Children, rocking chairs, Niagara Falls... We're going to do it all, don't worry about it. This can't stop us from hoping, from living in the moment."

Sara sighed. "I think I just want to go home. And, thank you... for being, you know, my friend."

"You too." Kyle smiled sheepishly. Despite their physical intimacy and close friendship, he had insisted for so long that they were only friends. But, something that day (perhaps the frightened look in Sara's eyes, or the sound of her shaky voice) resonated in his heart. For, as with death he had also put love out of his mind lest he struggle intimately with the loss of his parents; but now the two— love and death—were conjoined in horrific beauty.

\*\*\*

The following day Sara skipped school and stayed home to watch TV, paint, and cry. Kyle called her once in the afternoon to check up on her, but she didn't want to talk for long, and he was headed for band practice anyway. Her friend Jen texted her a few times wondering where she was, but Sara only said she was sick.

"bummer," Jen wrote, "sale @ mall, going after school, sure u don't want 2 go?"

Sara looked at the message a few times, then after an hour wrote back:

"ok... meet at bubbasubs 2:30"

At around 1:30 p.m. Sara got up from the couch, showered, and dressed. At 2:30 p.m. she met Jen at Bubba's Subs to get a sandwich and talk. The two brought their food to a small table in the food court and sat down and over the next ten minutes Sara told Jen about her diagnosis.

Jen's jaw dropped. "So there's no pills you can take?"

Sara tossed a soggy piece of lettuce over her shoulder onto the floor. "Not according to the doctor. And who knows what it would do to the baby?"

"What did your parents say?"

"I haven't told them yet."

"What?!" Jen's eyes widened. "You have to tell them, Sara!"

"I know. I tried last night when they called but, I don't know, I guess I didn't want to hear myself say it. I knew they'd flip out and come home, and then my grandma would be left alone, and I don't know, it just wouldn't come out of my mouth. They're coming back in a couple days; I'll tell them then."

"I mean, like, you look fine."

Sara pushed her sandwich away from her. "I feel like garbage."

"Does it make you nauseous?"

"No, I think it's this sandwich. You want the rest?"

"Not really. Oh no!" Jen peered over Sara's shoulder. "Hey, come on, let's walk and talk. Marcy Simmons is coming down the escalator and she's probably going to bug me about something. Throw that out and we'll go look for jeans or something, unless you're ready to leave."

While Sara's ghost haunted the mall, Kyle was in the musty, poster-covered basement of his friend Jay's house. He had gotten out of work early and headed over there for band practice.

"Dude," Kyle's friend and bassist Steve said, "you alright? That's like the fifth time you screwed up the bridge."

"Yeah, everything's cool. My fingers aren't working right, I guess."

"C'mon, let's try it again. Jay, give us a four count."

After four taps on the hi-hat, Kyle's band Sticky Wicket attempted another recording of their new song. It was the last one they needed for a five song demo they were giving to Steve's older cousin, Brian, who co-owned an independent music label.

"Yes!" Steve yelled when the song was through. "That, my friends, is how it's done. My cousin's going to love it. Now all we need is Mark to come record his vocal tracks and we can pass this out all over the place. Hey, I'm thinking we should upload some tunes on the internet, or create a website or something."

Kyle quietly turned off his amp, put his guitar in its case, and began to walk to the door.

"Whoa!" Steve said, "Where ya going?"

"I thought we were done for the day." Kyle turned around with case in hand.

"No way, dude, I got some more ideas I want to run by you guys. Got this cool thing I've been working on. It's early still."

"It's almost six o'clock."

"And? It's not like you got school in the morning. Stick around."

Kyle walked to the door. "Listen, I'll catch up with you guys later or something. Sorry. Really."

# ❄ Chapter 4 ❄

## EDUARD ACCUSES LUDWIG

"I know, strange isn't it? To bed with a storm, to day with the sun. Odd April we're having." Eduard stood in the doorway on his way out to work the next day, admiring the victory of spring over winter's last gasp. The pedestrians walked sprightly by his house in between horse drawn carriages, careful to avoid the thawing dung. "But, my silver snowflake ever glistens."

Nadine's dimples appeared. "Alright, you've polished my apples, now get along or you'll be late."

After one last blown kiss, Eduard began his walk down the slushy roads to his office. Passing by the Tower he noticed the man from the day before sitting on a bench next to another. Eduard stopped and glanced over the fence to see if he was alright, or showing any signs of abuse, but he had no black eyes or broken bones. In fact, he was talking calmly to the other man while the other slept. Eduard was surprised that the doctors had let him out again. He concluded that the man could not be very dangerous, but then Eduard noticed an orderly standing at the front door ensuring the man did not try to flee again (which was unlikely since his hand was chained to the bench). The man rambled on to his sleeping friend while Eduard listened:

"Boris, I'm glad you came here. Not many folks to talk to. Can I tell you something? Great. I don't want to be like this anymore. No, no, I'd feel this place had gotten the best of me if I killed myself. Besides, I miss her, and don't tell anyone, but that's where I'm going when I leave." On and on the man talked at the unconscious patient next to him until he caught sight of Eduard out of the corner of his eye. "What the devil are you looking at?!"

Eduard turned away and pretended to pick something up off the road. Tipping his hat to the two guards at the Tower's front gate, he walked away. He arrived at work about ten minutes later (twenty minutes late). The two steps up to the door had fresh tracks in them that told Eduard that Ludwig had already arrived. He took a deep breath, turned the knob, and entered.

"Oh my! Eduard, are you alright?" Ludwig rushed over to Eduard who had taken only three steps in before slipping on the wet tiled floor. It had previously been wood, but the building's owner was refurbishing his properties in the latest cosmopolitan styles. The grout was too thin according to Eduard, who had wanted to pick up some extra money by doing the job himself. Now the hard grey floor itself mocked him.

"Yes, I'm fine." Eduard waved away Ludwig's extended hand and rose to his feet.

"Well, it's good to see you." Ludwig said as he sat back in his corner of the sparsely decorated room.

Eduard now draped his wool jacket over his chair. "Ludwig, before we get started today I would like to talk with you about something."

"Here I am, partner. Even brought my ears today."

The cloud of smoke in the air around Ludwig's head wobbled and dispersed when Eduard approached his desk. Ludwig smoked a lot more since Austria Tabak opened a few years prior. Unfortunately for Eduard, who hated the smell, Ludwig was also sent copious amounts of the leaf from his brother who was employed there. Now Ludwig had never married, but recently found a love interest in an old maid at his church. This, thought Eduard, might finally motivate him to quit. And this, thought Eduard, might also motive him to steal—to impress her, or help her out with her finances.

"Take a look." Eduard opened up the ledger sheets on Ludwig's desk. "Now look at these here."

Ludwig put on his spectacles and scanned down his nose at the sheets. After a moment, he shook his head, removed his spectacles and said, "Sloppy. A lot of mistakes it seems."

"Or theft."

"Eduard, I don't understand. I know times are difficult, but you and your family have always done well for yourselves. If you're telling me what I think you are, then I... I'm not sure how to react. Have you been purposely making transpositions in order to... dear me, I can't even say it."

"What?!" Eduard stood up straight. "No, it's you who has been stealing! You! The lining of your hole is putting a purse in my—"

"Me?" Ludwig interrupted, slamming his pipe onto the desk. "I think you've gone and lost your mind, sir."

"Is that not your handwriting?" Eduard tapped the ledger relentlessly.

"No! That is your writing."

It was true that the two had nearly indistinguishable handwriting when it came to the ledger— a result of their shared need for order and uniformity. Both crossed their sevens, slanted their nines to the right, and slashed their zeroes. It was virtually impossible to tell who was responsible for the number switching, and neither was going to budge in the maintaining of his innocence.

"Unconscionable!" was the last thing Eduard would say to Ludwig that day. He returned to his desk, and only lifted his head when clients arrived. Even during lunch, Eduard did not offer Ludwig his usual unwanted pickle which Nadine insisted on packing for him. At last, when Eduard left for the day, he said no goodbye, but gathered up his belongings and slammed the door. He was glad that Ludwig stayed behind because not ten steps away from the building Eduard tripped again, and this time landed hands first in a puddle of slush and urine. It was humiliating, but he quickly got up and continued his stride before Ludwig could exit.

"I'm nobody's fool," Eduard counseled himself. "And to think, he tried to accuse me! Well, I'm not—what's that you say?"

An old man walking next to Eduard on the crowded street looked over at him. "I asked if you said something to me?"

"Oh... no sir, just talking to myself. Sorry."

The old man turned into a store while Eduard continued muttering his way through the crowd. "I'm not taking the blame for it. I'll direct our clients and their outrage to him, and the authorities if necessary." Eduard's rant was only just warming up when he arrived home.

"How was your day?" Nadine called from within the kitchen. Hearing no reply, she walked over to the foyer and gasped.

"Dear me! What happened?"

Eduard paced in front of the fire as his temper flared. "I fell... twice! It's not a big deal. What is a big deal is... is Ludwig! Do you know what he tried to do today?"

"Well, did you injure yourself?"

"That man tried to place the blame on me. Can you believe that? I showed him the discrepancies, and suddenly I was the one on trial. Outrageous!"

Nadine helped Eduard take off his sopping jacket. "No doubt it was an honest mistake, whoever did it, so why not work together to figure it out, instead of fighting over it. Ugh! This jacket is foul. I'll need to wash it."

"What's there to work out? I don't make mistakes, dear, not on the ledger, and certainly not that many times. I'm a professional, am I not?"

"I don't know what to tell you," Nadine said, "but I think it would behoove you both to calm down, and for your clients' sake try to work through this."

"Our clients are going to be up in arms if they find out their money is missing." Eduard slumped into his chair and rubbed his temples. "I can't even think about it anymore. I'm so tired."

Nadine massaged his shoulders. "Well, you haven't been sleeping well. You just sit there by the fire and I'll warm some milk."

"Fire?" Eduard questioned. He hadn't noticed it up until this point. "I thought you weren't going to build one with the windows open."

"What was that?" Nadine called from the kitchen.

Eduard looked from the fire to the open window near it and shook his head. "Never mind."

"What was that?" Nadine called out again in between a whistled tune.

"Never mind!"

Eduard rarely yelled, even at the children, certainly never at Nadine. Were he not so exhausted he would have felt worse about it. Nadine, however, was not exhausted at all and placed the milk on the table next to him. "Well, here is your milk sir, let me know if you'll require more."

"I didn't even want this one."

For the rest of the night Eduard's "silver snowflake" was icy. She would serve him dutifully, yet with all the coldness of the roadside slush. It wouldn't be until late that evening that Eduard would apologize.

As the two lay in bed listening to the quiet clack of horse hooves on the street below their bedroom window, Eduard said into the darkness, "I'm sorry, Nadine. It was wrong of me to lash out like that."

"I don't understand what's going on with you lately, Eduard. You're not yourself. The last few months have been very odd; maybe it's just age, but you've been forgetful, clumsy, irritable, and mostly just in another world. It's not so unusual for a man to yell at his wife, but it's unusual for you. Needless to say, I didn't appreciate it."

"I know, it's been..."

"It's been downright frightening at times, Eduard, and I'm trying not to worry or nag, but you're making it very difficult and I don't..." Nadine lowered her voice, remembering the children. "I don't know what to do."

"I've had work on my mind and other things. Yes, getting old too, I suppose."

"Perhaps it's time for a vacation. Maybe Ludwig can function for a week while you get some rest. Why don't you ask him? You can even spend the time fishing if you fancy; you'll hear no complaint from me. But, you really ought to consider it. It's not good for your health to be so weary, and certainly not good for your temper."

"Dear, I can't ask him for time off. First, I barely even spoke to him today, and tomorrow will doubtless be the same; and third, he's pilfering like a pirate. Can't imagine what he'd do with a whole week to himself."

Nadine turned on her side, rubbed Eduard's chest and said, "You worry too much, it's not like you. For our sake, the children, for you, take some time off."

"I'll consider it," Eduard said merely to discontinue the conversation.

With the street below now quiet, only the sound of their youngest daughter Julia playing "War" down the hall could be heard. And, although she should have been in bed, it was strangely therapeutic for the couple to hear the sound effects accompanying the epic battle in her room.

"Our son Julia," Nadine joked. "She'd have made an excellent boy."

Eduard breathed deeply. "A boy. Yes, it'd be excellent, you know, to have the Strobl lineage carry on. I feel like I let my father down as the last male in the family. Perhaps though...perhaps we could try again sometime."

The Strobls had, in fact, had a son a year after Anna was born, but it was stillborn. For some reason Eduard felt guilty for its death, as though God knew of his great desire for a son and caused the tragedy on his account to teach him contentment.

Nadine placed her leg over Eduard's. "Maybe tonight we could try."

The next twenty minutes were frustrating for Eduard. This was the first of many more nights to come that

27

despite his eager heart, Eduard's body was too exhausted to follow suit.

"Yes, that was fine, goodnight." Nadine finally mumbled half asleep. Clearly she was in a dream, for there was nothing "fine" about that night.

At last, Eduard rolled over on his back and stroked Nadine's leg. Once again alone with his thoughts, he amused and aggravated himself until four o'clock.

# ❈ Chapter 5 ❈

## A BITTERSWEET BIRTH

"Your mommy and daddy were in an accident tonight," Kyle's aunt and uncle explained to the eight-year-old after receiving a phone call from the police.

It was a warm July night nearly ten years ago when his parents left for a romantic weekend getaway after dropping him off. It was nearing his bed time and he was already in his pajamas finishing a movie in the living room. He had heard his aunt call for his uncle after the phone rang, and heard them talking, but the movie was far too engrossing to pick up on the breaking apart of his aunt and the quiet discussion of how and when to tell the boy.

"Your mommy and daddy have...," his uncle explained, "they've gone to heaven to be with Grandpa and Grandma and Cricket."

Cricket was Kyle's green parakeet. It had died a few months prior, and was more devastating to the boy than even the death of his grandparents two and three years earlier. He had gone to its cage one Saturday morning and found it lying on the bottom, unresponsive to his poking and flicking. He took the bird from the cage and ran with it into his parent's bedroom.

"Mommy!"

"What is it, Kyle? Oh no, did Cricket die? Poor thing." His mother took the bird and placed it in a box. "Don't be upset dear, we can buy you a new bird. As soon as your father comes back from fishing we can go to the pet store."

"I want Cricket."

"Oh honey. Cricket was tired. So tired, in fact, that he needed to sleep a very long time. That's what happens when animals get old or really sick. People too, like Grandma and Grandpa and even that boy from school. But, they're okay. And, even though we'll miss Cricket, he would want you to give another bird a nice loving home. But, only when you're ready, honey."

After a few days, Kyle was over Cricket's "sleeping," but rather than buy a new bird, his parents got him a hamster, which he named Ralph after a character in a book about a mouse and a motorcycle. This same hamster was now spinning his wheel in a cage set upon a table in the living room while Kyle's aunt and uncle explained to the boy that his parents were gone.

"They died?"

"Yes, honey," said his aunt, "So you're going to stay here for a little longer. Ralph too."

"But, all my toys are home."

"I know, honey, Uncle Pat is going to go to your house and get your things in the morning, don't you worry one bit. We love you, Kyle, and we'll make sure you have everything you need."

"Why did they die?"

"I don't know, honey, it was just their time. No one knows why these things happen, they just do. It's a part of life. But it'll be alright, I promise."

As his uncle left the house, his aunt took him to the room that would be his bedroom from that point on. He lay on his bed and closed his watering eyes while his aunt stroked his head. He didn't know what was wrong with himself, he just felt strange and empty. But, the more he thought of his parents, the more he thought of Cricket. He had practically forgotten about that bird. How could he have? Yes, that was death—being forgotten. Would he someday forget his parents too?

Yes.

As soon as possible, if he could help it.

No.

Never!

Kyle's aunt and uncle were up all that night making phone calls and numerous cups of coffee to say nothing of the many times Kyle got up to sit with them (only to be carried back to bed asleep ten minutes later). Barren, they had always wanted to have a child, and now had no choice but to accept the bittersweet birth of their new family.

# ❄ Chapter 6 ❄

## VACATION

When on the next day Eduard returned to the office, he and Ludwig spoke not except about necessary business. Around lunch time, Eduard got up for a walk around the block, but was stopped before he left the office.

"Eduard, hold on a moment." Ludwig put down his quill and took up his pipe.

Eduard took his hand off the door knob. "What is it? I already told you, if Mr. Bieler stops in, tell him I'll be back momentarily."

"No Eduard, it's about those discrepancies."

"Have you something to confess?"

"Well," Ludwig said as he fumbled with a match, "I was looking again at the days in question, and I'm not trying to accuse you, but..." Now quickly blowing smoke into the air he continued, "Look Eduard, each one occurred last month, and if you'll recall, you were out sick a few times then. Do you remember which days?"

"Of course I do." Reluctantly, Eduard returned to his desk, and shuffled through a drawer, "I write down every day each of us misses work. I already looked at that."

"Might we look again?"

It was ludicrous that he would make such a simple error, but if it would help, Eduard would humor him.

"Here you are." Eduard tossed the absence log on his desk.

Ludwig scanned the log for a moment. "Again, I'm not accusing you of anything Eduard, but look at this..."

Ludwig proceeded to point out that if one were to move up each entry a day ahead on the days Eduard was absent, then compare them with the receipts they kept, the numbers worked out perfectly and the negative balance they thought they had actually evened out. No clients had been cheated, and no one had stolen the money, but only on the ledger was there a discrepancy.

Eduard shook his head. "Such a simple mistake. I'm a fool."

"It's alright Eduard, it could happen to anyone."

"No! I should not have accused you, dear friend. I should have known better."

"Eduard, my good man, it's alright, you were just looking out for the clients."

"Yes, but... No! It's inexcusable."

"Tell me something," Ludwig said, "if you don't mind me asking... Is everything alright at home? I mean, far be it from me to pry, but as of late you've been, well..."

"I never used to make silly mistakes like this." Eduard rubbed the stubble on his chin. "I'm at a loss for words."

"Well, like you said, it was a simple mistake."

Eduard picked up the ledger and began to walk away, but stopped.

"Ludwig,"

"Yes, Eduard."

"I have... well, a favor to ask."

"Certainly, what is it?"

Pulling up a chair to Ludwig's desk, Eduard explained, "Nadine thinks (and I'm starting to think) that I could use some time off, maybe a week's respite. Would you be able to handle things without me? I hate to impose, but..."

"Eduard, of course you can take a week for yourself. I'll be fine. Get some rest, my friend, and return refreshed. Forget about this place for a while, it's not going anywhere and neither am I. Sadly."

"Are you sure? I promise that when I return I'll be thinking straighter, and if you want some time, I'll gladly let you take even two weeks."

"Eduard," Ludwig patted his partner's knee, "You're a good chap. Take your lunch, and I don't want to see you around here for another week, understand?"

"It's a deal." Eduard stood and shook Ludwig's hand. He then returned to his desk, removed some files and other things necessary for Ludwig to function on his own and plopped them on top with a thud.

"I think this is all you'll need, but if not, feel free to go into my desk to look, or send for me."

"Thank you Eduard, now get going. And, tell the wife I send my greeting.'"

At the door, Eduard raised his finger in the air and declared with a smile, "I shall return a new man, Ludwig." He then walked out, but returned a moment later.

"Well, that was a speedy week," Ludwig joked. "I do wish I'd gotten more done!"

"Here," Eduard handed Ludwig the pickle Nadine packed for lunch.

On his way home, Eduard whistled and waved to familiar faces along his route. Spring had finally melted all the untimely slush away, leaving behind evaporating puddles and friendlier souls. The faces and buildings, however, soon became unfamiliar, at least as far as his route was concerned. After twenty minutes, Eduard realized he had taken a left instead of a right at the end of the road on which his office resided.

Upon noticing what he had done, Eduard laughed off the mistake and headed back with his whistle. Ten minutes away from his house, he came upon the Narrenturm. As he passed the Tower on the right, he noticed a cat on the roof. It crouched on the ledge of the five-story building to stalk a bird. Eduard whistled to the bird to warn it, but the cat sprang. Eduard cringed when the feline pounced, but then smiled when it fell off the ledge to the yard below leaving the bird to fly away to safety. The unfortunate cat landed on it's back with a thud, startling a nearby patient, who subsequently punted the dead, broken creature towards the fence.

"Not his lucky day, I guess." said Eduard to the patient, but was ignored.

It was not uncommon for patients to be let out into the yard after lunch in order to get sun. They were, however, closely supervised, and not allowed to interact with the passing pedestrians. There were about ten patients in the tiny yard that day, some of whom were noticeably more suited to the asylum than others. Two patients seemed to be talking to each other, but really just happened to be facing one another. Another man spun in circles, and after stopping, began making circles in the air with a stick.

Eduard watched for a while. What particularly intrigued him was the man whom he had now seen twice, now sitting on a bench, then falling over on the ground, then sitting back on the bench, only to fall down moments later. What the devil was his problem? Odd fellow, indeed. Finally upright again, the man looked at Eduard, but this time Eduard did not walk away.

A few times the man began to mouth something, but inevitably fell forward. At last, the man stood up and tried walking toward Eduard, but fell back upon the bench. He was a larger gentleman, with a muscular frame. Instead of trying to rise again, the patient began to say something, causing an orderly to jog over.

"Lukas!" the orderly yelled while standing in front of him wagging a finger. "You're pushing your luck. You should be glad the good doctor von Croy still lets you out after the other day. Frankly I don't think all the fresh air in the world is going to help. Now leave the pedestrians alone."

"You don't think at all, you grunt," the man snarled before falling over and sliding off the bench. His face hit the ground, but his hand (being still chained to the bench) held half of his body up.

After a moment, Eduard shivered and left, trying to reason why the man seemed so familiar. Was he an old client, or a member from church? It would have been hard to forget such a large, brawny fellow, but he couldn't place him. He then heard the sound of someone calling his name and turned to look, but found no one.

"I'm tired," the voice spoke again. And, again Eduard looked about. Was someone following him home? Maybe one of the orderlies wanted to speak with him? Well, there was no one seeking his attention. Then, suddenly the same voice repeated its drowsy refrain, but this time it came from Eduard's own lips as he swayed home. "I'm... so tired... so—"

Eduard crossed the threshold of his door and fell to the floor of his foyer.

"Is that you, Eduard?" Nadine called from upstairs.

Eduard wiped the blood from his nose onto his shirt sleeve. He then wobbled up the stairs and into the bedroom where Nadine was rising from a nap while the children were at school. "My turn," he said and crashed down to bury his face in his pillow.

"Darling, you're bleeding!"

"I fell."

"Again? Goodness me! So klutzy... Eduard?... Eduard?"

"... Merely a pickle, Ludwig... she'll never know..."

Noticing her husband drift, Nadine quietly crept downstairs. The children were due back from school, and she did not want them to disturb their father. When they at last came home, she hushed them and took them back outside for a walk over to one of their friends and neighbors, the Trommlers, for a visit. Although her intentions were good, Eduard only napped for about a half an hour. When he woke and found his family missing he became anxious that something had happened to them and clumsily wandered the streets for them. However, his groggy sway and blood smeared face caused people to avoid him rather than assist, and after about an hour of pacing through the neighborhood, a police officer stopped him and asked where he was headed.

"See, officer, I was asleep," Eduard explained, "and when I awoke, my family was gone. The children should have been home by now."

The officer continued to question him until the interrogation was interrupted.

"Eduard! Eduard!"

When Nadine and the children reached Eduard, she confirmed that he had not been drinking, and that they had merely gone to a neighbor's house so that he could sleep. The officer let them all leave together, but not before Julia was embarrassed by some passing students from school.

"*Faulenzer!*" the three boys yelled, and then ran when Eduard motioned after them. He put his arm around his daughter's shoulder, but felt a tension that told him to remove it. Understandably, she did not want any more of her friends to see her with a "drunken beggar."

Julia and Anna walked ahead of their parents toward the house. Julia was happy the following day was Sunday Sabbath -- hoping her schoolmates might forget about the incident. But, they were boys; they'd remember.

Eduard checked behind him to see if the police officer was still watching. He was. He then turned to Nadine. "I'm glad you came when you did. Please next time let me know. Leave a note or something."

"I'll will, dear. Now, let's forget all about this and try to enjoy the evening. The children will no doubt need some cheering up."

Eduard agreed wholeheartedly. "We could all use some cheer. Hey, I know! Tonight, we'll have a puppet show. That should do nicely for our spirits. How does that sound children?" Eduard called to his daughters' back. "A puppet show tonight? Julia? Anna?" The girls continued into the house with their heads down.

# ❋ Chapter 7 ❋

## SPILLED MILK

"Thank you Pastor, I appreciate your prayers. Perhaps the Lord has a miracle planned. Yes, you too. Take care." Sara's mother put down her phone, and took the popcorn out of the microwave to salt and butter it.

Sara had told her parents about her disease on Tuesday night when they came home, and after a sleepless night, first thing on Wednesday they called to set up an appointment with Dr. Anderson. Now Thursday, they would have to wait three more excruciating days until they could all go to the office to question the doctor's findings. In the meantime they had talked to friends and family and looked for support wherever they could. Pastor Hancock had called to find out how Sara's grandmother in Virginia was doing, but while on the phone, Sara's mother told him about her daughter's foolish mistake with "some boy" as well as the shocking news of her diagnosis.

As expected, the pastor was empathetic, but Sara's mother was reluctant to accept his counsel, including the part about treating Kyle as family. Sara's older brother Scott, who was away with the Navy, had also called and was angry about both pieces of news, and swore he was going to kill Kyle if he ever saw him again.

Sara's mother walked back into the living room where she was watching television with her husband, Sara, and Kyle. This tiny, white, Colonial home on the outskirts of the New York City had become filled with thick tension ever since Kyle was caught sneaking out of Sara's window last summer. This was one of the first times in a while the four of them had been in the same room together. Sara's parents noticed her snuggle up close to Kyle on the couch and kiss his cheek.

"What did the pastor say?" Sara's father said, ignoring the display of affection.

"Well, he was very encouraging, and talked about—Sara, are you listening? The pastor talked about how these things are meant for our benefit even if we don't understand; that it's not God's anger but his love that brings these things about."

Kyle squeezed his arm around Sara's shoulder. "I think he's right, Carol."

"I suppose so, but it doesn't make it any easier, Kyle."

"Kyle, you're a philosopher now?" Sara's father kept his eyes fixed to the television.

Kyle chuckled, "Good one, Jim."

"It's Mr. and Mrs. Riley," Sara's dad corrected Kyle.

Sara and Kyle began to share whispers and giggles. Finally, Sara squeaked as though someone had pinched her under the blanket. Her father looked over with aggravation. "You two should—"

Sara's mother placed her hand on her husband's arm. Whatever he was going to say, she really did not want to hear it. The news of Sara's disease yesterday had devastated her parents. They suddenly found themselves wondering what kind of restrictions they could possibly impose upon their daughter who was not only an adult now (and going to be a mother), but also destined to be taken from them soon.

Kyle, on the other hand, was not viewed so generously. Sara's father had never liked him since the two kids had become friends in the eighth grade. At first, he was concerned that Kyle's rebellious attitude would rub off on his daughter and hurt her grades. Indeed, she had missed a lot of school since September, and he suspected it was because of too many late nights on the phone. His concern grew to other obvious areas, as well. Although Sara told her parents they were only friends, they knew better than to trust a rebellious teenage boy around their daughter.

The concern of Sara's father, however, had not been justified until the past summer when the two teens began to spend more time alone and 'joke around' by kissing and touching. Their intimacy had progressed more than the two could anticipate, and now her father's fears were realized in the expanding of his daughter's belly and the giddy laughter induced by the skinny boy next to her on the couch (with his feet on the coffee table again).

"Hey, I have a surprise for you." Taking her by the hand, Kyle brought Sara up the stairs to her room while her parents looked on.

"Okay, what is it?" Sara hopped up onto her bed, sat down, and bounced in excitement. Her bedroom had pink walls, old stuffed animals piled on a shelf, photos of friends from school wedged in the frame of her dresser's mirror, and hair products strewn about on the floor among scattered articles of clothing. On her walls hung drawings that she had sketched over the years.

"Well," Kyle said as he picked a shirt off the bed and twirled it, "I took Friday off from work."

Sara snatched the shirt and threw it on the floor with some others. "Wow, that's great! You're so lucky, I got a stupid math test on Friday; I wish I could get out of it."

Kyle had dropped out of high school at the end of September when Sara first told him of the home pregnancy test. A tense conversation with his aunt and uncle resulted in them giving up trying to convince him otherwise, and he had begun working at his uncle's garage. He enjoyed having a bit of money for once, though not enough to please Sara's parents.

"That's not all," Kyle said, now playing with a hair tie, "I talked to Vice Principal Marsha."

"Oh? Did she complain about me missing so much school lately? (Don't stretch my hair tie out, I need it)."

"Nope. But, now you have tomorrow off too."

"What?! Oh Kyle! You're awesome. Was she mad?"

Kyle shot the hair tie across the room to the dresser. "It's fine. Believe it or not, the ol' bag was happy to help, especially when I told her where I was bringing you."

"Sara scooted closer to Kyle's face and smiled. "And where is that?"

"Niagara Falls!"

"Shut up!" Sara pushed Kyle.

"We're leaving tomorrow morning. Should take about eight hours to drive."

"But, I have my appointment on Monday, remember."

"We'll be home by Sunday night."

"Kyle, you're too much!" Sara fell back on her pile of pillow.

"So after dinner you need to pack. I'd like to leave by 7 a.m. if possible."

"My parents aren't going to be happy."

"I'll take care of it."

Sara sat back up. "Crap! I think my mom's coming."

Kyle could hear the sound of steps down the hall and got off the bed. With a gentle knock Sara's mom opened the door. "Okay Romeo, time to go."

"No problem, Carol, I was just leaving. Oh, and thanks for the movie and for dinner. That ugly hunchback dude really had some heart. Good stuff."

"You're welcome, Kyle. Goodnight."

With a short wave of the hand, Kyle said goodbye to Sara and her mother and left for home. Half way home in the car he remembered that he didn't say goodbye to Sara's father, whom he hadn't seen on the way out. "Oh well, he was probably in the bathroom or something and didn't even notice I left."

... But he did.

"So how's my little girl doing?" Sara's mother sat on the bed next to Sara.

"I'm alright."

"You want to talk?"

"Not particularly. What about?"

"I don't know... About things... anything."

"Things are fine."

Sara's mother nodded and took a deep breath. "Sara, I know you're trying to be strong, but it's okay to be upset. There's plenty of time to be strong, but you have to allow yourself to cry too. You're going through a lot right now and I want you to be able to share your feelings. We're all shocked by this."

"I'm fine, mom, really. Tired as usual, but alright."

"Well, I can make you some warm milk if you'd like."

"Nope. That's alright."

"Would only take a minute."

"No thanks."

"I could put chocolate syrup in it like you used to have as a kid."

"Mom, seriously, I'm fine. I don't want milk right now."

Sara's mother sighed again. "I'm sorry, honey, I didn't mean to upset you."

"I'm not upset."

"Well, you seem upset."

"Holy crap, mom!" Sara sat up quickly, then landed back on the pillow in front of her, "Yeah, I'm getting upset now 'cause you're like trying to make me drink milk and I don't want milk right now. I'm fine. Really. Seriously. I'm okay."

"Well, I was just trying to help."

"I know. I just don't want any right now. It's no big deal."

"Did Kyle say something to upset you?"

"No!"

Sara's mother got up from the bed, "Well, I can see you're not in the mood to talk now." She closed the door as gently behind her as when she had opened it. Sara could hear her return downstairs, the argument with her father that soon followed, and the slamming of the front door indicating her father was going to the garage to tinker with something and sneak a cigarette. Sara turned the light off by her bed, and after a half an hour fell asleep listening to her mother crying in the next room.

At midnight Sara awoke. Nearly an hour had passed when she finally got up to use the bathroom and to update her status on-line at the computer in her room. "I'm spilled milk." she wrote, "No need to cry."

After reading through her other friends' posts and commenting on her friend Jen's new photo album, she put the computer to sleep and returned to bed where she lay for another two hours.

# ❈ Chapter 8 ❈

## CONFESSION

"I don't much care for these songs." Anna said to her mother in the back pew of St. Stephen's Cathedral.

"They're new, sweetie, you'll take to them."

Under Joseph II, the Catholic Church had undergone a lot of unwelcome changes. The Emperor styled himself as the guardian of the living faith, and often criticized the Pope for what he saw as antiquated hindrances to worship. Perhaps the most notable change for the congregation was the music during the mass.

"Is the service over yet?" Anna rested her head on her mother's arm.

"Soon, now try to settle."

Father Kraus continued from the pulpit, "And let us remember our Emperor, let us remember to pray for his patience, and mercy, that he will see the great needs of the Lord's church and encourage its growth, and use his power for good and not evil, that he will help preserve the traditions of the holy Catholic faith and Her ministers..."

The chief annoyance of the clergy was Joseph's reduction in the required tithes, as well as the number of priests and nuns. This left fewer priests to do more of the work, and there was much work to be done. Father Kraus in particular had his hands full, having to visit more congregants during the week than was reasonable to expect. Some said the Emperor—responsible for the *Patent of Tolerance*—even had Protestant and Jewish tendencies.

The Emperor's reforms, in fact, irritated all the nobility throughout his kingdom, particularly because they were the target of most of the taxes. By 1789, Belgium and Hungary would revolt, and when at last the Emperor would die in 1790, his humble and overstated epitaph would read by his request, 'Here lies Joseph II, who failed in all he undertook.' The lower classes, however, would mourn the great Emperor, especially the serfs, though they were soon thereafter reduced to their former status.

"... May justice flow like a river in our streets," Father Kraus continued, "that our landowners will not be penalized, that our labor will not be in vain, and that the love of money will not conquer the love of our Lord and the ever-blessed Mother of God. *Ite Missa est*," concluded the father at the end of that morning's St. George's Day mass.

Despite the Emperor's mandate that the clergy use German, Father Krauss insisted upon Latin during portions of the service. He received threats and ultimatums from Joseph for it, but the undeterred priest appealed to the authority of the Pope. This further incited the Emperor towards the Vatican, and particularly Cardinal Migazzi who oversaw the Church in Vienna.

Father Kraus, donning his holy garb, lastly read a passage from *The Gospel according to John*, said a prayer, and invited the faithful to stay after for confession.

"I'd like to stay," Eduard said as Nadine gathered up her belongings.

"That's fine. I'll take the children home and see you after."

Eduard sat back in the pew to pray until the rest of the congregation filed out. His prayers were disjointed. They mostly concerned his family, and his inability to sleep.

The night before he had only slept for three hours, and was finding it harder to concentrate on even the most rote tasks. Four times he had to look up verses that he had memorized as a child. Even the 23rd Psalm was a chore. As he sat blinking his eyes, a stocky man in a robe wearing a crucifix around his neck approached.

"Eduard," Father Kraus said, "it's so good to see you today. Was the family able to attend?"

Eduard lifted his heavy head. "Hello Father. Yes, but they left."

"And you stayed?"

"I was hoping to speak to you about a few things."

"Would you like to enter one of the confessional booths?"

"Very much."

Eduard arose from the pew and took the long walk up to the front right side of the cathedral. After entering the dim room, a slot opened from the other side.

"Father," Eduard said, "bless me, for I have sinned. It's been two weeks since my last confession and I have been impatient, angry, selfish, and cruel. I falsely accused my neighbor this past week and so broke the seventh... no, I'm sorry, the eighth commandment."

"Go on."

"It was my partner at work (he's a Lutheran); no matter, I accused him of stealing, but it turns out that it was my failing."

"You mean that you stole the money?"

"No Father, I mean that I made a mistake on the ledger, and I just assumed it was his fault."

"'Love believes all things, and hopes all things,' my child. Try to assume the best of people."

48

"Yes Father. I was very unloving, but he forgave me. I just need to know that God forgives me too. For this sin I'm truly sorry."

"God will pardon the contrite heart, which you have. I'll pray for you and you also must pray. The saints delight to intercede for us, and our blessed Mother never fails to show mercy. Do you believe this?"

"I do."

"Tell me more, or is that all?"

"No, there's more. Yesterday I embarrassed my family by wondering around like a lunatic in the streets. I felt so terrible for my son, and I hope that he can forgive me."

"Son? Did I miss something, Eduard?"

"Did I say 'son'? No, sorry, I meant my youngest, Julia."

"Did you intend to embarrass her?"

"Not at all. It just happened. I was looking for them, and I'm afraid I was not in the best shape at the time."

"Elaborate."

"Well, I had awoken from a nap, and my nose was still bloody from a fall. I went out into the streets, and I suppose I appeared as a drunkard and was nearly arrested."

"It was a mistake, child. I will not require anything from you for that, nor does the Lord."

"Still," Eduard said, "I felt horrible."

"That's understandable. You should talk to her later, and try to explain."

"Thank you Father, I will."

"Is that all then?"

"No, Father. I also have been forgetting my Scriptures lately, even the simplest ones elude me."

"When the word is sown," Father Kraus quoted from the Bible, "the devil quickly comes to take it away."

"What shall I do?"

"*Resist him, and he will flee from you.* Today we celebrate Saint George, who valiantly rescued the sacrificial maiden from a river. Did you pay attention to the homily?"

"I was a little distracted. I apologize."

"Well, with his sword *"Ascalon"* Saint George wounded and then bridled the dragon so that the princess of Lasia might lead it around as a horse. When the people of the town who offered her to the beast saw her yet alive and leading the dragon they feared for their lives, but the venerable saint promised to slay it if they were baptized. After they received the sacrament, he slew the dragon, and in that very place the king built a church where a spring emerged from the alter—curing all diseases. You are not a saint, dear child, but you must learn from their example."

"Yes, Father. But is it true that at midnight on this holy day all evil things have their way. Will the city be haunted? Should I be worried? Am I not already in grave danger?"

"It's true, my child, that tonight is a very dangerous night; however, the spirits still must submit to the authority of the Church, and so as long as you are protected by Her, you needn't fear for your life. We are buffeted, but not lost. Nevertheless, I do recommend staying home tonight where you can beseech the Lord. 'Tis not a night for chances."

"Thank you Father."

"Is that all?"

"Yes... well no, there's one more thing."

"Go on."

"Well, I haven't been getting any sleep lately. Over the past few months it's become much worse—from seven hours a night, to six, to five, to four, and last night I only slept three hours, if that. Wouldn't be such a bother if it weren't interfering with my employment and domestic duties, but I've tried everything and it just gets worse, and—"

"The Lord gives rest to the faithful," Father Kraus interrupted, "but there is no rest for the wicked. Your conscience has been defiled, but ye can be transformed by the renewal of heart."

"But what have I done? I've prayed many times for the Lord to aid me and reveal my heart, but no transgression comes to mind. Like the Scriptures, my heart's intentions escape me."

"The Lord opposes the proud, but gives grace to the humble."

"Yes, Father, but, what shall I do about it?"

"My child, you will need to pray for this spirit (perhaps a demon) to leave you, and if that does not work, then it will be up to the Church to handle. Vienna has become a city full of unclean spirits that fly from one person only to enter another. Here is a new prayer you can pray and teach your children: 'Now I lay me down to sleep, I pray the Lord my soul to keep, and if I die before I wake, I pray the Lord my soul to take.' You will pray this week and fast, and then I will see you next Sunday to check on your progress."

"That's a beautiful prayer, Father, thank you. I took the week off for respite. I'll spend my time contemplating the grace of our Father in Heaven, fasting, and praying to our Holy Mother."

"Very good, my child, and I'll also be thinking about you and your family. Now, is that all?"

"Yes, Father."

"Very good. For the sin of falsely accusing your neighbor I now pray: "God, the giver of grace, through the death and resurrection of his Son, has reconciled the world to himself, and sent the Holy Spirit among us for the forgiveness of sins. Through the ministry of the Church, may God grant you pardon and peace. I absolve you of your sins, in the name of the Father, and of the Son, and of the Holy Spirit. Amen. May the Lord's grace be upon you."

# ❄ Chapter 9 ❄

## ARTIFICIAL LIGHT

After one flat tire, six bathroom stops, and an argument with a tollbooth operator, it was around eight o'clock when Kyle and Sara reached the Niagara Falls area. Having checked in at the Crowne Plaza Fallsview Hotel, the two headed out to the Rock N Roll Café for a late non-candle-lit dinner.

"You drive too fast."

"Okay, we're here." It was probably the tenth time Sara had commented on his driving that day, so Kyle ignored it, parked the car, and hopped out. He was excited about his first time at one of these famous museum/restaurants, which was full of interesting music memorabilia.

Sara waited a minute before opening the car door. After all, why couldn't he be a gentleman and open it for her? Kyle was standing around looking at the entrance of the restaurant, but finally looked back and opened the door for Sara.

"C'mon, a little rain never hurt!" Kyle took Sara's hand and the two ran up to the restaurant to wait for a table.

"Lennon? Party of two?" called one of the waitresses at the front after twenty minutes.

"That's us!" Kyle motioned for Sara to come along.

"Lennon?" Sara whispered on the way to the table. "We can't take someone else's seat."

"Thank you," Kyle said to the waitress after being handed two menus. After she left, he leaned over the table and said, "Yeah, you know, like John Lennon? The Beatles? I thought it'd be funny. Maybe they'd think we're related to him."

"Um, I doubt that."

"Yeah, you're probably right. Anyway, look at this place. Isn't this awesome? We got autographed pictures of all the greats. And guitars too.

Sara nodded and smiled as though any of it truly meant anything. "Well, maybe someday your guitar will be up there, and some young boy will sit in this same seat and say, 'Wow! That's Kyle's guitar!'"

Kyle laughed. "I'm working on it. If that stuff with Steve's cousin pans out, then I'm on my way. I'm trying not to get too excited about it just in case it falls through, but man! That would be a dream. I'd be able to buy that Fender Twin amp, and that sweet Gibson ES-335...Vintage Sunburst... rosewood fingerboard and pearl dot inlays... nickel tuners... ABR-1 bridge... oh, and aluminum stop bar tailpiece. Yeah, baby!" Kyle pumped his fist.

"I see you haven't put much thought into it, huh?"

"What do you mean?"

Sara smiled. "Just kidding. But hey, you can do it, Kyle. If anyone can."

"I appreciate that. Here, I'll give you my first autograph." Kyle took a napkin and a pen on the table and scribbled his name, then handed it to Sara.

"Hold on a second." Sara took a piece of gum from her purse and began chewing wildly.

"What are you doing?"

After the gum was moist, Sara took it from her mouth and stuck it to the napkin, then after looking around quickly stuck it to the wall next to a framed picture of a rock star "There! Now my boyfriend... um, sorry 'friend'... is famous too."

"You're nuts, man."

"A little. Anyway... what are you ordering?"

"Not sure. Hey, we should have gone to the Canadian side and got some drinks. The drinking age is eighteen over there."

Sara rubbed her belly. "No alcohol for me...but that lady's dinner over there smells incredible. What is that? Yeah, I think that's what I want."

"Fajitas, I think. Go for it. I'm getting theeeee..." Kyle perused the menu with his finger, "... the 'Open-Faced Sirloin Sandwich' sounds good."

Dinner was just as Kyle had hoped—the beginning of a fun, stress-free weekend where the two of them could relax and just be young and foolish. Not once did the topic of Sara's disease come up, and only briefly did they talk about the baby. For the most part they talked about art, music, friends, and their least favorite teachers. After the bill was paid, they left the napkin on the wall and hurried out back into the rain to watch cable TV at the hotel, knowing that they would probably make love instead.

Around 12 p.m., Kyle awoke in the disheveled bed to the sound of the roaring Niagara waterfall mixed with sniffles and feverish typing on his laptop.

"What's the matter, can't sleep?"

"Sorry," Sara said from the desk. Her back was to the bed, but the blue glow from the monitor lit her silhouette. "Yeah, I was thinking about stuff. I know I should relax until we meet with Dr. Anderson on Monday, but I was curious."

Sara wanted to know more about the disease she was suffering from, and so she had gone online to research it. As acceptance of her fate was slowly sinking in, she rebelled against the mystery of the disease. In characteristic defiance, she determined to know her opponent rather than let it afflict her in timid anonymity.

"Sara," he said, "stop looking at that stuff and come to bed. It was a long drive, and we got a lot to do tomorrow. I want to go on the Maid of the Mist. You can ride right up to the Falls and get soaked. It'll be a blast. Anyway, you can't trust anything on the internet."

"The Maid of the Mist isn't even open now."

"Of course it is. Where did you hear that?"

"Right here on this 'untrustworthy' website. It stops running in October. It's almost December. That means it's not running."

"Really? That stinks."

"Hey, check it out. There's a pub in Toronto called the 'Ferret and Firkin,' but it used to be called the 'Sticky Wicket.' Maybe they heard of your band. Where'd you guys get that name anyway?"

"I don't know. Jay came up with it. It means a difficult situation, a cricket reference, I think."

"Like the insect?"

"No, like English baseball, I think. Sooo... you coming back to bed?"

"This is interesting. I'm reading here that as the disease progresses the patient becomes paranoid, even suspicious. Your memory gets worse, and you can become very irritable. It says the patient will often hallucinate, and even hear things that aren't there. Isn't that freaky? I hope Dr. Anderson has stuff for that."

"Sara, c'mon. Come here." Kyle got out of bed to gently pull Sara away from the screen but she shook his hand off her shoulder.

"Stop it, I'm trying to read."

Kyle tried it again and got a slap on the hand. "Fine, have it your way." Kyle rested back on the bed. He almost made a joke about the 'irritable' part being right, but caught himself. Instead he said, "You know, I had to go through hell with your father to bring you up here. I told him we'd get separate rooms—not that it matters now—but I don't think he believed that one for a second. I think he was more upset about you taking a day off from school, and I'm thinking, 'what does it matter' well, my point is that I want you to have a good time and try to forget about things for now."

Sara clicked the computer mouse and leaned in to read the screen.

"Hello, anyone there? I said I'd like for you to forget about things and have a good time." By the movement of Sara's lips, Kyle could tell she was still reading, but he was determined to get her attention. "Sara, I probably should have told you sooner, but, I ate your cat... Sara, I'm a Russian spy... Sara, the bed's on fire!"

Sara yawned and said coolly to the computer screen, "What do you want me to forget about, Kyle, that I'm pregnant, or that I'm dying, or that even if I lived I'd be an unwed mother? Sorry, they're all kinda big deals. You can't just tighten a screw or change a filter to fix it. You shrug off your problems, but this can't be shrugged."

Kyle sat stunned for a moment at her coldness. She could have at least yelled at him for bugging her. No, instead she calmly rebuked him like a child. Feeling helpless Kyle then foolishly said, "Well, I can fix at least one of those."

"And what's that?" Sara clicked onto another website.

"I mean that you don't have to be 'unwed' if that's such a big deal to you."

"Is that so, Kyle? Are you asking me then?" A video began to play, but Sara stopped it and turned to Kyle.

"Um... Yeah....Sure, why not? I've always liked the *Chicken Dance*. We can have the reception at a Rock Café and my band can play too."

"Yeah, because it's not like you'd have to spend the rest of your life with me anyway. No, I don't think so, Kyle. I want a wedding, not a pity party, and that's the only reason you're saying this. You always tell me how we're such 'close friends', and so maybe that's how we should stay. And... and maybe we should have gotten separate rooms."

"But, you... I mean, you're having my kid, right?"

"Hey, anything for a friend." Sara turned back to the computer and un-paused the video. "Anything else I can do for you? Tuck you in, maybe?"

"Well jeez! Sorry for trying. I didn't mean to upset you. I do care about you and I... I want to help. So, what's with the attitude all of a sudden?"

Sara wasn't sure why she was feeling so irate, and didn't care to figure it out. After a moment she said toward the screen, "Well, what kind of guy proposes without a ring anyway? That's so unromantic."

"You don't need a ring to love someone, Sara." Kyle defended the ambiguous emotion he had seen in romantic movies.

"No, but you do need love, and so there's two things you can't give me. Lucky me."

"Look, I never said I didn't love you."

"You never said you did (at least not like you meant it)." Sara turned to him again and continued, "You know something, after all these years, you're still just a scared little boy, Kyle Hertz. You're afraid to love anyone because you might lose them like your parents. You're the world's orphan and everyone owes you an extra bowl of slop. Well, guess what, Oliver, you're going to lose me too, so why should I expect more?"

Kyle rolled over and pulled the covers up to his neck. "I'll be asleep if you need me."

Sara returned to the luminescent screen and raised the volume all the way—a better choice than throwing the computer at Kyle and storming out of the room. Neither noticed the tears of the other, nor the Niagara River falling and shattering upon hidden rocks below, colored by artificial lights of red, blue, and gold.

The next day was Saturday, and although they could not take a boat up to the Falls, they stood near a railing and watched it for a while in silence. The silence was not so much from contemplating the majestic wonder of the water fall, but from the unresolved argument the night before and wondering who would be the first to apologize?

"I was a jerk last night," Kyle said, "I'm sorry."

"Yes you were." Sara's gaze broke from the river to look him in the eye. "I was just trying to look something up and you practically assaulted me."

"Whoa!" Kyle backed away. "I gently grabbed your arm to bring you to bed. How is that an assault?"

"I didn't want to go to bed."

"Well yeah, I got that, but it wasn't 'assault'. But, don't worry, it won't happen again, you can count on it. Oh, and don't tell your brother (that jerk already wants to kill me)."

"Don't you call my brother a jerk."

"I just called myself a jerk too."

"Because you are."

"Whatever."

So went their sparse conversations throughout the day. The Canadian side of the falls which they visited afterwards could not aid their perspective; the Wonder Museum and its four-leafed clover exhibit could not help their luck, and the long ride home on Sunday where at least ten ballads played on the radio could not change their dower mood. When Kyle finally dropped Sara home, she grabbed her bags from the back seat, and said, "Thanks for the ride."

"See you Monday?" Kyle called out of the passenger window as she walked to her front door.

# ❋ Chapter 10 ❋

## FISHING THE LAKE OF FIRE

"A demon?!"

Nadine was shocked when Eduard informed her that evening of the priest's counsel. They sat in the living room together on a plush pink couch, a replica of popular French décor. With half a bottle of wine left between them, the two talked late into the night about Eduard's spiritual malady and his plans for the following week.

"I'm not sure I agree with the Father's advice," Nadine said, "but if it helps you feel better, then I suppose it's fine."

"What's not to agree with, dear? The man knows God better than anyone."

"What were you telling me about Job's companions the other day?"

"You shouldn't say that, Nadine. I need to believe this can work, to trust the Lord with all my heart, and lean not on my own understanding, in all of... in all of..." Eduard clenched his eyes as he thought. "I can't remember the rest of the verse!"

"Eduard!"

"See, I probably do have a demon."

Nadine stood to go to bed. Eduard reluctantly followed. As usual, Nadine fell fast asleep, but Eduard scanned with wide eyes the dark corners of the room for hours trying to spot any sign of demonic hosts released after midnight, bringing Saint George's Day to a frightening close. He then lit a candle and read more from the book of Job. Finally, he slid off of the bed onto his knees and prayed.

"Now I lay me down to sleep, I pray the Lord my soul to keep, and if I die before I wake, I pray the Lord my soul to take."

The prayer must have worked, because after getting back to bed, Eduard fell asleep. That was around 4:30 a.m.

In his sleep, Eduard dreamed that he was in St. Stephen's Cathedral. It was nearly empty, but Father Kraus was at the pulpit repeating a line from Dante's *Divine Comedy*.

"So full of sleep when you abandoned the true path! So full of sleep..."

Father Kraus lifted his hand, and pointed to Eduard in the back pew. Suddenly, Eduard found himself sitting in the front. He coughed on incense, and noticed it was coming from—

"Oh Ludwig," Eduard said, "I thought that was you up here."

Ludwig sat by the priest's feet with bloodshot eyes smoking the incense in his pipe. On his forehead was an accusation burned into the flesh by an angel who had taken a coal from an altar of burnt sacrifices.

"Thief?" Eduard read the accusation in horror. "No, no, no, it wasn't him, Father Kraus, it was all just a misunderstanding."

Ludwig picked at his forehead and put some skin in his pipe. The fragrant smoke became putrid. The peeled skin revealed his white skull, or was it marble?

"Father," Eduard continued, "What's going on? Why is Ludwig here? Why won't you talk to me? What did I do?"

Father Kraus pointed to a hole in the tile floor and said, "Descend!"

Eduard looked inside the hole and saw that there was a ladder made of bones. He hesitated, but was pushed in by one of the sanctuary's statues. Eduard felt the push from behind and wondered if it were one of the twelve Apostles? Perhaps it was a Mason upset about the removed tile? Maybe it was the ever-virgin herself?

When Eduard felt a good grasp of the ladder, he turned his head to see. Behold, it was a contemporary missionary named Clement Marie. Everyone in the city knew of him, but why was he so angry with Eduard? Why was he even here?

But, he's not even dead yet! Eduard thought, as he hung from the first rung of the ladder. Why is his flesh of marble? Why is everything becoming marble? Why? Why?! Eduard did not say these things aloud, nevertheless the missionary answered him.

"We're all dead, yet made of stone until we're broken. Wholeness is in the sanctuary of divine mercy. Now, descend and be broken, Eduard Strobl, that you might become a fixture in the Temple of Christ."

Eduard began to climb down, but the smell of flesh grew stronger. "What if I stay on the ladder?" he protested.

*"Their foot shall slip in due time,"* Father Kraus recited. Then the bones of the ladder became slippery with water and blood.

Eduard looked at the priest and back to the missionary. His heart raced. "But..." Eduard again sought to protest, but his footing faltered.

He lost his grip...

"Help!!!"

Eduard was falling quickly down the pit, passing layers of Hades, Gehenna, and Tarturus, catching glimpses of the damned. The lustful, the gluttons, the heretics, and the hypocrites whipped their heads only to see him disappear from sight.

"God help me!" he screamed, but the roar of fire was his only answer.

Despite the resistance of the air, his speed increased. Nothing could stop the force pulling him downward. His hair and cheeks flapped in the blistering wind. His eyes watered and his shirt frayed. His insides began to hurt and his bones crack.

At last, he crashed down upon the bottom and all his bones shattered.

"Broken!" Eduard cried out, believing his penance to be complete. "I am broken, Clement! Thank you, God!" He then waited to ascend and be ministered to by ravens and angels like the prophet Elijah. It was a terrible anguish to endure, but it was over as quickly as it had begun and was therefore, he concluded, well worth it.

"For our light and momentary affliction," Eduard stammered, "which is but for a moment, accomplishes for us a far more exceeding and eternal weight of glory." Eduard sighed in relief that he remembered these words from Saint Paul to the backslidden Corinthians. Even the Christ's cross was temporary, he reasoned, and though containing an eternal weight of sorrow was replaced with surpassing splendor. Yes, it was good to have gone through this ordeal and to have glimpsed the damned, but at last..."It is finished." He would now be laid in green pastures protected by the Shepherd's staff. Sleep, blessed sleep.

Suddenly he began to rise. However, he was not being carried up, but pulled upright by his wrists. Now standing, he began to walk involuntarily. Ropes attached to his arms and legs moved him down a dark tunnel which smelled of sulfuric rotten eggs. He could not see where he was going, but he walked onward.

"Wait!" he called out at the entrance, "This isn't the right way!" He wept as he travelled further and further into the darkness, and when he could weep no more, the echo in the tunnel kept the sad noises in his ear. Every gasp and sob remained with him as fresh as when it had been first sounded until frustration evoked more. At last, to overcome the noise, Eduard forced out a loud laugh, the echo of which caused more laughter until all around him was a strange mix of hell-induced weeping and hilarity.

After traversing miles of stony road, he saw a dim light. It grew brighter until at the mouth of the tunnel he saw molten waves crashing upon a beach of ash. Happily, he stepped out of the noisy tunnel. All was quiet except for the waves upon the infernal beach. The solace it brought tempted him to kiss the ash ground or dive into the water. Were he not restrained by the ropes, he just might have.

When Eduard heard the faint return of laughter, he became nervous and looked around for an escape. For sanity's sake, he could not return into the tunnel. But, it wasn't the tunnel from which the laughter came. He soon noticed that to the right of the mouth of the tunnel was an angel chained to a bolder much like the man at the Tower of Fools had been chained to the bench. It was Raphael, and he was being prodded and poked by a giggling goblin who took no notice of Eduard.

"There was nothing I could do," the archangel said to Eduard. "This is the way it must be accomplished."

"But, Raphael," Eduard pleaded, "You are the patron saint of healing. Please heal me!"

"I am."

"Is this then a dream?"

"It's time to go, Eduard. You will be saved, but only through fire."

"But, good angel, why do you allow that thing to hurt you so? If you cannot save yourself, how will you save me?"

"I restrain myself for its sake," said Raphael, "as the Lord of Hosts has done for you. I placed this chain upon myself as a reminder; otherwise I would smite this baneful irritation. And you, sir... are you not God's goblin?"

Eduard trembled. He frantically recited the prayer of Saint Gertrude the Great:

"O most holy angel of God, appointed by God to be my guardian, I give you thanks for all the benefits which you have ever bestowed on me in body and in soul..."

"Cease, Eduard!" the angle instructed. But, Eduard continued:

"... I praise and glorify you that you condescended to assist me with such patient fidelity, and to defend me against all the assaults of my enemies. Blessed be the hour—"

Eduard's prayer was cut short when the ropes turned him abruptly toward the sea, where a small black boat, like a Venetian gondola, awaited. Over the side of the boat, many worms crawled out and onto the shore. A headless man stood at the back with a long paddle clenched between coiled fingernails—nails which had not stopped growing since the day of his death. On a seat in front of the man was a fishing pole, a bait box and his shriveled head, its skin taut and leathery with white hair, which had also grown long since his death. The hair draped over the side of the boat where it was singed, otherwise it might have trailed the boat for miles.

On the shore near the boat was the beautiful and chaste Dymphna, the patron saint of sleepers, runaways and the insane. She had been murdered by her father in the seventh century in the heat of his passion and anger, but here she was a bulwark and a goddess. She wore a scarf around her head and a thick green dress—much too thick for the unbearable heat, but her sweat never broke. She was like ice in fire, a rose among weeds. The ropes moved Eduard forward to the bank, but the compulsion was unnecessary as he was already tugging at them to move toward her.

"Madam," he said when he reached her, "does your presence mean that I'm sleepwalking?"

"Behold!" the woman said, "Your legs move not of their own accord. All walk in sleep until awoken; all men are sleepwalkers, and every dawn begins in darkness. You must board the boat and become a 'fisher of men' or else be the worm they consume."

"Madam, does your presence mean that I'm in heaven?"

"If it is in you, then you are in it."

"But, who is that at the stern? Where will he take me? Why is his head removed?"

The saint explained, "In life his name was Damon. He was my father, but desired me as a wife after my mother died. I resembled her and he lusted for me. When I refused, he took off my head and took my body's virginity. My soul, however, floated above his thrusts, and looked on as surely as my head gazed from the table. I was not alone, however, but with the souls of my mother and a dozen others."

"But, I detect no hatred in your eyes," said Eduard, "no bitterness to speak of."

"To be sure," Dymphna said, "I watched above him with anger as he fulfilled his desires, until another soul approached me. It was a young boy. 'Mother,' he said, 'let your anger turn to pity.' To which I responded, 'I am no mother, as surely as my own mother stands here beside me.' The soul then pointed back to the earth below and said, 'No mother, for a fleeting moment your body conceived and your lifeblood fed me so that our Heavenly Father could raise me. I have, indeed, arisen. On earth I would have been to you both brother and son, but here I am only your eternal brother.' From that moment on, the boy referred to me only as 'sister' and 'friend' and a truer friend I have yet to find among men and angel."

Eduard was moved onto the boat for a journey that would last seven years. As he and the headless man set off from the beach, he asked Damon many questions, but his head never spoke, except as Dymphna disappeared from the horizon.

"Dearest daughter, I will love you always."

"Your head, sir?" Eduard said. "Is this the punishment for your crime, for decapitating her while yet alive?"

The head said nothing, but kept his gaze fixed on Eduard.

"Sir, are we almost there?"

Again, the head said nothing.

"Sir, what are these things below us?" Swimming in the infernal sea below were large fish with heads like men. They would rise to the surface, eject fire from their lungs, and then plunge back beneath.

As they moved into deeper water, Eduard saw another strange phenomenon on the water surface in the distance. The surface seemed to move. Perhaps a mirage from the heat—a trick of the eyes as the hot air waved and wiggled. They were approaching this mirage quickly, but it was not dissipating. Eduard could hear a hum accompanying the sight. It grew loud and methodic until Eduard discerned the voices of humans—millions of them.

At last, the boat was close enough for Eduard to see the cause of the illusion. Sticking up through the sea were millions of spears with flailing bodies upon them. They wiggled face up above the red cresting waves. They lifted their hands and praised a large beast in the sky above them, shouting, "Dragon! Dragon!" and some in Latin, "*Draco! Draco!*" Each was given the name '*draculea*' or 'son of the dragon.' It was difficult for the boat to navigate through these protrusions, and not a few times did Eduard feel a kicking leg or shuttering arm skim the singed hair on his head.

It was the ghastliest scene of inhumanity Eduard could ever have imagined (if he were inclined to imagine such things), and it was the only occasion when Damon provided any answers.

"Whatever could a man do to deserve such a fate?" asked Eduard.

The head coughed out a plume of dust. "Plunged through and above, neither beneath nor below. Saint George could ne'er salvage from this almighty lake and her patron serpent. Here the dragon claims his sacrifice. Here he pierces and bridles the daring and leads them as goats to a wellspring of disease. Yet, for all of this, these have been spared worse."

"Is the dragon bitter this night over the wound he suffered at Saint George's hand? Were these the company of the good Prince of Wallachia, Drakulya? Was not his impaling necessary? The zeal of righteousness?"

"They're the blessed ones who ne'er made it across. Pierced, but unconsumed."

Those were the last words the head would utter for a while. As his journey lingered on, Eduard began to despise the silent head, even attempting once to toss it in the sea along with his host in order to turn the boat around. The ropes, however, pulled Eduard back to his seat where he sulked again in silence.

"Sir," Eduard finally said after three years, "Have you been here since your death?"

The head said nothing.

"Sir," he asked after four, "do you ever sleep?"

The head said nothing.

"And how does your body move without being connected to your head...? Do you miss eating...? Have you tried stitches? Perhaps you can sew it back on. Fishing line might do the trick."

The head said nothing.

"Excuse me," he asked after five years, "but... oh, never mind."

The shock of the sea had worn off after years of travel, and Eduard even grew bored. The draculea would not speak to him either, so he began making a game out of spitting on their bodies to watch the saliva steam and bubble, but then this too grew old. Finally, he decided to try to catch one of the fish-men in the burning sea for companionship. Perhaps, he thought, a fish out of water would at least yell at him.

"Sir," he asked the head after six years, "can I borrow your pole and bait?"

Eduard didn't wait for an answer, but moved to the back of the boat, grabbed Damon's gear, and brought it to his seat. Thank God, he thought, the ropes had allowed this. He unlatched the hook from the third guide and opened the bait box. He took a worm from the box and hooked it through twice. His first cast got hung up on the ropes attached to his legs, but after untangling it, he cast the line again.

"Darn it!" Eduard reeled back in. He put another worm on.

"Darn it!" Eduard yelled after another disappointment. "Damon, did you ever catch one of these things? Come on, worm, stay still!" Again he baited the hook and cast into the sea.

After a few hours, the pole bent down and was nearly pulled from Eduard's hands. "Got one!" Eduard set the hook by pulling back quickly, then began to reel. The fight lasted for days but Eduard was not tired. The man-fish banged his head on the side of the boat and thrashed, but

Eduard leaned over the side, took hold of his gills and pulled it into the boat.

"Let me go!" the fish screamed and writhed. "I'll die."

"You want to go back into the fire?" Eduard said.

"Yes!"

"First, tell me your name." Eduard's heart raced with excitement over his new friend. Any creature that would talk to him he considered a friend.

"I have no name. I am a pit, a void, the destiny of all who come here. I will consume you and your name will perish from the Earth."

"Sorry, but I'm bound for the shore," Eduard said. "Were you once a man?"

Eduard pressed the fish for more, but it was no use, he was as silent as the head. At last, Eduard lifted the fish to the edge of the boat. He managed to push its top half over first, but while he got behind the tail end, it whipped its back, slashing Eduard's face, causing blood to splatter the water. A frenzy of tiny fish surrounded the boat in hopes of more, but left after a few hours. Eduard again sat silent, except one last time when he tried to turn the head away from him and got reprimanded.

"Don't!" is all it said.

\*\*\*

Only a minute had passed in Eduard's sleep, but in his dream he had reached the end of the seventh year, as well as the opposite shore. He fell to his knees when he left the boat, out of joy, and because his legs were weak from sitting so long. There, a skinny doctor with a long nose approached him in a red jacket.

"This way," the doctor said.

Eduard was mesmerized by his voice, even aroused. At last his loneliness had ended. The ropes pulled him up, and he followed the doctor from the beach and into a wooded area behind it. Not ten minutes later, a clearing in the forest appeared, and in it a merry coven. The sight pleased Eduard, for everyone was cheerful and naked.

"Where am I, doctor? Have I, at last, reached heaven?"

"It is not. It's all in your mind; careful analysis will show this. It's all here in my—oh, I forgot my journal again."

"Will I be okay?"

"Eduard," the doctor assured, "don't worry, everything will be fine."

"What's going to happen to me?"

"You'll feel a little pinch. That's all. It'll be over before you know it."

Just then, a boy approached the two. He looked to Eduard and spoke sweetly. "Hi daddy." The boy then turned to the doctor and complained of a sliver in his finger.

"Not to worry," the doctor said with a smile, "a simple procedure. Now turn your head and look toward the woods."

As the boy turned his head, the doctor pulled from his bag a black powder pistol and shot him in the temple. After holstering his pistol again, the doctor continued, "Alright, Eduard, I have to find that journal of mine, so you stay here and I'll be back." He then stepped over the boy, and headed into the woods.

Eduard leaned down to get a closer look at the child, but was pulled back by the ropes to join the festive gathering.

In the woods, he saw thousands of torched marionettes dancing in a circle around the perimeter of the clearing. He pushed through the crowd and into the center of the ritual where a deep pool of maggots squirmed to the amusement of the taunting spectators. He then noticed that above the pool hung a marionette. It screamed and strove to break free. Finally, its ropes were cut, and it dropped into the pool to the applause of all. Then another from the crowd was lifted up and dangled over the pool until he too was cut loose.

One after another, these puppets from the crowd were lifted and dropped in similar fashion, yet for each one lost, another arrived on the shore. Immeasurable time passed for Eduard until he also began to find the whole scene amusing. After thousands of marionettes were disposed of, he began to cheer along. In his hysterics, he ripped off his clothes and absorbed the freedom around him. He wondered why the pool was never satiated and now hoped it never would be. But, he then felt a tug at his own ropes and looked around.

"Doctor, is that you?"

Eduard was suddenly lifted high into the air. His stomach sank. He struggled to break free, but the ropes became so tangled that he could no longer move his limbs. Now hanging helplessly over the pool, Eduard cried out, "*Eloi, Eloi, lema sabachthani?*" to which came a whisper in his ear, "*Why do you seek the living among the dead?*" Eduard's ropes were then cut. Dropping from over a hundred feet, he now became entangled in fear.

He screamed as he flailed through the air, awaiting the hungry maggots. However, when he plunged into the pool, the maggots did not consume him. No, the maggots merely entered him. His sinuses, eyelids, and tear ducts bulged at their filling, making it hard for him to breathe or close his eyes. The pores in his cheeks were invaded, as were his ears and lower regions. Even his lungs filled when he tried to breathe. However, his flesh was not dead, and so the maggots had nothing to eat. They merely positioned themselves for the inevitable.

Eduard swished around in the churning caldron, flapping his arms to swim to the surface. But, an unbearable hunger developed, causing him a sudden change of direction. He now struggled with the maggots to reach the bottom of the pool where he sensed food and the smell of Ludwig's flesh tobacco.

When he reached the bottom, what he thought was a pit turned out to be, in fact, a deep hole. The hole was so crammed with worms that they were suspended, but now at the bottom, he dropped from the ceiling of one realm into a wasteland—the bottom of hell, or at least that was what was written on a charred sign.

"Hath God said, 'an abyss without end'?" said the most beautiful creature Eduard had ever laid eyes on. It was an angel of sorts, but more beautiful than Raphael and Dymphna combined. It stood two stories high, and had three faces, but spoke with one voice. It was both male and female, god and animal, and wore only a thin black robe over its androgynous frame. Its eyes were pearls, and its crown an intricate weave of gold vines.

"May I look at you," Eduard said, "...forever?"

The creature patted Eduard's head. "Someday. For now, survey my estate. This will all be yours."

Eduard looked out and viewed boundless desolation. When he looked back, the creature was far away, herding goats to itself—allowing the youngest to nurse from its many breasts. Craving milk, Eduard tried to run after it, but was only able to crawl. He looked down to see if his legs were still wrapped in rope, hoping he might untangle himself, but when he viewed his body, he saw that it was long, yellow, and wiggling. He had no arms or legs, but was rather a tubular form.

His hunger now returned greater than ever. Instinctively, he pushed himself along the soot and the yellow, crystalline brimstone until he found food. It was the body of a German woman. Did he know her? Maybe, but he was hungry. She cried out for a man named 'Eduard,' but he was no longer him. Crawling up upon her ankle, he fought his way past others down to her foot, where he began to gnaw her carcass until it looked as though she had melted.

The blood that pooled around his dining area reflected a macabre image. His face was no longer his own, but that of a maggot. Yet, he cared not, for hunger drove him on for all eternity, from body to body. As he and his companions gorged themselves, a chant accompanied by a great iron bell repeated itself in the air, "*Vermis eorum non morietur! Their worm shall not sleep!*" Thus he remained for thousands of years, forgetting who he was and any memory of his past life.

At last, a large hand picked him up, and placed him in a dark box with others, where he remained for another thousand years. He wiggled around in the box, crawling under and over the others, and even made friends with one, though they could not talk. Finally the roof of the box opened and light appeared. His friend was taken, and the box soon closed again. Then, outside the box he heard a familiar voice.

"Darn it!" it said. It seemed more than the curse of frustration, but of prosecution.

After this, the ceiling of the room opened again. The large hand now grasped him and removed him from the box. He looked around and saw the lake of fire, the edge of a boat, and a man without a head. The more he struggled to get free, the tighter the hand's grip became. Finally, he twisted his body enough to see who was holding him.

I know that man, he thought.

"Damon," the man holding him said, "you ever catch one of these things?" After this the man addressed him personally. "Come on worm, stay still!"

"No, don't do it, Eduard!" the worm shouted in his mind. Then a hook attached to a line pierced his abdomen and he was cast by his own hand into a fiery lake to be devoured by one of the fish-men he had seen when he first arrived. While in its mouth he saw his friend, the other worm that had been lost. It motioned for him to come near and so with great effort he writhed to the other side of the mouth where the other wrapped itself around him as if to protect him.

Soon the mouth opened and the two fell out into the boat while the fish argued with the one on board. His friend brought him to other to end of the boat where a headless man sat. They crawled into a nook in the wood where they stayed for years until the fisherman was dropped off, and the headless man returned to where he had begun his journey.

When the boat ran ashore on the ashy beach, the other worm now led him onto the edge of the bow. There the two were picked up by the hand of the angel Raphael who said, "Eduard, your penance is complete, as is your companion's. The goblin no longer taunts, and the chain will no longer bind. Your hunger shall be filled."

Eduard wanted to ask about the other worm: What was his name? Why did he help? Would they both be restored? But, all he could do was lie helpless in the angel's arms and be carried back through the tunnel and up the pit he had first fallen down. By the time he arrived back at Saint Stephen's Church it was empty. But, no! It was filled. However, everyone had turned to marble to remain forever situated in the company of saints.

"I'm tired," Eduard thought, "but what can I do?"

"You have now arrived at the house of God," said Raphael, "where the worm *does* sleep. The same prophet has spoken, saying:

'The righteous perish, and no man takes it to heart: and merciful men are taken away, none considering that the righteous is taken away from the evil to come. He shall enter into peace: they shall rest in their beds, each one walking in his uprightness.' *Requiescat in pace*, Eduard. Surely, you and your companion may now rest in peace."

Eduard and the other worm crawled to the foot of a statue and fell asleep facing east, while Raphael continued to chant with a tolling tenor bell, "Réquiem æternam dona ei, Dómine. Et lux perpétua lúceat ei. Eternal rest grant unto him, O Lord. And perpetual light shine upon him."

# ❄ Chapter 11 ❄

## SUPPORT

Sara slammed the door when she got in the house, causing the nearby key rack to fall. "Aghhh!" she yelled.

Her parents were watching television as usual, but her mother came to the foyer. "You're home! Everything okay, honey? How was your weekend with Kyle?"

Sara threw her scarf on the floor next to her shoes and the key rack. "Why are guys such idiots?!"

"Things didn't go well?"

Sara's jacket joined the scarf in the pile. "It was horrible."

"What happened?"

"I told you we shouldn't have let her go," Sara's dad called from the other room, "but no one wants to listen to me. That Kyle is bad news; I've said so from the start."

"Do you want to go upstairs and talk?" her mother continued gently.

Sara rubbed her forehead to ease a developing headache. "It's okay, mom. I'll be fine. I'll be upstairs."

\*\*\*

"Hold on, it's the cops." Kyle quickly concealed his phone in his lap as he drove home after dropping Sara off. After passing the police, he put the phone back to his ear. "You still there, bro?"

"Yeah, dude," Steve answered, "just putting new strings on my bass. So what's up? How was the weekend?"

"Man, that girl is nuts. I don't get it. You try to do something nice and it never pays."

"That's why I'm single. Did she complain all weekend?"

"I mean, it started out alright, but then she got all moody and offended at everything, and I was like 'someone kill me already! Anyway, did you guys work on the mix this weekend?"

"Yeah. Sounds alright. Needs some solo dubs when you get a chance. Maybe tomorrow?"

"Maybe. I was thinking of going to the hospital with Sara, but I'm not sure anymore. But, next time I'm over I'll lay down a track or two.

"Music will never whine or complain. Priorities, man, priorities."

"Yeah, I know. Anyway, I'll see ya later. I think I see another cop up ahead... Ugh! I'm being pulled over. Alright, talk to you later, bro."

# ❄ Chapter 12 ❄

## EDUARD'S FIRST DAY OFF:
## THE FASCINATING STRANGER

Nearing 7:00 a.m. Eduard awoke in a cold sweat to the sound of Nadine and the children downstairs eating breakfast. After catching his breath he stretched his limbs in relief, "Today, sweet psalmist, *I am a man and no worm, the doe in the morning.*"

As he leaned up, his Bible slipped off his chest onto the bed beside him. He picked it up and reread a passage in Job from the night before: 'Am I the sea, or the monster of the deep, that you set a watch over me? When I said my bed will comfort me and my couch will ease my complaint, even then you frighten me with dreams and terrify me with visions.'

Eduard sighed, put the book down, and got up. After relieving himself in the bed pan, he rinsed his face off with (what he thought was) the other pan of water on the table near the window, and went downstairs for some bread and tea.

"Have a good day at school," Eduard said as Anna and Julia shut the front door. "Do you think perchance they're still angry with me?"

"They're fine," Nadine said. "I'm sure their classmates have long forgotten about Saturday... You smell peculiar, dear."

"I do hope they forget."

"Pay no mind," Nadine said as she cleared the table, "they're children, they'll recover. Adversity builds character. So, what have you planned for your first day of vacation in what?... Ten years?"

"I'm not quite sure, but I think I'd like to finish that wood burning picture I began a while ago."

"Splendid, I was so hoping you would someday. So much secreted talent; it's a pity to keep it so. *No one lights a candle to put under a bowl.* Let me fix you some breakfast."

After a half hour, Eduard gathered together from the back of the closet a pointed metal utensil and a flat plank of wood with an image of Christ on the left reaching out to nowhere. In the nowhere was to be an image of an open tomb, and a man coming forth wrapped in funeral dressing. The finished part was done by the fireplace, and Eduard decided that since it was a nice day, he would take a hike up a nearby hill overlooking the city, make a fire, and enjoy the solitude of nature's sanctuary.

It was a ten minute walk to reach the hill. Eduard stopped once to talk to a client who was unhappy to hear that Eduard was taking a whole week off for himself. Eduard reassured him that Ludwig was more than competent, but the client was nevertheless perturbed. After that, Eduard stifled the cursing under his breath, and walked the rest of the way. When he reached the base of the hill he sat to rest.

"No, I'm fine, thank you," Eduard said to a man descending the hill, "just a little short of breath. Yes, beautiful weather. Good day, sir."

Eduard at last reached the summit and looked out over the sprawling city. So full of culture and architectural genius was his beloved metropolis, demonstrated chiefly by the grand Tower in his foreground. His nerves calmed, the complaints of his clients dissipated, and for the first time in a while he felt near to Heaven.

He looked around for kindling, and found logs left in a camp fire from others. They were burnt, but mostly whole. With a few trips, he grabbed some old coal to draw with, and relocated the wood and rocks to the place he had been before. It was a better view, and more conducive to creativity. He had forgotten to take flint with him, but after a few minutes of rubbing sticks together, the dry pine needles ignited under the small branches. Soon, the larger sticks caught, and then the logs. It was a perfect fire, and would be hot enough for his utensil in no time.

The rough coal drawing was coming along well, and Eduard enjoyed the solitude. Because it was a weekday, there were few disruptions from others—only the occasional hiker, or young lovers looking for a secluded place in the forest. Eduard greeted them politely as they passed.

"I say, what a fascinating illustration," said one particular woman as she strolled by with three rambunctious boys. She had blonde hair that had been hurriedly pinned up, and wide blue eyes as youthful as her brood. Her figure and dress were immaculate, and the breeze spread her wisteria scent throughout the woods. Her children ran around the hillside after blue butterflies, but the woman came closer.

"Thank you ma'am," replied Eduard. "It's been a while since I've worked on it, but I think it's coming along well."

"Is this how you earn a living?"

"Oh no, I am an accountant in the city. I assist mostly landowners, equestrians, and other businesses in the area... a bookkeeper of sorts."

"What a fascinating profession."

"I suppose. Keeps food on the table and allows me to live in the city."

"I see. We live in the country, about thirty minutes from here, but we love to visit when we can."

"Yes, well enjoy your visit; beautiful day for a stroll."

Eduard turned back to his work while the woman checked on her children. He expected her to hurry after them but instead she looked back at Eduard, then leaned her head in to observe his progress.

"So does your wife fancy the city?"

Eduard was flattered by the inquiry. He never said he was married, so he reasoned she was either a widow, or divorced and looking for a suitor—she was clearly not dressed for hiking through the woods. "Yes," he said, "I think she does, ma'am, thank you for asking. My children enjoy it too. We actually live in the outer Alsergrund district on the edge of the busy Innere Stadt, where I work. The inner city is fine, but can be a bit crowded for the family. Nadine, well she likes the bustle—always been a bit adventurous. One time she even—"

"Fascinating," the woman interrupted, "I'm not sure I could live here myself."

It was a lie, thought Eduard, for never was there a woman who would rather live in the country than in the vorstädte. Vienna's suburbs were envied by the world as much as the city itself. But, he accepted her gracious way of ending the conversation and bid her farewell.

She called to the children and they would all continue on the path, but not before Eduard fixed a final glimpse of her. He turned his head quickly as she turned back, but she caught his eye, and smiled. His blushing cheeks gave away any pretension of gentlemanly innocence, but to his relief she was soon just a distant voice reprimanding three energetic boys for hitting each other with sticks.

"Oh Lord, forgive me," Eduard prayed quietly. "I didn't want to look. But, that's a lie, because I did. Forgive me for lying, for lusting in my heart. How will I ever escape the long purging flames of Purgatory? Truly, I am a worm and no man."

An hour had passed and the embers in the fire were glowing, as was the memory of the woman in the woods. Satisfied with his outline, he moved over to the fire, stuck the long pointed metal utensil in the midst of the coals, and once again stared out into the city. To the left was the Danube River, which he planned on visiting later in the week, and straight ahead in the distance were steeples—one of which belonged to St. Stephen's.

"Hail Mary, full of grace!" he said, followed by a few 'Our Fathers'. Last of all, he prayed the prayer his priest had taught him to pray before going to bed. The prayer must have worked, for he soon drifted asleep.

When Eduard awoke half an hour later, the fire before him was still burning, but steamy, and the charcoal drawing he had just finished was dripping from a light rain. The thunder around him, however, was heavy and echoed through the city. Lightning struck a metal pole relentlessly atop the Narrenturm tower. This pole was placed upon the tower to transfer electricity to the facility's newest electroshock devices. In the British Colonies, Benjamin Franklin had invented the lightening rod in 1753, but a year later in a small garden in Primetice, about ninety-two kilometers north of Vienna, a Czech inventor named Prokop Divis had developed this technology. Ever the one for innovations, Joseph II implemented it at the Fool's Tower soon after.

"*Soli Deo Gloria*," he said in reverence as he tossed the plank into the fire, leaving the hand of Christ beckoning nothing but the hopeless Tower in the distance. How presumptuous of him, he thought, to attempt a depiction of the Lord; how proud he had been of his ability to capture God on wood as though He were a landscape, a gull, or a cathedral.

By now it was almost lunchtime, but Eduard was not hungry, so he wandered off into the woods behind him to look for the woman. What was he to do when he found her? He hadn't thought that far ahead. He spent the better part of the afternoon listening for her. He often heard her voice saying this or that was 'fascinating,' but was disappointed when his search ended fruitlessly. At last, he abandoned the hunt, but it took him nearly two hours to find his way back to the trail and the fire he had left burning. By that time his picture was severely charred but still recognizable, and he regretted his hastiness. He picked up the picture by one of the cooler corners and carefully walked the trail down the hill toward home

\*\*\*

"You're not hungry?" Nadine said later at the dinner table.

"No, not really."

"Does that mean we don't have to eat?" Julia said, hoping to find relief from the fermented cabbage.

"No, your father will eat later; he's just a tad weary now. Finish what's on your plate."

Eduard stared at his own cabbage, listening to the argument. "Finish your food, Julia."

"Dear," Nadine said, "how did... Eduard!"

Eduard looked up quickly from his plate.

"How did your wood-burning come out today? Were you able to finish it?"

"The wood-burning? Oh yes... I mean, no. I mean that I still have some work to do on it, but it's coming along just grand. It's really, um... fascinating."

"That's wonderful, dear."

Eduard knew that Nadine would not understand (or at least support) the religious zeal that led him to surrender the wood-burning to the flames, and figured he would save himself the trouble of explaining it. She was devout in her own way, but did not share the intensity of his religious fervor. As for himself, he would begin tomorrow by rekindling a new flame of zeal, which would assuredly result in the Lord's rest. And, as for the picture, it ended up back in the closet, covered with a blanket.

# ❄ Chapter 13 ❄

## PRIONS

"I'm sorry I ruined the weekend." Sara took Kyle by the hand in the doctor's waiting room Monday afternoon. The two hadn't spoken all day, but Kyle showing up at the doctor's office was enough for Sara to put the it all behind her, especially since he brought her chocolates. She needed him to be there, and the thought that he would still be upset and so stay away devastated her. It was the first day of December, joyful Christmas music played from the receptionist's radio, and Sara's parents sat stoic, skimming through magazines.

"You didn't 'ruin' the weekend, Sara," Kyle whispered, "I just wanted you to enjoy yourself. But, if you feel that bad, we can always go back. It was beautiful wasn't it?"

"Yeah, it really was."

"So," Kyle said, "after we finish up here I want to take you out to dinner."

"That's sweet of you, but let's see how this goes. I may just want to go home."

"Fair enough. These places creep me out. Oh, here he comes."

Dr. Anderson walked into the waiting room and greeted the family. He then escorted them into a room where he had a file full of information and pictures. The family sat down, except Sara's mother who was so nervous she preferred to stand. It was her feeble attempt to combat the feeling of lost control.

"Now, I need to explain this to you," the doctor said, "and though it's not easy to hear, it's important that you know so you can prepare yourselves for what might come."

"We understand, Dr. Anderson." Kyle said and nodded along with Sara.

Sara's father shot him a look.

"I already know a lot, doctor," Sara said. "I read about phobias, and panic attacks, and worse."

"Well, I'm not sure what you've read," Dr. Anderson said, "or where you read it, but that part—"

"I told her not to trust those sites," Kyle interrupted.

"Listen," Sara's father said impatiently, "just let the doctor speak."

After an excruciating pause, Dr. Anderson continued. "Well then, let me begin by showing you the picture from your cat scan." Dr. Anderson took a picture from his file of one the many tests Sara had undergone and placed it on a lighted board upon the wall. He pointed out one area of the picture and said, "Do you see this region of the brain? That is the region of the thalamus, which regulates sleep. You'll notice here that there is a blotch. That's the beginning of a protein buildup similar to what occurs with *Bovine Spongiform Encephalopathy*."

"I'm sorry, what?"

"'Mad Cow Disease,' Mr. Riley. Now, what happens is that insoluble proteins—or rather a plaque-like buildup of prions—clump up in the brain and destroy nerve cells. You see, most proteins 'fold' one way, but prions can fold two ways. When a prion mis-folds, or mutates, it takes on the properties of a virus; however, unlike a virus you can't kill a prion because it's not alive. You can get rid of them with bleach, but there's no safe way to administer that; and *formalin* (which has been tried before) only makes it worse, as does alcohol. Inducing a coma is also dangerous and in the end doesn't stop the disease."

Sara's mother pulled at the top of her blouse to cool down. "I need to sit." Kyle tried to bring her to a chair, but she refused his help and so became the pale and reluctant center of attention for about five minutes until her breathing calmed and color returned.

"I know this is difficult on everyone," the doctor said, "and diseases like this one can really strain emotions and relationships. But, you're all in this together. Sara needs all the support you can give, and not one person can give all of it. You all need to try a for Sara's sake. Now, there's much more I need to explain."

Sara's eyes stayed upon the doctor. "Thank you, Dr. Anderson. Please go on."

"You're very courageous, Sara," replied the doctor, "and I'm telling you all of this so that you can get the correct information. Now, some symptoms are common to all sleep disorders," Dr. Anderson explained, "but insomnia is the most common 'disorder'—actually it's usually a symptom itself of something else—and nearly sixty-four million Americans suffer from it on a regular basis. It can lead to restlessness, fatigue, jumbled thoughts, and anxiety. Weight loss and loss of appetite can also occur, immunity to other illnesses lessens, memory loss occurs, and the ability to make decisions decreases.

"Depression, hypertension, increased cortisol levels, high blood pressure, and slurred speech are also things you may experience, though not necessarily all at once. You may also suffer rebounds of R.E.M., and therefore dream more when you do sleep. Again, it's important to remember that you are your own person, and that you may not suffer the same symptoms as someone else, but I'm running down this list so that you're not caught off guard."

"I appreciate that doctor," Sara said. Then in another spirited attempt at optimism she said, "I suppose it could be worse."

Dr. Anderson smiled, and didn't contradict her, but he knew that this disease would ravage not only her body, but also her mind, that the prions would enmesh themselves into her until they were at one with the host, that she would likely suffer all of them and to such a degree that most people could never comprehend. If she survived the entire span of the disease, she would be left as a mere shell of a girl—a cathartic soul trapped behind glazed eyes without the ability to speak or express her pain, but fully aware of her situation. He knew that her plunge into this bizarre torture had just begun.

# ❄ Chapter 14 ❄

## EDUARD'S SECOND DAY OFF:
## THE DANUBE

After two hours of sleep the previous night, Eduard went downstairs and sat by himself in the dark hours of dusk.

On the wall in the dim moonlight, Eduard gazed at a musket with a bayonet that was mounted over the mantle. It had been used by his grandfather in the War of Quadruple Alliance at the turn of the 18th century, and oh how the old man loved to talk about it. The war spanned to the far ends of the earth such as Pensacola, Florida, but the worst of it was on European soil. Over eleven-thousand Austrians were either killed or wounded fighting the Spanish over their right for self-governance, including his grandfather who had lost his hand due to an infection. His fingers were shattered by a musket ball, and a piece of wadding stuck to the muddy round imbedded itself. Over the course of a week his hand turned greenish black and had to be removed.

"Prime and load!" Eduard could still hear his grandfather yell as he told one of his many war stories. "Cartridge!" his commander would instruct the line of soldiers, "Prime!" and the men would pour powder in a small pan near the trigger, "About!" and the young men poured the rest of the cartridge powder along with the ball and wadding into the barrel, "Ramrods!"

"And let me advise you, young man," his grandfather said, "when he yelled 'Ram!' you better be sure you had that pole in the barrel and be packing it down, cause if the Spanish didn't kill you, your commanding officer would. And, don't go in half-cocked. No, after you prime it, then you cock it all the way back, like this..." The boy sat at his grandfather's feet mesmerized while he demonstrated it. "Ram!" his grandfather yelled, forcing the long pole down the barrel. "Present!" he yelled again, and in a flash of rigid discipline the butt of the rusted and unloaded gun was up to his shoulder, aimed at the boy's face. "Fire!"

Eduard remembered the strange feeling he had when his grandfather yelled this last command. Up until that point his heart had been racing, and when he looked down the barrel of the gun he envisioned a lead ball exploding from the end and into his head. Even though he knew it was not loaded, nor was there any primer on the pan, it was still thrilling. However, at the command to fire, the boy's heart calmed. He looked for the pulling of the trigger, but found only a stub at the end of his grandfather's wrist.

His grandfather put the musket down and smiled. "Did I alarm you, boy?"

"No sir."

"No?"

"Sir, your hand."

His grandfather looked down at his stubbed wrist and laughed. "Well, I suppose I should have used my bayonet."

His grandfather then sat back down in his chair and motioned for Eduard to sit on his lap.

Eduard rested his head on his grandfather's shoulder. The thought of people killing and making war, especially his grandfather, did not so much sadden him as it did confuse him. "Did you really shoot a man?" he asked.

"I wouldn't know," replied his grandfather, "they just had us line up in a row and fire in the general direction, hoping for the best. Never can tell where the balls ended up. First the front would shoot, fall back, then the second row would move up, and so on. Rumor has it that the English are working on a two row technique. Less kneeling involved. Not sure why we don't use the riffled barrels and just hide in the woods, but what do I know?"

Eduard's fond memory was interrupted by a knock on the front door. He got up and walked over to turn the handle, but stopped.

"Who is it...? Hello. I say, may I help you?"

Perhaps it was just the wind. Eduard sat back down and looked back at the musket. His eyes then fell to the mantle where off to the right sat a cornice plane. It was a carpenter's tool for shaving and shaping crown molding. It was his father's, and had cost him a good deal of money. However, in the years that passed, he was able to make a handsome profit by exporting his work to other parts of Europe, as well as Vienna, where he eventually moved his family. Although Eduard had picked up tips and skills from his father over the years, he had no desire to advance in the carpentry profession, and so placed this tribute on the mantel when his father died six years prior.

Again Eduard heard a knock on the door and went to answer it.

"Hello?" Again, there was no answer. Eduard then went to a window to look around, but there was not a soul to be found, so he sat once again.

On the opposite side of the mantel was a top. This was not any ordinary top, but one that whistled when spun. The rounded body was green with a hole cut in the side for the wind to pass over, and the stem on top was red. Attached to it by a string was a fashioned stick that one pulled in order to set the top in motion. It was given to him by the son of a client whom Eduard had helped out of financial trouble years ago. The father could not pay for Eduard's accounting services and the son overheard his parents arguing about it one night.

The boy came to Eduard's office with his only toy to offer. Eduard tried to give it back, but the boy refused. Later that day Eduard dropped it off at the boy's house and talked to his parents. The father broke down in front of his wife. Eduard felt sorry for the man and not only wrote off their payment, but lent them money of his own. Later that year, after the family was back on their feet, they moved to the country somewhere, but they left on Eduard's door an envelope of cash they owed him and next to the envelope was the green top.

"My word!" said Eduard to himself when he heard another knock at the door. "Hucksters, no doubt." This time he crept to the door and opened it quickly and found the sun peeking over the horizon. He walked out and around the house but saw no sign of footprints. He then reentered his house and closed the door, standing by it for a few minutes with his hand on the knob, but not another knock was heard. Again he took a seat.

Light began to beam through the easterly windows; the pale orange and pink glow revealed specks of dust floating in the air. In his mind, the dust took the shape of his wife.

"I don't understand it, Nadine," Eduard whispered to the dust. "I just want to lie in bed next to you... like before—even if waking in the night, I could perceive you breathing, dreaming, basking in twilight's calm. Now night becomes as day."

"Ah, there you are." Nadine said as she came down the stairs in her nightgown. "I thought I heard something down here."

Eduard was startled. "Oh, was that you knocking upstairs?"

"No, not me, maybe one of the children. What's going on?"

"I'm leaving, dear."

Nadine laughed. "Was it something I said?"

"No," Eduard said, "I just have to get out of here. Been sitting all night, need to go somewhere else."

"Where to?"

"Not sure, maybe inscribe my journal by the river... take a nap." Eduard slapped his knees and stood.

"Did you sleep well last night?"

"Grand. Never better."

Eduard put on a light jacket and hat, and then grabbed a quill pen, ink, and a journal, which like the wood-burning he had neglected for years.

"Very well, my dear, I'll miss you." Nadine waited for Eduard's kiss goodbye, but he walked out the door with other things on his mind.

After a fifteen-minute walk, Eduard arrived at the Danube. Even at such an early hour, it was busier than the hill and forest, with pedestrians walking the bank, swallows cutting through the air, and boats traveling along the waterway. All of this added to a charm that neither Homer nor Isiod could tell, though they had certainly tried. He passed a group of painters carefully trying to capture with oil the twisting and winding waters that surged into the Lobau floodplain. He admired their work, hoping also to pick up a few pointers.

"It's not green, sir, it's chartreuse," one student replied to Eduard's question.

"And this one?"

"Turquoise."

"Fascinating," returned Eduard, "and that brush you're using, what's that called?"

"A knife, sir."

"Alright then, carry on, young man."

At last, Eduard sat in the chartreuse grass and admired the cobalt blue, turquoise, and silver river before him. He waved to a group of fishermen passing by in a small boat. They saluted back with raised glasses of wine and a recently caught sturgeon. The sturgeon also appeared to wave.

It was not uncommon to see people drinking in public, or even on the job, for clean water was not as easily come by nor as convenient to carry as a bottle of cheap wine. Of course, canteens and jugs were filled from wells, and used for drinking, washing, and boiling, but unless one wanted to frequent a well for fresh water, or drink the warm insipid water that hung around in a jug for the day, or even take a chance with the river's water, it was preferable (particularly for a fisherman) to keep a bottle of wine around, or else another liquor to add to one's water.

Eduard had taken neither wine nor water with him, but was not thirsty or eager for an intoxicant. Hoping to keep his mind clear for prayer he drank nothing, but raised an imaginary toast back to the men. Then undoing the ties of his journal, Eduard laughed as he read to himself one gushing entry:

"The wedding will be held at St. Stephen's Cathedral in the afternoon. We're expecting many guests. It's very late, can't sleep, thinking about Nadine. How can I describe her? She is my *regis* and I her *rex*. She is a snowflake; no other resembling her singular beauty. She caught me with her penetrating eyes like a fish on a golden hook. She destroys me with the most blissful agony, an edifice torn asunder.

"How will it feel to make love for the first time? Is it right to wonder such things? Will I die when I touch her, as Uzza was smote when he reached out to the arc of the Lord? Surely it will be a most pleasant demise (forgive me, God). Will I find myself panic stricken in the inferno, or in God's cool garden covered with the dew of Paradise, her Tigris running like a river over fertile land to spill into the sea. Turbulent waters to quench my thirst like crystal cataracts down sturdy mountains. No, rather I will ascend to the very bell tower of heaven's cathedral to be fed by seraphim.

"It is difficult not to think about her, I have done so often since we made acquaintance at my uncle's farewell party. He took leave for the 'new world,' and I discovered my own in his yard. We were so youthful then, keeping in contact through letters and brief meetings for the ten sore years when she returned to Germany, leaving me torn asunder like flailing tapestry in a frigid storm. But, the warm wind of change has now blown my way, and our banner is united again in a woven union of silk skin, divine magic, and the dizzy craze of unrefined affection. It was a miracle that she refused so many suitors before me. My candle is low now (as is my ink), but tomorrow I will be lying next to Nadine, the occupation of my dreams from this day onward."

Eduard laughed and turned randomly to another old entry of his journal.

# ❄ Chapter 15 ❄

## DAYDREAMERS

A few days had passed since Kyle, Sara, and her parents had visited the doctor. Kyle was trying not to let it depress him and so focused more attention on his music. Music was the only thing that had saved him from debilitating depression when his parents had died, and it had been there for him ever since as a panacea, or at least an anesthetic. He took Thursday off from work and stayed in his room all day to practice scales and chords, and in the afternoon went to band practice. Steve's cousin, Brian, was coming to observe the band that day, and so Kyle tried to concentrate on playing well.

"I love it. Loud and melodic, you guys really got something here. I'm impressed." Brian nodded his head in approval after listening to Sticky Wicket play their five original songs in Jay's basement. "I especially like that tune... what was it called? *Never Grow Old.*

"Thanks man," Kyle said as he retuned his guitar. "I just wrote that a few weeks ago. You think it's alright?"

"Yeah! You should hear some of the junk bands send me. This is actually pretty professional sounding, especially for your age. I've signed bands with a lot less talent than this, and they've done pretty well. You guys could be hot. You got the whole dark thing with a fun edge. It's working, man, really working. And, this guy here,"

Brian pointed to the singer, Mark, with his thumb, "man, the chicks are gonna dig him."

"Well, we appreciate you coming by," Steve said. "I told these guys you'd like it. So what's the next step? Where do we sign?"

Brian put his sunglasses back on. "I gotta talk to my partner, Bruce, first. I gave him a copy of your demo and he liked it, which is good for a dude who's mostly into metal and prog, but he's going to want to see you guys play a show, see how you work a crowd. See, it's all about live performance these days with all the file sharing and streaming on the web. Concerts and merchandise are where the money is at, and that's what a label is looking for. If you can't put on a good show, it's a waste of time."

"Dude," Jay said from behind the drums, "We rock live! Won the last two battle of the bands at school. Did a crazy light show with strobes, lasers, and dry ice."

"I don't think they care about that, Jay," Kyle said. "High school is for kids. This is adult stuff, man."

"No, that's cool," Brian said, "I can respect that. It shows you're competitive. I like that. But, Bruce is a tough nut to crack, and yeah, he's gonna want to see you at a club with an older crowd that's not just your friends. Not that you can't invite friends, of course."

"We've played a few clubs already," Steve said, "that won't be a problem, bro."

"Great. You guys book some shows, and let me know your schedule, and I'll talk to Bruce."

After Brian left, the four band mates looked back and forth at each other in disbelief until Mark finally yelled into his microphone. "Ladies and gentlemen, the hottest band in the land: Stickyyyyyy Wicket!!!"

The other guys started screaming like a crowd. This was followed by a cacophony of guitar, bass, and drum solos filling the imaginary stadium while Mark provided the sound of various pyrotechnic explosions:

"Boom!

Buuuush!

C'boom!

Get your hands in the air! I wanna hear you scream for me!"

"Hey! Hey! Hey!" The room came to a sudden halt when Jay's dad came into the room waving his arms in the air.

"Oh hey, Dad." Jay quickly dampened the ring of his cymbals. "What's up?"

"Jay's mother is trying to work upstairs on her blueprints. Now, we don't care if you guys want to practice, but if you're just going to make noise down here then at least turn down the amplifiers."

"'Amps', Dad; no one calls them 'amplifiers'."

"Hey, Mr. Simmons," Mark said and gave Jay's father a cool thumbs up, "We're gonna be famous, dude. Ain't that awesome?"

"That's great, then you can buy me and Mrs. Simmons some earplugs."

"You got it, dude."

Jay's father shook his head and went back upstairs.

"Man," Kyle said, "your dad is cool."

"Eh," Jay shrugged, "he's alright. I guess you guys should probably turn down a notch before he has another heart attack."

"Anyway," Steve said, "we gotta book a real good show for my cousin and his partner. I'm thinking we play a few more dives to get more exposure, then we go for a show at The Pulse."

"Dude, that's a hard club to get into," Jay said, "my brother's band tried a couple times, but couldn't."

"That's because they play all that jazz junk no one wants to hear," Mark said. "But, if we're really, really serious about this now, I may be able to pull some strings." My ex is friends with the owner's daughter."

Kyle and the others lit up. "Really?!"

"The only problem is that she hates my guts for breaking up with her."

"Oh great," Steve said, "now we'll never play there."

"Well, here's the thing," Mark continued, "I'm thinking that maybe I can call her and 'patch things up' for a bit... at least until we play The Pulse. I mean, she's a royal pain, but she's pretty hot. I could put up with her for a little while if it helps the band."

"See," Steve said, "that's what I like to see, a little sacrifice for this band. That's commitment, bro."

"Sounds like a scummy thing to do, Mark." Even Kyle was shocked to hear himself be such a downer.

After tiring of the quiet hum of the amps and the room, Jay finally said, "Hey guys, let's concentrate on getting this gig and getting out of this basement and into a tour bus before we kill each other, alright? We need lots of practice.

## ❄ Chapter 16 ❄

## FLOAREA REGINEI:
## QUEEN OF FLOWERS

"Why has the Lord made us to suffer?" Eduard read from his journal. "It was not my intention to hurt Nadine, but I can't take back what I said. No, she is a wonderful mother, and I am a fool for criticizing her handling of Anna. Tomorrow is the first of Oktober; I will buy Nadine something special for our anniversary. She likes shoes, or maybe I'll get her a necklace."

Eduard looked up from his journal and his mind drifted again when he saw a young couple strolling along the bank. He remembered one of the many times during their courtship that he and Nadine walked about the Danube. The breeze blew strands of her hair into his face— how he longed to run his hand along her hairline to brush them back. Why was he so afraid to touch her?

How they enjoyed those walks together and the talks they had until the early morning hours. Sometimes serious, sometimes trifling, the content didn't matter. One night they talked very little, but Eduard tried to teach her how to juggle and jog at the same time—anything to make her smile. Another night they sang songs together and joked about touring Europe as stage performers. Still another night they lay under the night sky on a blanket, waiting for shooting stars, nervously hoping their hands would accidentally touch. Somehow they always did, and neither bothered to move away, but instead tingled anxiously, wondering if the other realized they were touching.

Eduard was always careful to have Nadine home when her father specified, but he could have stayed up all night with her—every goodbye, a fresh affliction. Even in the same room she was too far away, for they were often accompanied by friends and relatives that would have taken issue with their too frequent smiling. It took so much effort to mask the enjoyment they felt together. From that time on, their courtship blossomed. Eduard had felt friendship towards women in the past and desire, but with Nadine it was different. Yes, he felt both of these things, but there was a third element—a desire to be with her for her own sake. In this condition, he did the only thing he could: he banished the thought of ever being without her.

The most recent entry he had written in his journal was also about Nadine. It was a simple unfinished poem he had wanted to give her on their anniversary, but it had needed editing and a fitting end:

*Green upon white, grass on ocean shores*
*Your eyes steer me like emerald oars*
*Upon your waves I ebb and flow*
*To pleasant lands where Edelweiss grow*

*Floarea Reginei you are to me*
*The milky moon and silver sea*
*The cresting tide at noonday bright*
*The placid Danube's reticent might*

*Pale skin as soft as down*

*Enchanting spell from feet to crown*
*Vienna's glory, found in you*
*In every shade and vivid hue*

*In your meadows I walk for days*
*Short of breath, a glad liaise*
*Brilliant trophy, my heart you keep*
*Through waking hour, and ...*

Eduard thought about fixing it now, but not feeling terribly inspired, he began a new page and tried to ignore the strange sights flashing in his mind and before his eyes. Shaking his head and dipping his pen he began,

"Tuesday. At the Danube now... tired... pleasant weather. God is good. No wine, but drowsy. Prayers reach half way to heaven, return like rocks thrown to the sun. Skimming along this life like a stone upon a lake, but the water will sink me. The fish in the deep will not have me, so I lay motionless in Purgatory until my edges are smoothed. The arm of God will reach into the water and skim me across the heavens until I sink into the light of His star.

I begin to see what is after me—ghosts, elusive melodies. Should I flee, or continue to write until they pass? I tell myself they are not real, but they return to me in ghastly form. One peers at me in a passing boat even now, raising a toast of blood to me. Does he know I am writing about him? Oh Lord, he just smiled and waved. Perhaps they are angels in disguise, for a demon would mask his true intent. A test perhaps? Maybe they will go away."

Eduard put down the quill quivering in his hand. The vision he had just seen was gone. "I don't know, little fellow" he said to a passing *wolpertinger*, "could they be real? I'm not mad, I know that. I could ask someone else if they saw him, but who would admit it? Did you see him?" The rabbit shook his antlers side to side then flew away after a finch. "Well, there you have it. Of course, what would a Bavarian know?"

He remembered a treatise he had read a few years ago by Charles Ferdinand de Schertz (and flippantly dismissed as enthusiasm). He now wished he had paid better attention to it. In it, the author discussed the reanimation of a pious woman who had died in a certain village but haunted the living for several months, appearing as a dog and sometimes a strangler. The 'ghost' wounded man and animal, and tied together the tails of cows for amusement. Finally the woman's fresh body was exhumed, revealing no decomposition.

When her body was burned, it flowed with new blood, and the corpse let out a shrill scream until it at last turned to ashes. Silesia and Monrovia were the most commonly haunted areas, but Vienna was known to have hosted not a few vampires and such. Eduard tried not to entertain the idea, and so trained his mind back onto prayer and writing.

"Lord, I have tried to serve you," he wrote, "I have tried to placate your anger, but there is no rest for the wicked. Make me acceptable in your sight—like land to a lost ship, like wine to a drunkard, or turn your gaze away from me that I might smile again. You say an early morning blessing will be taken as a curse, and I greet you in the early hours before the roosters announce the suitable time. But, I cannot restrain myself, and you sleep not. It is only in this that we are alike; a similarity no man desires. Restrain the devil for my sake. Restrain the Sabeans, the strike of lightning, the raiding Chaldeans, the mighty wind, and the sore scraped by pottery shard. Send only Elihu; send the flogging whirlwind with restoration in its wake."

Eduard was nearly out of ink, but didn't wish to return home. He tried to clear his mind and enjoy the sound of a quartet that had set itself up nearby. He recognized the song as one from Vienna's rising star Wolfgang Amadeus Mozart. The famed composer had recently come to the city to work, and was filling up halls, churches, and the homes of noblemen. Here were four brave men adapting one of his more popular numbers from the opera *Die Entführung aus dem Serail* for four stringed instruments and doing their best to perform it to the author's specification. When they finished, they continued with the composer's dedication to Joseph Haydn entitled *Dissonance*.

Eduard recalled that one of Mozart's operas was being performed the next night at the Burgtheater. People sometimes fell asleep at these symphonic events, so perhaps it would be just the thing. Before he returned home that day, he would stop by the theater to purchase tickets. For now, the quartet would do. He lay back on the ground and closed his eyes, but the passing spots floating beneath his eyelids in the pink and green glow caused by the sun's piercing gleam annoyed him. He could not focus on any single spot, for the dots would race across his field of vision. He temporarily amused himself by squinting tightly then releasing his muscles to see what shapes would develop. As he squinted he saw mostly black, but when he relaxed, phosphorescent reds, greens, yellows, pinks, and purples took odd forms.

Eduard opened his eyes again and looked at the clouds. These also seemed to long for shape and identity.

He complied with their wishes, and gave them names like *Adam in the Garden of Man's Dawn*. A companion could be found among them, though one looked like a dog, and another a man with a cane. A tree stood in the midst of the sky with one long branch reaching to the horizon. There was no child nearby, or it would no doubt have climbed upon it, or have tied a swing to hang upon. The closest thing to a tree dweller was a small cloud on the other side of the sky resembling a squirrel. He sat in a puff of grass where he surely had found a nut last autumn. Perhaps, thought Eduard, he would fill himself up on nuts before the day's end, and then drop himself down upon the earth in the form of rain.

"Rain." said Eduard to himself, "Overflowing, wet..."

He felt the urge to relieve himself; otherwise he might have lain there well into the night. It was approaching 4 o'clock, and though he had gone the whole day without relieving himself, he now felt enough annoyance in his bladder to sit back up from his reclined position and look for a tree to go behind. He stood up and felt dizzy, but the urge in his bladder was agonizing. He staggered along the riverside lightheaded, until at last he tumbled over to his left and slid down a short bank, landing in the shallow water.

Eduard was dazed, but was lying down again with an empty bladder, and in some way, he thought, it was less an accident and more a gracious act of providence. Eduard lay there in the water for a moment finishing his business.

## ❄ Chapter 17 ❄

## EDUARD'S THIRD DAY OFF:
## PHANTASM OF THE OPERA

"Haste dear, we're sure to be late." Nadine called from downstairs.

Eduard had spent Wednesday morning and the afternoon lying down in futile prayer. He prayed on his back, on his stomach, and on his knees, wavering between which posture was most humble. It was now seven o'clock, and the two were leaving the children home for a rare visit to the Burgtheater to see Mozart premier his new production, *The Marriage of Figaro*.

Eduard arose from his knees and walked into Anna's room where she and Julia were at play. He admonished them to be on their best behavior for the sitter—reminding them that one of the neighbors would also be dropping by sometime in the evening. Anna stood up from the floor and gave her father a hug and kiss. Julia, however, simply waved goodbye.

"Alright dearest, onward." Eduard said to Nadine as he descended the stairs.

"Planning to give a show of your own, are you?" Nadine pointed to Eduard's long underwear.

Eduard returned upstairs, and finished dressing.

"Are we ready?" Nadine asked when he returned.

Eduard stopped at the bottom step and stared at Nadine in a mixture of admiration and confusion. She smiled and spun around to show off her yellow gown and receive the inevitable and obligatory fawning of her escort.

"What in the devil is on your head?" Eduard said.

"It's a hat, of course. You like?"

"I mean what's that sticking out of it?"

"Feathers, and flowers... they're dyed. I bought it today to go with my dress."

"Looks like the bird perched up there."

"If you're trying to be complimentary, Eduard, it's not working. This is the latest style, and if you took me out more often you might know that. Now, if you're through insulting my attire, I think we best be off."

"Do I look alright?" Eduard asked.

"Button your vest."

Instead of taking a coach, the two took a leisurely stroll under the smoldering glow of the setting sun. The air was warm, and the conversation eventually pleasant, even delightful, after Nadine's aggravation cooled.

"No," Nadine laughed, "I was the one that first said, 'I love you,' and you didn't say it until later that evening when you returned me to my cousin's house. Before that, you had only written me a note saying you 'fell for me,' but that's hardly the same thing. Besides, I think you drank too much, or the singing and dancing at the party went to your head."

"I could have sworn I said it that time we visited the Black Mountains."

"Dear," Nadine said, "we've never been to the Black Mountains."

"Are you sure?"

"Positively."

"Well, it's what I meant when I said that I fell for you. I meant that I loved you."

"You barely knew me."

"And yet, I still feel the same way."

"So, what if I had married someone else? You would certainly have found another. Or would you spend the rest of your life in lonely despair, never to love another?"

Eduard thought for a moment how to answer this. Finally, he said carefully, "For the sake of conscience and the tenth commandment I would have to put you out of my heart, but only with the greatest reluctance. However, because we are meant to be fruitful and multiply I would look to love another, and in finding a suitable mate I would be compelled to love her according to Paul's exhortation to love one's wife as Christ loved the Church."

Nadine laughed. "Well, if we hadn't married, you'd have made a good priest."

Eduard didn't respond. Why would she say such a hurtful thing? Why, thought Eduard, bring up his recent failures in the bedroom? But no, clearly it was lighthearted banter instigated by his overly thought-out homiletic response. Or was it? Maybe it was because he could not give her a son? That wasn't his fault. Or was it? Perhaps God really wanted him to be celibate and was punishing him for not entering the ministry. Eduard's mind contorted in analysis over Nadine's cryptic comment.

"Father Kraus could not have given a finer sermon," Nadine finished.

The couple at last made their way down the cobblestone road and saw a crowd lined up near a lone lamppost centered in the middle of the road, and the domed building nestled on the corner of the street.

"You were right," Eduard said, "Apparently all of the women have birds on their heads. I guess I should take you out more often."

Nadine responded with a jab of her elbow to his side.

The theater they entered was stately, with pillars, and a roof adorned with statues. It had remained in disuse until 1741, a year after Eduard was born, when Maria Theresa commissioned its use as a theater. Since its refurbishing, and particularly Joseph II's assistance in 1776, it had hosted only the finest artists in Christendom.

Mozart, in fact, had previously premiered his *Die Entführung aus dem Serail* here, and its rousing reception told him of the great future he might have in Vienna over his old commission in Salzburg. Other than Joseph II's rumored jibe that his opera had too many notes, the crowds filled the composer's ears with accolades and ovations. Even performers such as Ludwig Fischer (with his famous low "D" vocals) had become household names due to the composer's ambitious work. The city was abuzz to see what new delight this master and his partner Lorenzo da Ponte had in store that night, and the guests were excited to be in the company of the Emperor himself.

Now sitting in their seats, Eduard and Nadine winked at each other in anticipation. This was the first time they had seen a play or opera together in years, and it was only by chance that Eduard was able to find tickets (though he paid double the price). He had bought them the day before from a man on the street near the theater after the man saw Eduard disappointed that no more tickets were being offered. Tickets were usually reserved for aristocrats. Eduard had not questioned whether the tickets were forged, and luckily neither did the hosts at the door that night.

Regarding the play, there was a great deal of controversy already surrounding this sequel to the *Barber of Seville*, for the composer had written it based on a comedy by Pierre Beaumarchais, *La folle journée, ou le Mariage de Figaro*. That play, written in 1784, was previously banned in Vienna for its criticism of the aristocracy; therefore, the crowd would keep a steady eye on the Emperor and take their cue from him when to applaud. That Joseph II allowed it to be performed at all was a testament to his musical taste and admiration for Vienna's rising star. Neither Haydn, nor von Gluck would dare such a performance, but consequently neither of these contemporaries would achieve such great celebrity in Eduard's beloved city.

After the opening act, which featured a lighthearted play involving two lovers dressed as birds, one of the theater's seventeen directors addressed the audience. He began with a few jokes, as well as some expressions of gratitude for honored guests. Then, 'without further greeting,' he reverently called for the young composer.

Emerging from behind the side curtain, Mozart took his seat at an ornate piano. Covered in mostly black keys with white keys for sharps and flats, and boasting an incredible five octave range, the Viennese piano was about to emerge victorious as the instrument of choice for composers. Particularly after this groundbreaking performance, the new *pianoforte* would virtually replace the harpsichord and organ.

"Can you believe we're actually here?" Nadine whispered to Eduard as the orchestra finished tuning.

"A transposition," Eduard mumbled, "Why didn't I think of that? Ludwig probably thinks I'm an idiot now. But, how—"

"Eduard," Nadine counseled, "enjoy yourself. Forget about work. Be with me... Be here."

The room fell silent as the curtain opened, revealing a lone chair in a room. After a moment, the composer nodded his head to cue the orchestra. A maiden on stage, played by the lovely Ann Storace, began to complain to her fiancé about some Count who was making advances to her. She was not pleased with her room, nor the prospect of having her aristocratic host sleep with her before her wedding night, as the law might allow him to do. Figaro was also apparently upset by this.

"What did he say?" Eduard whispered to Nadine.

"Dear, I'm trying to watch."

Eduard sighed and looked around the theater. Everyone was absorbed in the music and the drama. He wondered if half of them even understood it. Eduard tried again to concentrate.

"Oh, so this Figaro gentleman works for the guy who wants to sleep with his fiancé?" Eduard whispered.

"Yes, yes,"

"And Count Almaviva is the guy trying to steal Susanna from him?"

"Will you please keep quiet?" said a man from behind Eduard.

"You're embarrassing me," Nadine shot from the corner of her mouth.

Eduard leaned his head back to listen to the music.

"*Non so più cosa son!*" sang the distraught countess, "I don't know anymore what I am!" She was obviously upset about her husband's lust for the maiden.

Eduard's eyes became heavy. The last words he remembered hearing were, "Non piú andrai... No more gallivanting," before being woken by applause at the end of the first act with Nadine pulling on his shirt.

"Wasn't that marvelous?"

"Oh yes, beautiful, dear. Do you think there'll be an encore?"

Nadine's smile dropped. "That was only the first act, there's three... Oh, never mind."

"Of course. I just meant at the end of the fourth act, do you suppose there'll be an encore?"

Nadine stared at Eduard. "Where are you, Eduard?"

After this, the two sat silent until the second act began.

"Goodness!" Eduard said, "She told the Countess about it?"

"Sir, please!" whispered the man again from behind.

Eduard stayed awake during the second act, and remained quiet until the intermission, when Nadine quickly clarified the plot for him. Then, with a bow to the Emperor and a nod of the head, the illustrious composer began the third act. Eduard's head also nodded. His dreams mingled with the play, and he softly muttered, "Foolish girl, why did you make me wait so long," subsequently receiving a pinch from Nadine. After twenty minutes into the third act his dreams abandoned the theater altogether in favor of more bizarre imaginings about the seduction of the Emperor's first wife, Infanta Isabella of Parma, who had died years earlier. In his dream, she had not been resurrected, but remained a corpse. She brought him to an empty room.

Infanta began to sink her teeth into Eduard's neck. His heart pumped his soul out from his veins and into her mouth. She was swallowing it in gulps except for that which dribbled through her rotting cheeks to trace down her onyx and ruby necklace. After she had finished her meal, a small child was given to her and it began to suckle.

At last, the Empress rocked the demon in her arms until it spit up black blood. Somehow Eduard understood that there was something foul about his blood. The Empress also began to vomit, until the floor around him was stained. She became angry, but then fearful. Pale and drained of life, Eduard looked into her eyes which shamed him for putting her demon child's life in jeopardy. What was wrong with his blood? he thought. Was it too holy? No, that was not it. In fact, it was too evil—even for this seed of Satan.

The crowd in the theater was enjoying an aria with the sad refrain *"Dove sono i bei momenti...* Where are they, the beautiful moments?" when suddenly, heads began to whip around...

Nadine shook her husband, but waking him only intensified the nightmare he was having. The actors upon the stage stopped and stared out into the dark crowd, and the distinguished composer ceased playing his piano altogether.

All eyes now beat down upon the intrusion. Two of the theater's directors could be seen calming the furious emperor in the balcony. Quickly the protests came, and Nadine shook Eduard more violently.

"My blood! Not my blood! Not my blood!"

Eduard yelled as he awoke. He was then taken hold of by an usher, and dragged out of his seat kicking and screaming to the entrance, Nadine crying close behind. He was thrown out onto the road where he sat disturbed. Still disoriented, he dashed his head from side to side looking for an escape. Nadine ran over to him and placed her hand on his forehead.

"Darling, it's me," she pleaded. "You're alright. Please stop! Please get a hold of yourself; it was only a dream. You're going to get us in trouble."

Vampires were a common fear in Vienna at this time, and most believed in their existence, which made Eduard's outbursts not only embarrassing but incriminating. '*Magia Posthuma*' was the phrase coined around the Habsburg Empire to describe the wiles of these diabolical un-dead. Though a controversial practice, dead bodies that did not decay and whose spirits were seen tormenting the living after their burial were dug up and burned for good measure.

One of the numerous guards outside the theater came over to question the couple. "What's the problem here?"

"Oh sorry, sir," Nadine said. "He was just having a dream, and needed to leave the theater. I'm taking him home now."

Nadine helped Eduard, while disgusted pedestrians stared and the music in the theater sounded forth again. Back on his feet, Eduard shuffled next to his wife with his head down like a child. When they arrived at home, Eduard slumped into his chair by the hearth while Nadine went upstairs to check on the children. Both were fast asleep, so she returned downstairs to make a final attempt at conversation.

"I don't want you to feel bad about tonight," Nadine said, "I just want you to talk to me about it."

Eduard shook his head slowly and smiled. It was the smile similar to that of a mourning father who can no longer cry at the death his child and so chooses hysteria to cope. It was similar to the smile of exasperation, which one might misinterpret as disrespectful during a sad occasion, as natural and as odd as a mother crying at a wedding or her son's homecoming. Breaking apart, he was like a shattered wagon wheel down a stone covered mountain, dragged by stumbling horses.

"Tomorrow," Eduard finally whispered. "Tomorrow."

# ❄ Chapter 18 ❄

## DROPPING OUT, DIGGING IN

It was the second week of December, and about four weeks since Sara had learned of her disease. She was still getting about five hours of sleep a night, and possibly a half hour nap during the day. However, she was having many more dreams due to stress and what Dr. Anderson called "rebound," when R.E.M. increases over time. Due to the resulting lack of concentration and anxiety she took an extended leave of absence from school to rest at home.

On the enclosed back porch of her house, she sat at an easel wearing sweats and sunglasses. The world outside had become brighter, or at least she was squinting more. Strands of her strawberry hair had come loose from her ponytail, and her lips were chapped. She didn't notice. On the canvass before her was a man on the roof of a skyscraper. The people on the street below looked up and stared.

"Hello," she mouthed and waved through the window to her neighbor. Mrs. Cohen was shivering in the sun on her own back patio and waiting for her dog to finish his business in the woods. The old woman, who had watched Sara grow up, play in the streets, and who had made the Sara's family countless cakes and breads over the years, waved back with her wrinkled hand and then returned inside.

Sara could never have imagined envying her old neighbor. After all, who would want her thin grey hair, arthritic steps, polyester pants, and three children that only visit on the holidays? Who would want to live knowing that you and your husband had—at the most—ten more years to live? Although Sara was young, beautiful, and her strong legs walked with the smooth grace of a ballerina, she did— she wanted to be like Mrs. Cohen and have ten more years to live.

Taking up her brush, Sara looked at her smooth hand. Her rings were looser now, and none of them gold or diamond. Framing the hand was a watch she had bought at the mall three years earlier. The band and battery were worn, but still it refused to stop ticking and perhaps freeze her in time like a still-life painting of fresh fruit -- never to rot or be eaten. It's persistent hands brought her and her baby ever closer to spoilage, to rot, to the human compost pile down the road dotted with headstones.

Kyle, meanwhile, was finishing up his usual morning hours at his uncle's service station. He was rubbing his hands under the warm water in the bathroom when his uncle walked by the open door and said, "See me when you're done."

"Sure thing, Pat. Hey, we're out of that orange soap; I can't get this stuff off." Kyle had never been comfortable calling his uncle "dad," and "Uncle Pat," didn't feel right either, since he was like a father. Instead, he settled on "Pat." Now finishing with the paper towels, Kyle walked back into the garage where Pat was under a lift fixing an exhaust system on an old car.

"I told Harry not to buy this hunk of junk," Pat said. "The parts are near impossible to find."

"That's why they call you the 'car wizard,' Pat. If anyone can rig this thing, it's you."

"Well, this is a wrench, not a magic wand. But, Harry wanted it, so here I am. I should make him come in on his day off and help."

"Sounds good, Pat. Listen, I gotta run, but I'll be home for dinner."

"Hold on a second. I wanted to talk."

"You want to talk right now?"

"Yeah. Mitch is working the counter, and it's slow. Besides, we don't see each other any other time—between my working, your band, guitar lessons, and Sara. I'm glad you're busy, but it doesn't leave a lot of time."

"So, what do you want to talk about?"

Pat paused and replied, "How are things going?"

"Going great," Kyle was quick to answer, hoping to make it a short talk, "I mean, the band's working on more songs, playing shows soon, and we even have a chance to get signed. Told you those lessons would pay off."

Pat smiled. "That's great to hear, Kyle. And how's things with Sara?"

"Good."

Pat paused. "I called her parents a couple times recently and left a message, but haven't heard back. Everything alright over there?"

"Oh no, why'd you do that?"

"I just figure we should get to know them since you kids are going to be parents. We're going to be family. Grandparents. Not trying to intrude or anything, just want to be a part of what's going on in your life. We love you, kiddo."

"Well, her parents aren't the most friendly people in the world, so I wouldn't hold your breath on them calling back."

Pat laughed and continued working. "Can you hand me that screwdriver? Nope, the one with the red handle. Thanks." Giving the screwdriver a few taps with the wrench, he continued, "So, Sara -- haven't seen her much either. She okay? You know, you could bring her over to the house for dinner. I think I saw her more before you two were dating."

"She doesn't eat or sleep like she should, but she's got a good attitude at least. I think she's in denial or something. I know I'd be freaking out if I were her. She's a great girl, but we're not exactly dating... just good friends, I guess."

Pat huffed. "Yeah, *very* good friends, I guess."

"Oh boy, here it comes."

"Kyle, I may just be old fashioned, but when I was your age we called that 'dating'. Heck! We called that, 'marriage'.

"Yeah, you're old."

"Thanks. Hey, hand me that greaser, would ya? See, I'm just saying... and I'm not trying to pressure you, or come down on you... I'm just saying that you're going through a lot right now and have a lot to think about, so if you need to talk, your aunt Gina and I are here for you. And yeah, we're old, but even old folks can give good advice once in a while. You haven't had the easiest childhood, Kyle, and it's okay to be upset about things, and about Sara. Don't hold it all in all the time."

"I get it, Pat. I appreciate it. Sara's a good girl, but I'm too young for marriage."

"I see. But, not too young to act married?"

Kyle sighed. "See, now this is why I don't ever want to talk. I feel like I'm always on trial."

Pat got off of his stool and walked up to Kyle. Putting his hands on his shoulders, he said, "Kyle, you're the only son I've ever had and I'm proud of you. You got that?" Pat slapped Kyle's shoulders and got back on his stool. "That's really all I want you to know. I'm not the best listener, but I need the practice. Now, get out of here and tell Sara that your aunt and I say 'hello.'"

Kyle grabbed his jacket from the office and hurried out the garage. He drove over to Sara's house blasting the awkward conversation away with the radio and the new speakers he installed the previous month. After screeching into Sara's driveway, he went through the house and out to the porch. "Who's that...?" he asked, looking over Sara's shoulder at the picture she was painting.

"Oh my goodness!" Sara jumped in her seat. "You scared me!"

"Sorry."

Sara pulled Kyle down to kiss his cheek. "It's okay. How was work?"

"Work was pretty good." Kyle scratched his cheek, leaving a streak of oil and grease from his not-so-well-washed hand. "New painting? Looks good. So who's the guy on the building?"

"Not sure. It's not very good, but I like the colors."

"Nice sunset."

"Sunrise."

"Cool. So hey, do you want some lunch? I picked up some Chinese on my way over." Kyle held up a bag.

"Maybe later."

"You gonna be here for a while?"

"Yeah."

"Cool, I'll come join you; let me go grab a plate." Kyle turned to walk back into the adjoining living room, but not before saying, "Oh yeah, I also have something important to ask you."

# ❄ Chapter 19 ❄

## EDUARD'S FOURTH AND FIFTH DAY OFF: WINE AND SPRITS

It was now Thursday. Where Eduard was going, he didn't know, but before long he entered St. Stephen's Cathedral and sat in his usual back pew to pray. It was both easy and hard to pray—easy because it was much like talking to oneself, which Eduard was doing more often these days, and hard because his mind was easily distracted by things he thought he heard and saw.

"Confession?" said the angel, then a demon, then at last the priest near his pew.

"I really need to talk, Father Kraus," Eduard said, "but I don't know if I can confess."

"Have you been saying the prayers I gave to you?"

Eduard gazed straight ahead at the massive crucifix in the front of the church with its painted blood dripping from the thorny crown. "Yes, Father, all week—morning and night."

"And?"

"Nothing has changed. I don't understand; something's sucking the life out of me."

"When you say, 'something,' what do you mean?"

"I mean, I feel like there's an invisible force against me (a ghost perhaps) that taps me on the shoulder every time I begin to drift. Yet, at the same time, I feel like my life has become one long dream. I can't function anymore, I hear things, I see things, and I think things. I don't know if I want them to be real or not, I don't know which is worse."

Father Kraus stroked his chin. "What sort of things?"

"Out of the corner of my eyes, I see people, people with large heads, like melons. They have tiny bodies with tails, large horned skulls, and round, red eyes. I hear music too. I hear violins, and talking. Sometimes it's beautiful, or repulsive. Nadine sings a lot, but it's not her."

"You 'think things' you said?"

"This is a bit embarrassing, but... yes. I think about a woman I saw on top of the hill at the edge of town. I think impure thoughts... What it would be like to be with her—to have her sons as my own."

"You thought she was a beautiful woman?"

Eduard continued to stare at the crucifix before him. "I thought more than that...but yes, she was very beautiful. Her hair was dark, her face was bright, and she smiled at me. She showed me herself when she bent down. Why did you make her do that? I didn't want to look, but I did want to. I knew it was wrong, but I couldn't help it. She wanted to talk to me, and was sad that I was married."

"Eduard, look at me. Did you confess this to your wife?"

Eduard turned his eyes from the crucifix to the priest. "No! Do you think I should?"

Father Kraus sat down near Eduard. "Yes," he said, "you need to cleanse your soul through penance, and that will be your first step. After that, you will pray, and not give rest to your eyes. The Lord has kept you awake because he desires your attention, and so you must give it to him, fully."

"I will, Father. Tonight I'll pray, without ceasing."

"Very good! I want to see you again on Saturday. Tomorrow you will meditate on the Blessed Virgin, and then you will sleep soundly tomorrow night. Is this understood?"

"Yes, Father."

"Go and do as I have instructed."

"Yes, Father."

Eduard left and returned home, sat in his bedroom, and looked out the window at the pedestrians below. He told Nadine that he would be praying for the rest of the day, and so he remained with only minor interruptions. Eduard finally spoke to his wife as she lay herself down for the night.

"Nadine," he said toward the window in his chair, "I have a confession to make."

"To me? Why don't you come to bed and tell me all about it."

"Yes, Father Kraus told me I needed to tell you."

"What could you possibly have done to me—besides ignore me all day?"

Eduard was embarrassed to say it. He watched an old couple passing by below. The man helped his hunched wife walk beside him. They looked content in their fragility. They were a paradox, being both strengthened and weakened by the same passage of time—hunched, and yet standing taller for it. Eduard reconsidered his confession, but how could he disobey the instruction of Father Kraus?

After a moment Nadine said, "Well, go on then."

Eduard sighed. "I sometimes... I occasionally... I often think of another woman, a woman I met on the hill earlier this week."

"Is this a mistress? I mean, have you been seeing a lot of her?"

"I only saw her once, but I can't stop thinking about her. You're so beautiful Nadine, I can't even imagine—"

"Eduard, why are you telling me this? Just come to bed."

"Father Kraus, he thought that I should, that it would cleanse my conscience, help me to sleep."

"Did you touch her?"

"No!" Eduard stood from his chair and turned. Hanging his head he continued, "But, I wanted to."

"Well, it sounds to me like you're pretty normal, dear. Be ye forgiven. Amen." Nadine made the sign of the cross in jest, then fluffed her pillow and rolled over on her side.

"Aren't you upset?"

"A little. Yes. But, I'm sure this isn't the first or last woman you've ever looked at that way. The Lord permitted many wives in the Old Testament, and some say even the New. Should I get upset that you're a man? All men look to be fruitful and multiply, it's just what they do. Even Father Kraus, I'm sure, has looked. And besides, women look too, you know."

"Do you really?"

"I'm sure I have."

"At who? Diederich Trommler at the store?"

"Eduard, it doesn't matter. We both love each other, and I didn't marry you because I wanted a priest. I'm quite sure you didn't want a nun. It's not important. But, if it helps you sleep, then I forgive you. Now come to bed. I'll help occupy your mind."

"I can't."

"Why is that?" Nadine sat back up. "Please Eduard, you have to at least try."

"I told Father Kraus that I'd stay up all night to pray."

"Why, Eduard?"

"Because he recommended it. He said that God wanted me to spend more time in prayer, that's why I can't sleep. He said that if I give God my time then he will give me his rest."

"This is not a good idea, dear. Besides, if God punished every person for not praying, no one would ever sleep."

"I need to do what he said. I must." Eduard carefully planned his next rebuttal.

"Goodnight Eduard." Nadine laid her head back down. "And, tell the Lord I'd like my husband back one of these days."

Eduard brought a candle near to the bedroom window and sat back down. His mumbling did not disturb Nadine, nor did his occasional outbursts of laughter. What was so funny? Everything, anything, and nothing at all. The melon-headed parade that passed by on the street below, the black cat from the Narrenturm that stuck its forked tongue out at him, the lady from the woods with two dozen legless children, and the empty fishing boat paddling itself down the road. These all served to break up the monotony of his first droning Pater Noster.

As the night wore on, the beads in his hands felt heavy as he hailed Mary full of grace:

"Ave Maria, gratia plena, Dominus tecum.

Benedicta tu in mulieribus,
et benedictus fructus ventris tui, Iesus.
Sancta Maria, Mater Dei,
ora pro nobis peccatoribus, nunc,
et in hora mortis nostrae.
Amen."

*That would make a beautiful song*, Eduard thought as he adored the Virgin. But, somewhere along the way he switched to his native language; and, although it was currently authorized in Vienna for such purposes, it still felt strange and rebellious.

When he reached what he thought was the traditional hundred and fiftieth prayer (it was only the tenth, but his hand slipped down the beads), he began to count over, meditating on the great mysteries of the faith. The Virgin, the woman in the woods, and the Empress became one in his mind until he began to think of the woman in the woods as the ever-virgin queen. This posed problems for him, for he was not less attracted to her for it. Guilt plagued him, so he prayed more earnestly. His thoughts were on the virgin, the boat, the melon-heads. He held her hand on the boat while the melon-heads watched. Down the streets of Vienna they admired each other; the cat from the Tower perched upon the bow.

The boat stopped near the Danube and the two walked onto the water. They were clothed but they were as free as Eden, and their hands were bound together by rosary beads. They walked upon the surface together but stopped in the middle. There were no stakes or flailing victims protruding from the water this time, but candelabras providing a sheen. A table set with plates ascended through the water, but there was no food. The woman climbed upon the table to dance and Eduard held her hand from below.

As a waltz played they danced, and the shape of the woman's face shifted to the appearance of a leopard, then a sow, then a doe, and at last back to a harlot. She sang to him in strange melodic tongues.

They continued to the other side of the river where a black carriage awaited. After the two had entered the carriage, an old man wearing a coxcomb cracked a whip upon the horse's back, and they drove off into the cold night.

The carriage rattled over roots and rocks, slowly shaking the woman's top lower. She didn't bother to pull it up, but let it continue to inch downward until she was nearly bare. Eduard looked away. He then saw a bottle of wine on the seat next to him and raised it to her.

"Ah, look! Care for a glass, madam?" Eduard looked around and found only one glass on the seat next to him and laughed. "Care to share?"

The woman reached out and snatched the bottle.

"It's stuck," Eduard said, "Perhaps the driver can assist." Eduard leaned up out of his seat to call for the driver's help, but the woman kicked him back with her bare foot. She then gripped the neck of the bottle with her right hand, steadying it with her other at the base.

Eduard could see her hands tightening around the bottle. She squeezed and squeezed the neck until it crushed in her hands—causing wine and blood to spill. Eduard looked on in shock as she put the broken bottle to her lips and guzzled liquid and shards—letting it flow down her neck and chest to pool in her seat. Blood began to rise to their ankles, then to their knees. The woman kicked and waded in it like a child at a pond. The cab quaked in place. Eduard felt himself being pulled backwards. He instinctively looked for ropes around his limbs, but there were none. He tried the door handle to escape the rising blood but it was locked.

It was not just him moving in reverse. No, the whole carriage with its neighing horse struggled to continue but was being dragged against its will by that 'invisible force' back over the river, through the streets, then to the front of his home. Eduard gasped for breath at the roof of the cab, waves of blood now swishing back and forth at his neckline. At last when the carriage door opened, the blood dumped out into the street and Eduard panted for fresh air. He was then pulled by the force from the carriage, through his front door, up the steps, into his bedroom, and back to his chair while the woman looked on from her seat, disappointed that something or someone had come between them.

"Darling, I said are you alright?"

Eduard turned quickly, causing drool to fly off his mouth. "Yes! I... I'm here."

Nadine tied a bonnet to her head. "You were yelling about something. I thought you were hurt. Didn't mean to wake you."

"I must have dozed off. What time is it?"

"About seven. The children are gone, and when I left the room you were still awake praying. That was about an hour ago."

"Then I failed."

"Don't be dramatic. You didn't fail, you stayed up all night. Today is a new day, you just... well, you just took a nap this morning, that's all."

"My eyes hurt."

"Well, I can't imagine why."

"I should go for a walk; I've been in this chair long enough."

"Eat something."

"I'll eat later. I need some air." Eduard stood up from his chair, began to stumble out of the room, but turned again to Nadine. He approached her and gave her a long hug. "I love you. Please always remember that."

Nadine patted his back. "I love you too. It'll be alright, you can't stay awake forever. It's still only Friday, and you have at least two more days off. After your walk, why don't you come back here and lie down with me."

Eduard continued down the stairs and outside into the blinding sun. With no place in particular to go, Eduard walked to where he worked, searching for paddle marks on the road along the way. His hair was a mess, his jacket was buttoned improperly—each button inserted into the hole above its corresponding place magnifying his already slouched posture.

"Nice day for a walk." A friendly pedestrian said.

"Yes it—oh, greetings." Eduard stopped. "Don't I know you?"

"Eduard" the melon-head said, "it's me, your son."

"But, I don't have a son."

"Of course you do."

The two began walking together again. Eduard pondered this dilemma, then as he turned the corner to the street on which his office was located he said, "You've outwitted me, dear boy."

"So, where are you headed?"

"Thought I'd stop by the office, see how ol' Ludwig's doing."

"Oh him?" The melon-head kicked a rock down the road. "You know something, father, you should just stab him when you get there."

"Why would I do that?"

The melon-head shrugged. "I don't know, just for fun. Here, you can use my knife."

Eduard waved away the gift. "No thanks, you hang onto it. Now, you'll have to stay out here for a moment while I go inside."

The melon-head put his knife away and sulked.

"Good boy. Now I won't be long." Eduard hugged the air, opened the door, and slouched in the doorway.

"Eduard," Ludwig interrupted his business and said, "what are you doing here? It's good to see you. Come in. You remember Dietmar and Benjamin?"

Eduard wandered in. "Yes, yes I do. Good to see all of you again. How are the horses, gentleman?"

"Mr. Strobl," Dietmar said, "they're lovely, thank you for asking. We are hoping to purchase another American Stallion, and Ludwig was just helping us figure the cost and the shipping. Beautiful horses really."

"Very large testes too," Eduard slapped Dietmar on the back.

"Oh, well... yes," Dietmar said, "I suppose they are, Mr. Strobl. Keen observation. Have you an interest in breeding Stallions?"

Eduard glared on with a smile.

"An accountant, and an equestrian," Benjamin quipped to fill the silence.

"Um, Eduard," Ludwig interjected, "Is there anything I can do for you?"

"No sir, just taking a walk. Thought I'd come by to see how things were going with your testes."

The two clients looked at each other quizzically. Ludwig then rose from his chair, grabbed Eduard by the arm, and led him out the door into the street. "What has gotten into you, Eduard?" he whispered, "Are you drunk? These are very important clients, and devout men. I don't think they appreciate your humor."

"Oh Ludwig!" Eduard said, unconcerned with his own volume, "I was just fooling around, no harm in it. So, how have you been, ol' boy?"

"I don't have time to talk right now. You should be home getting some rest. Don't worry about things around here, everything's perfect."

"You still want me back on Monday, don't you?!"

"Of course, but not sooner. Sorry, I've got to go." Ludwig returned inside to apologize for his partner's behavior.

"He thinks he can run this place without you," the melon-head crept up and said. "He thinks he can just take over, drive you away, and take your clients for himself. You knew he was planning this."

Eduard grimaced and kicked the door. "Scoundrel!"

The men inside were startled by the noise, and Ludwig made up a story about neighborhood kids knocking on doors.

"Drunk? No, he's drunk!" Eduard consoled himself down the road. "Did you hear what that bum... Hey, where did you go?" The melon head was gone. "Wait a second, that's it! If bums drink and pass out, why can't I."

Eduard's pace quickened. He roamed about the streets repeating to himself, "heurigen... heurigen." A thirty minute walk to the west would bring him to an old vineyard in Ottakring where he could purchase a few bottles of wine and sneak off to medicate himself. He would have liked to purchase it in the fleischmarkt along with a morsel of dried meat and cheese, and bring it home, but he didn't want his family to see him drunk.

It was nearing 8:30a.m. by the time Eduard reached the Ottakring vineyard and its tavern. It was a beautiful estate. The vines were already showing fresh, small, spring leaves. There were at least a dozen men working the land—recently freed serfs enjoying the independence that came in the last five years. They pruned missed growth from the fall, and spread dung by hand for new vines. The worn dirt path leading to the main house barely had room for two carriages, which made it difficult during the busy wine season when nobles came to picnic with their families. Eduard had taken Nadine here a few times before they had children, but hadn't been back since. It was just easier to buy wine in the city and not fuss with making a trip.

"Here you are, sir." The owner's son said as he exchanged eight small bottles of red with Eduard in the tavern. "Bauernschmaus?" he continued, holding up a plate of frankfurters, smoked pork, ham and meatballs, "or perhaps some Leberknödelsuppe," now picking up a steaming bowl of beef soup and liver dumplings.

"Oh, no thank you, this will be all for now. I'm out of coins."

Eduard clumsily gathered up the bottles in his arms and left with a whistle on his lips. Finally, sleep was a few swigs away. He walked back down the driveway almost to the entrance, then looked about to see if anyone was watching. He then left the path and walked up a hill where the fruit trees were planted and sat down behind a tree in the thick of the orchard. It was a perfect place for a nap, he thought, and far enough away for anyone to notice.

Eduard struggled with the tapered cork, but finally pulled it out with his fingernails. He began to guzzle down the tannic liquid. Not stopping to feel the effects, he tossed the first bottle aside and began the second. As the first two bottles began to work, Eduard uncorked the rest of the bottles while he still had strength and sat them up in the grass around him. The third bottle was 'corked' (going bad from mold spores), but Eduard drank it all the same. He grabbed at the fourth on his right side, cursing when he knocked it over. By the time he was able to right it, the contents were nearly gone, but he drank what remained. On his left were the last four bottles. Eduard's eyes were now twitching and his vision darkening. The trees and the sky began to spin, making rapid half rotations then coming back to turn again.

Eduard stopped. He had never drunk so much before. He felt sick. His eyes closed, then opened wide, then closed again. It was for him a moment of victory, and he knew that he would soon pass out. He burped and heaved fluid into his mouth. He spit out the acidic vomit and placed his hands on the ground to steady himself. Moments later the vomiting, coughing, and gagging came in abundance.

His body rejected the liquor all over his lap. His eyes would not water and so they stung at the straining.

When he could vomit no more, he felt betrayed by the wine as though it had conspired with God against him. All of his hard work soaked into the ground. He grabbed the fifth bottle and began to guzzle. He managed to keep it down, and started on the sixth, but the contents fell more upon his chest than in his mouth.

Now rolling over on his right side he prayed, "God, the virgin is never riding in the parade... always my blood being spit up." It made no sense, but it was reverent. "And when the boat spills the wine, the clouds make a cork. Help me! Help! Now I lay me down to wake... the Lord my soul to take... if I die before I sleep... I pray Lord my soul to keep."

Suddenly the melon-head appeared from behind one of the trees, holding a knife. Then he was gone. Eduard sat up and then stood, then fell, and then stood again. He stumbled through the trees to find him, and then tripped to the ground again. He wandered around the hillside until he arrived back to where he sat before. Falling to his knees he gripped one of the remaining bottles and began to drink.

The melon-head approached him. "Father, what did you do?"

"I'm sorry; I just don't know what to do anymore."

"No. Look what you did to me."

"I just wanted a son, can't you understand? To carry on the name, to make my father and grandfather proud."

"You got a monster instead!"

"No, you're not a monster. I love you."

"I love you too, father, but now... now you have to die." The melon-head then stabbed Eduard in the chest, staining his shirt red.

Eduard screamed, "I'm bleeding!" He then stumbled to his feet and made his way towards the vineyard house. The serfs in the field looked, pointed, and laughed among themselves.

Eduard at last flew open the door. "I'm bleeding!"

"Oh my God!" The owner's son hurried over to Eduard, sat him in a chair, and called for his father in the next room.

"I'm bleeding, I'm...!" Eduard's eyes at last closed and his head fell. The owner of the vineyard hurried into the room to look at the injured man, but Eduard was unresponsive.

"He's not bleeding, you imbecile, the fool is soaked with wine. Get him out of here!"

"Where do you want me to take him, father?"

"I don't care; get him off of our land!"

The young man enlisted the help of two workmen and carried Eduard out of the vineyard. They dropped him over a stone wall down the road away from view of any incoming patrons.

"There you are. Sleep tight!"

Eduard felt himself hit the ground and became aware.

"It worked," he thought, "I slept a whole day. But, Nadine will be worried."

Eduard opened his eyes, and saw the world spinning as before. He rose to his feet and looked back toward the vineyard. His heart sank when he saw the back of the vineyard owner's son and two workers in the distance walking away. He surmised that it was not more than ten minutes that he had been unconscious.

"Hello father!"

"Oh no!" Eduard frantically took off down the road to return home and hide from the dancing melon-head waving his arms for attention. Turning a corner onto the main road back home, he ran into (or over) a woman. After helping his portly wife up, the husband of the woman ran after Eduard and pushed him to the ground. Eduard vomited again, and then noticed that all of his pursuers had disappeared. He slowly got up and brushed himself off.

Now walking as straight as possible, Eduard passed the Tower. It was nearing ten o'clock in the morning, and some of the patients were again outside. Eduard saw a familiar man on the bench. Like the last time Eduard had seen him, the man looked out onto the road with wobbling head. Feeling the same, Eduard concluded that the man was an alcoholic. A strange sense of kinship developed in Eduard, and so he called out to him.

"You there! I understand, brother!"

The man looked around to see if any of the nurses and orderlies were watching, then put his finger to his mouth to shush Eduard. He arose from the bench, then sat back down and nodded his head for a moment. Again he lifted his head, and arose from the bench to walk over to the gated fence.

"It'll be alright!" Eduard said to the man with a smile.

"You know that?"

"I do," Eduard slurred to the man, "I may be on the outside, but I understand the allure of the bottle."

The man laughed. "Not the bottle, but the bed; and you'll be here before long if you're not careful." The orderlies noticed the man walking toward the road and talking to the pedestrian. They rushed over to apprehend him. And with that, he slumped over to the ground five feet from the fence.

Another man began talking to Eduard from behind. He told him that his blood was no good, 'full of poison.' Eduard turned to look at the man but it was no man at all, but a cat from the hospital standing with an albino wolverine.

"Eduard," the white wolverine said, "Are you afraid of ghosts? Wait, come back!"

Eduard ran until he arrived home, slammed the door, hurried to his room, and crouched down in a corner shivering.

The children were not yet home, but Nadine was in the kitchen when Eduard arrived. She heard the slamming of the door, and his race up the stairs.

"Eduard!" Nadine walked up to the top of the stairs. "Eduard, is that you?" At last, she peeked into their room. Then hurrying over to him, she cried, "Eduard, look at me. What happened?"

Eduard shook in silence.

"Talk to me, dear. Tell me what happened."

"I keep seeing them," Eduard finally said. "I don't know why they want me... no, that's the thing, they don't want me."

"Who are you talking about?"

"Vampires and virgins, melon-headed monsters, they come for my blood, but my blood is no good."

"Eduard?" Nadine gazed hopelessly at her husband whose drunken pontification accelerated at a frightening pace.

"Neither the Lord nor the devil will have me, neither day nor night."

"Eduard!"

"On the inside looking out, toward the tower struck by fire. Lightening rod... Mighty God... falling man... cork in hand."

Nadine held Eduard until he stopped ranting. Her tears fell into his oily hair. She then removed his dirty clothes until he was naked. She went to his bureau, got a change of clothes and returned to the floor where he would continue to sit intoxicated for the rest of the day and into the night. At last, he stumbled to bed and fell asleep around 5 a.m. the next day. Nadine had let him rest and sober up alone, but checked on him frequently. Not wanting to scare the children, she told them not to enter the room or bother their 'sick' father.

## ❄ Chapter 20 ❄

# THE PROPOSAL

"Who wrote that?" Kyle returned from the kitchen to the sound of Sara's humming. He sat in the chair across from her on the enclosed back porch and dug into his Chinese food.

"What I'm singing?"

"Yeah."

"Brahms. I think it's his lullaby."

"Funny how songs like that just become a part of life and you never think to wonder how they got here. I wonder if I'll ever write anything like that." Kyle wiped some sauce from his mouth on his sleeve. "Probably not."

Sara put her brush down. "I had to learn it on piano when I was a kid. God, I hated those lessons."

"You're finished with your painting?"

"I'm getting tired. It's nice just to sit here."

"Well, glad to see the dude you painted on the building didn't jump."

Sara looked out the window up to the sky. "I guess."

Kyle reached across the table and took Sara's hand. "Don't go all gloomy on me." He then rose from his chair, walked to her side of the table, and put a box down.

Sara knew that Kyle had finally come to his senses. She had felt bad about their last conversation regarding marriage, and that she had been so hard on him, but it seemed to have paid off. Now that he had some time to think about it, his proposal would be more sincere, and she would gladly accept. True, her parents would probably be upset, but in light of her circumstances, they would keep their objections to themselves for once.

"It's an early Christmas present. Open it."

Sara slowly opened the box, revealing a beautifully manufactured plastic flower of yellow and pink.

"It's... a corsage."

"For the prom."

"I thought you said you didn't want to go?"

"I changed my mind. Surprise!"

"But, the prom's not until May, I think. I don't know if I'm going back to school. Heck, I don't even know if —"

"Stop," Kyle interrupted, "I'm asking you to go with me."

Sara looked down at the corsage. "Well, sure. Yeah, this is really... nice."

"Great," Kyle declared with the clap of his hands.

"So was there anything else you wanted to ask?"

"No, that was it... Oh yeah, are your parents coming home soon? I think I'm blocking the driveway."

"I think they're out for the day."

"Hey, why don't we go out too? We can go look around for some baby stuff, or something."

"You'd really do that with me?!"

"Sure. I'll clean up and get some sneakers on. Can I use the shower upstairs?"

"Yeah, but make it quick. I don't know how long I can stay awake."

# ❄ Chapter 21 ❄

## EDUARD'S SIXTH DAY OFF: DARK NIGHT OF THE SOUL

An hour later - at 6 a.m. - Eduard awoke with a headache and cold sweats. He could hear Nadine and the children downstairs eating breakfast. He hadn't eaten anything the previous day, but was not hungry. He was no longer intoxicated, but still felt as though the spirit lingered in him. He slowly put one foot out of the bed and rotated his body in preparation. Then with two legs hanging off the side of the bed, he sat upright. With his head hung between his knees, he heaved with animal grunts for a few minutes, but only scraps of bile presented themselves. After the heaving subsided, he very carefully made his way down to the chair by the hearth.

"Poppa!" Anna ran over from the table to hug her father. She squeezed him hard from the side around both shoulders, and he did his best not to heave again. "How do you feel, Poppa? Mother said you were sick."

Eduard rubbed Anna's head "I was, sweetie, but I feel much better now, thank you."

"Father," Julia said from the table, "would it be alright if I stayed with Benjamin this weekend? His parents are taking him and his brother on a boat ride to Pressburg after school today."

"Pressburg?! What's in Pressburg? We took the crown jewels years ago. Nothing left to see. Besides, tomorrow's Sunday, and you need to be in church."

"Please father, it'll only be for a couple of days."

"Dear," Nadine interrupted, "let her go, please. She's getting older, and needs to see life outside the city. It'll only be today and Sunday. The Goldstein's are a reputable family."

"Fine," Eduard said, "but don't make a habit of it."

"Oh thank you, Father!" Julia ran over to hug her father.

"Yes, fine. Is there any bread left?"

Julia ran to the table and fetched a piece. "I'll get it!"

Eduard ate it quietly as the children finished preparing for school. When the children had gone, Nadine sat down next to Eduard with a dish towel in hand and asked him again about the previous day. He explained to her his plan to pass out.

"What happened to relaxing and prayer? You're thinking too hard about it, dear; it's causing you more stress."

Eduard slapped his forehead. "Why didn't I think of that?"

Nadine draped the towel in her hand over her arm. "Well, if you're going to be rude, then I'll talk to you later when you're ready."

"I'm not ready now, I won't be later," Eduard threw the last bite of bread on the floor like a stubborn child. "I just want to die."

Nadine leaned down from her seat and picked up the bread. "Don't talk like that. Remember, you've a wife and family. Don't you dare leave me alone, Eduard Strobl."

"You'd survive."

Nadine wiped the floor with her other hand than sat back up.

Eduard looked up at the bread and towel in her hands and began to cry.

Nadine put her arm around him. "My dear Eduard, why are you crying? I'm sorry."

Eduard's head fell on her shoulders. "You're strong. I am not."

With her cheek pressed against the top of his head, she smiled. She recognized in his lament the sound of her children when they too lacked rest and fretted unreasonably. Like a good mother she squeezed him closer. "Now why would that upset you?"

Between whimpers, Eduard replied, "Because you shouldn't have to be. I'm a mess, and you shouldn't have to clean it up. I just want to lie down with you at night like a normal person and go to sleep."

"We will lie down together again, my love."

"I know. My time is coming."

"Of course it is," Nadine whispered to his ear. "Now, what can I do to help get your mind off things?" Nadine twirled the hair on the side of Eduard's head.

Normally Eduard would have whisked her away, but his desire did not produce the typical biological response or even the motivation to try. Instead he replied, "Maybe you could just watch the door while I lie down."

"Watch the door?" Nadine asked in confusion. "What am I watching for?"

"Just in case they come back for me."

Nadine began to tear up. "Anyone in particular I should look for?"

"Father Kraus says they've overrun the city."

"Alright, now," she said and wiped her eyes, "I'm going to lock the door, and watch while you lie down. Is that alright?"

"Thank you, Father, I will."

Nadine led Eduard by the hand to the bedroom and laid him down. He rolled over onto his chest and closed his eyes...

"Are you still there?" Eduard asked an hour later.

"I'm here," Nadine reassured, "everything's fine."

"I love you."

"Are you still there?" Eduard asked again sometime after noon.

"I'm here," returned Nadine.

"Are you still there?" Eduard asked after two o'clock

"Yes, I'm here, dear."

"Are you still there?" Eduard asked around two-thirty. "Nadine?" Hearing no response, Eduard turned over and noticed Nadine was gone. He then heard footsteps approaching the door and stood up out of bed. "Nadine!" he yelled. "Nadine, help me!"

Nadine opened the door and approached the bed. "I'm right here, don't fret. I just needed to help the children with some food. Come now, lie back down. Julia left for

Benjamin's and told me to tell you goodbye, and Anna went down the road for some milk, then she has homework to do. Come now, sleep tight, my dear."

"Sleep tight, yes, that's a good idea; yes, maybe that will help." Before lying back down, Eduard tightened the lattice ropes of the bed frame. He then eased back onto the down filled mattress and turned back over on his side. Nadine sat on the bed next to him and rubbed his back. She sang a children's song she had recently heard from her friend and neighbor, Regina Trommler:

> *Aber Heidschi Bumbeidschi bum bum.*
> *Aber Heidschi Bumbeidschi bum bum.*
> *Aber Heidschi Bumbeidschi bum bum.*
> *Aber Heidschi Bumbeidschi bum bum.*

"Could you stop saying that?" Eduard mumbled, "Doesn't even make sense."

"It's a children's song, it doesn't have to."

"Sing something else please."

Nadine breathed deeply and began to hum another song.

"I'm sorry," Eduard said into his pillow.

"I'm fine."

"I'm falling apart. I'm forgetting who I am."

"You're my love, Eduard. I'll pull you together."

These last words resonated in Eduard's ears until they disappeared into glorious oblivion and he slept for nearly a half-an-hour. Nadine did not dare to move during this time, not even to lift her hand from his back. When at last he stirred and woke again, she calmly removed her tingling hand and replaced it with the other.

"You fell asleep." Nadine whispered. "Good job."

"What time is it?"

"Don't worry; it's enough that you've slept. Now, let me sing you another song."

Eduard fell asleep again. This time Nadine was careful to lift her hand slowly from his shoulder when she saw his body relax. An hour passed, and Eduard stirred, then slept again. Another hour passed, and Eduard had slept nearly two and one half hours. Now nearing five o'clock, Eduard awoke.

"Did she lock the door?" Eduard mumbled into his pillow.

"What was that, dear?"

Eduard turned over quickly. "Did she lock the door?"

"Who?"

"Anna! When she came back home, did she lock the front door?"

"Yes, of course she did. Why are you getting so—?"

"I don't believe you." Eduard rose from the bed and ran out of the room,

... tumbled down the stairs,

... limped through the living room,

... scurried to the door, which was not only unlocked, but opened a crack.

He pulled the door closed and latched it. "Anna!" he yelled up to the second floor. Anna soon ran down the stairs with her marionette.

"Hello, Poppa," the marionette said, "I'm glad to—"

"Why didn't you shut this door?!" Eduard interrupted. "There are people in the world—thieves, murderers that take advantage of an open door. Now get back up to your room, and don't come out until I tell you!"

Anna ran back up the stairs whaling, being caught at the top by her mother who asked what was going on. Anna couldn't speak, but continued into her room and closed the door. Nadine then hurried down the stairs to the door where Eduard was still fuming.

"What happened? Why is Anna crying like that?"

"She left the door open," Eduard snapped, "and you lied to me!"

Eduard began to punch the door he had just closed. When his fist was sore, he walked over to his chair by the hearth, picked it up, and began smashing it down upon the floor. When that was shattered and splintered, he moved on to the next chair.

"I thought she locked it!"

Eduard raised the chair above his head. "No... no you didn't!"

Nadine fell to her knees. "What is wrong with you?!"

Eduard threw the chair down and stormed over to Nadine. Pulling her up by the arm, he tore the bonnet from her head, and yelled into her wet face. "With me?! Are you with them too?"

"With who?!"

Eduard shook his head in disgust and pushed Nadine away. "I'm not safe here." Grabbing his coat, Eduard swung it around himself. As he threw his hand down the sleeve, he accidentally struck Nadine in the face. As Nadine stood in shock, Eduard ran out into the road, being nearly trampled by a passing carriage. He then jogged down the road towards the hill he had started his week at, and where he might find the strange woman again.

***

When he at last reached the hill, Eduard fell to the ground and began crawling on his knees up the path. Where was she? No longer able to take the terror, he would allow the terror to take him. Panting hard, Eduard at last reached the summit and stood with his arms and face to the heavens.

"Here am I!" he shouted. "Here am I, take me!"

The sun was beginning to set and the warm spring air caressed his face. He turned, and turned, repeating his offer to whatever angel or demon would accept it. He then lowered his head and arms and looked out over the city. The orange beams shone from behind him, casting his fatigued shadow toward home.

"Sir?" her voice said from behind. Or did it? There was no one there when he turned. Still, he felt a kind presence in the air.

When Eduard arrived at his house later he was in better spirits—even whistling a tune. When he opened the door, however, there was no one home.

"Nadine! Anna! Hello! I'm home!"

He searched the downstairs, then the upstairs, and at last found a note from Nadine on his dresser:

*"Eduard, I am sorry and scared. I could not stay the night. Please forgive me. Anna is with me, and I will pick up Julia at the river when she returns. I love you dearly. Please don't look for me."*

Eduard dropped the note on the floor. He sought his chair, but noticed it in pieces upon the floor. He wandered into the bedroom to write in the company of ghosts. Journal in hand, he penned one last entry in the chair by the window. It took him most of the night to complete, and was filled with incoherence, but what he intended to write was the following:

Dear Nadine,

If I thought evil of you, it was not by design, for I have become an unmendable stocking -- twice unravelled, threadbare, and torn, bearing an endless night, abandoned by rest, by reason, by you. Yea, my heart is a moonlit sepulcher filled with schemes, melodies, and regrets. Unwelcome guests are these meditations upon my featherless pillow. Rude and lingering long, they are a boorish company prying open the eyes after wedging a discourteous foot in the door. Will their conversation never end? Will they notice the yawn and glassy eyes of the host? Will they eat every morsel in the cupboard?

Your leaving has ruined me and left me with these untimely visitors. Yet, I have already seen you leave me a hundred times during the night in our pillowed casket, covered in sheets like dirt, our headboard a tombstone. You are elsewhere every night, and where you go I cannot follow. But, there is a bed in which I shall best you to the slumber. There my name shall be lost to time, my heirloom will be bones, and despair the sake of my name. Yet, as I am purged I shall await you, for as a fool I remain,

Forever yours,
Eduard.

Eduard tore the paper from his journal and left it on the bed, he then stumbled back downstairs and took a seat on the splinter-laden floor.

# ❆ Chapter 22 ❆

## IT'S NOT FUNNY

Kyle and Sara spent that Saturday afternoon shopping for the baby and talking over what to name it. They weren't sure if it was a bot or girl and hadn't yet decided if they wanted to know, so rounding out the top of the list were 'Angela' (one of Sara's favorite names), 'Jen' (after Sara's best friend, and the child's god-mother), 'Kyle' (after the father), and 'Jim' (after Sara's father). Sara suggested naming it after one of Kyle's parents, but he said it would be a bad idea, that he didn't want the baby to 'remind him of dead people'.

"Besides," Kyle said, "no one wants to name a kid with an old fashioned name like 'Anne,' or 'Walter.'"

Later that evening at Sara's parent's house, Sara sat on one of the kitchen counters with her own laptop researching sleep disorders again, while Kyle peeled carrots for a salad. She had become distracted and agitated in the last three months, but this research acted as a type of therapy.

"It's actually quite interesting." Sara said.

"What's that?"

"It's an article on *narcolepsy* and *cataplexy*, and for crying out loud, will you please be more careful with that knife!"

Kyle flipped the knife in the air like a drumstick and moved on to the celery. "What are those?"

"Well," Sara said, "With narcolepsy the person is sleepy all day, and will fall asleep at inappropriate times. Cataplexy is something narcoleptics often have, and is brought about by emotional experiences. Now, if the narcoleptic gets excited in some way, he loses muscle control in his face or body, or will just fall over."

Kyle suddenly fell to the floor.

"Oh my God! Kyle, are you alright?!" Sara hopped down from the counter in a panic. Then seeing him smile she whacked him on the leg. "Get up, jerk!"

"Ouch! Sorry, I just got a little excited."

Sara hoisted herself back onto the counter. "It's not funny, Kyle, there are actually people in this world who have this. Would you like it if someone made fun of me?"

"I was just playing around. Go ahead, tell me more."

Sara hesitated, and then began again. "Okay, well, here's another one: 'Kleine-Levin syndrome', where you sleep for days or weeks, except maybe to eat or use the bathroom. Unlike narcoleptics, emotions don't affect them, because they lose their emotions all together."

"Sounds awesome, like sleeping beauty."

"Oh, hey," Sara held the computer closer to her eyes. "I think you might have this one. It says that males who have it can get real, well..."

"What?"

"Let's just say, 'aroused'."

"Oh yeah, got it for sure, and—oh no—I think my symptoms are starting." Kyle walked over and began feeling Sara's leg.

"Quit it!" Sara pushed Kyle away. "My folks will be home soon."

"Sara!" came a holler at the front door, "Tell Kyle to move his car, it's blocking the driveway again!"

Kyle smirked. "Speak of the devil. I'll be right back." Grabbing his keys from the table, he walked through the living room to the front door where Sara's father was waiting cross-armed. "Sorry 'bout that, Jim."

"Of course."

Kyle chuckled and strolled down the driveway twirling his keys around his finger. After moving it to the side of the road, he noticed Sara's father stomping towards the car.

# ❄ Chapter 23 ❄

## ONE HAND WASHES THE OTHER

Nadine and Anna stood on a worn and splintered dock on the Danube and watched as a brown stained boat owned by the father of Julia's friend, Benjamin, sailed in. Julia waved from the boat and tried to keep her balance. Benjamin's father tied the boat off with the thick rope and helped the two children and his dainty wife.

"Thank you again," Nadine said, quickly brushing back her messy hair at the sight of the exquisite woman and her tailored husband. "It was awfully nice of you to host Julia for the weekend. I do hope she behaved."

"Dear me," Benjamin's mother responded, "she's an absolute delight. The children had a marvelous time of it, as did we. I do believe my little Benjamin has quite taken to your Julia, ha! In the two years since we moved to Vienna this is the first time we've been to Pressburg. Fancy that? Perhaps next time you and your husband could accompany us."

"Absolutely! If it's no imposition (of course). I've not been there in years. I hear it's changed."

"Oh, darling, it's simply stunning... truly. Never more grand."

"Julia!" Nadine shouted to her daughter who had run off the dock with Benjamin in a game of chase. "Julia! Get over here!"

The children ran back to their parents, laughing and out of breath.

"What is it, Mommy?"

"Give Benjamin his hat back, and say 'thank you' to Mr. and Mrs. Goldstein."

Julia threw the hat at Benjamin and then smiled brightly to Mrs. Goldstein. "Thank you Mrs. Goldstein."

With a pinch to Julia's cheek, Mrs. Goldstein returned, "Any time, darling. Thank you for joining us. Charming little lady, aren't you?"

"Alright, dear," Mr. Goldstein said, swinging a scarf around his neck, "we'd best be on our way if we're to rendezvous with the Schreiber's. Mrs. Strobl, it was a pleasure to finally meet you. Do join us for dinner some evening—your husband as well. I've heard fantastic things about his practice, and may perchance enlist his services."

Nadine shook Mr. Goldstein's hand. "He's the best accountant in Vienna, Mr. Goldstein, and I'll certainly pass along the invitation. Good day to you all."

Nadine and her daughters left the dock while the Goldsteins set off again on their boat. It was not a fishing or cargo boat, like most on the Danube, but simply for luxury and recreation. Nadine walked with poise until they were out of sight.

"Mommy," Julia said while bopping along, "the big building was beautiful inside—big and bright, and... big! But, a lot of the things you hear about were gone."

"That's because they are here in Vienna now, dear. That's what your father was trying to tell you. We have the best of all worlds right here. We're Viennese, we Strobls, and have been for many years. People move here from all over the world, just to be around people like us."

"Like the Goldsteins" Anna said.

"Yes, Anna, like the Goldsteins"

"Mrs. Goldstein was beautiful," Anna said. "Did you see all the pearls she was wearing? I bet they live in a mansion. Julia is going to be rich when she gets married."

"Your sister's not getting married anytime soon, Anna; and money isn't everything."

"She was pretty too."

"Looks aren't everything either, dear."

"Mommy," Julia continued, "the priests use the big square building now for priest school."

"It's called 'seminary,' Julia."

"Yes mother, and there were a lot of priests too. It's so big, bigger than anything, and it had walls all around it. We went to the roof and I think I could see our house from there."

"It's possible. Bratislava palace is a castle. It's on a hill surrounded by walls so they can see invaders. That's where the queen used to live."

"Mommy, where's daddy? I got him this." Julia reached into her bag and gave her mother a copy of *Presspurske Nowiny,* the first Slovak newspaper. "Maybe he can read it to me."

"Hang on to this paper, dear. Daddy's home, but we're staying at the Trommler's tonight (and maybe longer)."

"But, I want to see daddy; I have so much to tell him."

"Daddy's mad," Anna said, offering her own maternal counsel.

"Anna, your father is going through a tough time," Nadine cautioned, "let's mind our manners. Now, pick up the pace so we can get back before lunch."

\*\*\*

"Now remember," Nadine instructed the girls before opening the door to Trommler's house, "we're guests here, and must be on our best behavior. Is that understood?"

"Yes mother."

"Good. And, wipe your feet. And, no running, Julia." Nadine then opened the door to find Diederich Trommler tuning a snare drum while his wife Regina spanked their four-year-old son, Dirk. Diederich owned a variety store on the fringes of the city and sold many of Nadine's dolls among other things, such as musical instruments. Nadine had helped out at the store part-time before having children, and worked a few hours here and there now that they were in school during the day.

"Oh, come in, come in!" Regina said and put her screaming child down to run. "Julia, little Dirk has been asking for you; wants to play; just ran to his room if you want to find him. Doris is around here somewhere too. And Nadine, I put some water on for tea, should be boiled any moment. Diederich! Diederich!"

Diederich ceased hitting the drum and looked up at his wife. "What now?!"

"Can you do that somewhere else?!"

Diederich shook his head and went up to his room to finish.

"Children," Nadine beckoned, "why don't you go upstairs and occupy yourselves. Mrs. Trommler and I will fix lunch. Be ready to eat when I call you."

Anna and Julia ran upstairs and played with Dirk and his twin sister Doris, while Nadine and Regina took to tea and conversation. Regina was a good church friend who loved to talk, and did most of it the rest of the day. It was good therapy for Nadine, who by now was tired of thinking about her own problems; however, by the time lunch, and dinner, and dessert, and cordials, and more cordials, and a nightcap were through, she was happy to sit alone downstairs while the others went to bed.

"Nadine, I'm saddened to hear about your misfortune with Eduard." Diederich came down stairs in his pajamas and robe.

"Oh, hello Diederich, you startled me. In my own world, I suppose."

Diederich sat on the couch next to her. "You are in a world of your own, Nadine. And, a good woman like you should be treated like a princess, not yelled at and abused. I've always thought you were too good for Eduard—no offense."

"Well, Diederich, I do appreciate your concern. It was just a broken chair really, but thank you anyway. Is Regina up too?"

"Sleeping like a baby, same with the children."

"Great idea. In fact, I should probably go to bed myself."

Diederich took Nadine's hand. "You have very talented hands, Nadine. Your dolls always sell well at the store; the children adore them. Your beauty and creativity shines through every one of them. I would love to have you work with me full-time during the day. I'd be willing to pay you hourly, plus a cut of what your dolls make. How would you like that?""

Nadine pulled her hand away and patted Diederich's shoulder. "That's sweet of you, Diederich, but it's really a just a hobby."

Diederich laughed and rubbed Nadine's knee. "Oh Nadine, so humble... so beautiful. You deserve someone who will treat you like the princess you are."

"Well, you're very kind, and I'll consider it...working at the store. You and your wife were very kind to let us stay here this weekend. Yes, perhaps I could spend a few more days at the store."

Diederich moved his hand further up. "Like they say, 'One hand washes the other."

Nadine smiled. "Diederich, you and your wife have been quite charitable yourselves over the years; in fact, I can't wait to tell your wife all about this conversation and just how kind you have been."

With a grin, Diederich slowly stood and adjusted his pajamas. "Indeed. And, now I'll be heading back to bed if you're feeling better."

"I'm feeling just perfect, Diederich, and thank you again."

Diederich returned to his room, and Nadine to her worries and sadness. Eduard, what would she do without him? The concern was not only romantic, but practical. She had children to care for. She couldn't stay at the Trommler's forever, but couldn't afford to stay in the city without her husband's income. Yes, she would have to return home even if it meant abuse. After all, what woman didn't received the occasional thrashing from her husband? Why should she be any different?

## ❄ Chapter 24 ❄

# GUYS ARE JERKS

"I don't know, Jen, he just never came back in." Sara sat on her bed talking on her phone later that night. "My dad said he just drove away, and now he won't answer his phone."

"Guys are jerks," Jen said, "probably just went to hang out with the band, or practice guitar. So immature."

"What if he got into an accident or something? He could be lying in the middle of the road somewhere bleeding to death for all I know."

"Sara, he's not dead, he's just inconsiderate like all guys. God! I can't wait to go to college and meet some mature men."

"I just have a bad feeling."

"Listen, I guarantee he's not worried about you right now. See, this is what guys want—they want to do what they want and have us there to worry about them. We sit by the phone crying, and they're out laughing it up. Wait, hold on, my parents are calling..."

As Jen answered the other line, Sara spaced out. In her mind she could see Kyle blasting music in his car as usual or talking on the phone. He wasn't paying attention to the road. He didn't see the stop near the doughnut shop. It's such a busy intersection.  There's always accidents there. Kyle was now laying on the cold pavement, his blood smeared in long lines, his skull cracked. He always forgot his seatbelt. It was bound to happen. The police were setting flares, and the EMS were scraping bodies off the street.

"Okay, I'm here." Jen came back on the line. "So, when do you want to shop for the prom? I found this gorgeous gown. It's deep blood red... *like Kyle's blood. So cold, but he can't shiver. Gone forever. You're alone. Your baby will die too...* with these sequins, and a sexy cut around the back... *like Kyle's body, cut up from the glass when he was thrown through the wind-shield...* and a matching purse... Hello? Sara? You still there?"

Sara sucked back a line of drool. "I... I don't know."

"What do you mean you don't know? You don't like sequins? I was going to try out another dress but this was love at first sight. I can't wait 'til Matt sees it; he won't be able to keep his eyes off me. Serves him right for breaking up with me. Let's see that Monica pull off a dress like this. Oh my God! Do you know what she said to me the other day? I can't believe it. I was like, 'first you steal my boyfriend, then you have the nerve to tell me...'"

As Jen rambled on, Sara's mind laid a rose on Kyle's grave and returned under an umbrella to her parent's car. She smiled as they turned off the hazard lights and drove away -- knowing that she and the baby would be back soon, and they would at last be together as a family.

## ❄ Chapter 25 ❄

## EDUARD'S LAST DAY OFF:
## DAY OF REST

As fascinating as the relentless ticking of the clock upon the mantle was, Eduard was finally ready to move. It was the first night that he had not slept at all, but it would not be his last.

He was supposed to return to Father Kraus that day. The thought scared him, however, for all of his prayers went unanswered, and he was ashamed to discover the reason. He walked slowly up the stairs and into his room to use the bed pan, but nothing came out. It hurt. He stood there for nearly ten minutes before giving up, then returned downstairs, took a bite of moldy bread and walked down to St. Stephen's.

Passing by a store, something shiny in the window caught his eye. Walking up to the window, he put his hands up to block the sunlight and tried to see past the dirty, wavy glass.

"For crying out loud," he muttered to himself, "clean your windows."

Eduard left the window and tried the door. "Hello!" he called out with a knock. He saw the owner inside moving crates, but the door was locked because of the Sabbatarian law forbidding business on Sunday.

Eduard knocked again. "Hello!"

The young clerk came to the door and opened it a crack "Sorry, but I'm closed, just getting a few things I left here yesterday."

"Sir, I just fancy something in your window. Might I come in for a moment for a look?"

The clerk looked back into the store at the many boxes left to move, then back at Eduard, back to the boxes, and over to a clock on the wall. He looked back and forth, then up and down the street, and finally said, "Fine. I'll allow you five minutes, then I need to leave."

"I'll be but a moment."

Eduard walked to where the object sat among colored glass vases and silver utensils. He picked it up to admire it in the light of the window. It was a silver snowflake pin for a woman's dress. Eduard remembered the first winter he and Nadine had spent in their home, how they cuddled together near the fire place, made love, and fell asleep in each other's arms. So peaceful was the memory of the snow falling outside the window, and the crackling of the fire before them. Nadine was just beginning to show signs of being pregnant with their first child.

"You like that pin, do you? It's not much; give you a deal if you'd like to come back tomorrow." The store clerk approached Eduard from behind. "They say no two snowflakes are alike. Never seen another pin like that either, I bet."

Eduard continued to examined the pin in the sunlight. "I'll always love you."

"That's a bit much," the clerk said with a snort, "but you're welcome."

Eduard spun around to the clerk. "Indeed. This would make her so happy. Oh glorious day! I thought I'd never see her again, but this... yes, this is a divine sign."

"Give you a good deal. It's used (if 'divine signs' can be used). Been eager to get rid of it for a while now. Painful reminder (if you catch my meaning)."

Eduard reached into his pocket for money.

Noticing Eduard come up empty handed, the clerk responded, "Sorry, couldn't sell it today anyway... Wait a moment, you go to St. Stephen's don't you?"

"Yes sir, my name's Eduard Strobl. I'm on my way there now. Can you save this for me; I'll come for it as soon as possible. I must have it. Please don't sell it. Please."

"Ah, I thought you looked familiar." The clerk then shook Eduard's hand, "The name's Adalbert Jaeger. Listen, Eduard, put that in your pocket, and pay me later. Just don't tell anyone about it—wouldn't want to get in trouble, or have customers taking advantage. Far be it from me to forestall divine signs for a faithful parishioner."

"Are you sure?"

"Absolutely. You're an honorable man. Besides, I know where to find you... back pew on the right. You're an accountant, right?"

"I am. And, thank you..."

"Oh, call me Bert."

"Well, thank you Bert. I... I've got to go now, but I'll come back as soon as I can to pay for it." Eduard shuffled to the door, grinning as though he had found buried gold.

"Here, let me get that for you. Sometimes the knob gets stuck. You take care, and tell Father Kraus I send my best, but you didn't see me here today, understand?"

"Will do, Kurt."

As Eduard continued down the road, he gripped the pin in his pocket so tightly it punctured his hand. He didn't notice the pain because the amusement of his surroundings and glee over his find, the likes of which he hadn't felt since his wedding. He entered the church laughing at the statues, then the windows, then the priest who hurried over to him from the front of the church.

"Eduard, you must keep the noise down. We just finished a service but there are others here still trying to pray. What are you doing here?"

Eduard slumped down into the pew. "You told me to come back, Father. You wanted to check up on me."

"Oh yes. Yes, I did. Well then, how are you?" Father Kraus motioned for Eduard to make room for him, and then sat down.

Eduard grinned. "Never been worse, Father."

"You seem fairly happy. What's so funny, Eduard?"

"Never been better. Kurt sends his greeting."

"Eduard, you don't look good. Did you confess your sins like I told you? Did you pray the prayers as I instructed? Did you stay up for a night and seek the mercy of our Lord?"

"Even better! I stayed up two nights, confessed my sins, and prayed all the prayers you told me. But, here I am, no better, but better off than you would think."

"Eduard, what did Nadine have to say about your confession?"

"That's what you think!"

The priest paused. "Eduard, I asked you a question."

Eduard slouched away. "You aren't going to get me," he yelled. "You'll be on the outside looking in!"

"Eduard, you need to keep it down.."

Blood spurted from Father Kraus's lip as Eduard struck him in the face. Father Kraus was stunned. He yelled for one of the deacons. A burly man ran over to check the priest's face, then called to Eduard who was now tripping over the pews to get to the door.

"He's gone mad," Father Kraus shouted, "he's going to hurt himself. Get him!"

Just out of his grasp, Eduard fled from the deacon out the double doors. A police officer noticing the commotion pursued him.

"Aghhhh!!!" Eduard yelled as the officer's baton crashed upon his spine, his legs, and chest until he could no longer breathe. Finally, it struck his head, but he was not knocked out. His vision went dark and he endured the pain. Five minutes later, Father Kraus arrived at the scene with the deacon, and told the officer what had happened. He reprimanded the officer for being so brutal, to which the officer replied with a disinterested shrug—spitting on the ground near Eduard's face.

"Eduard, are you alright?" Father Kraus cradled Eduard's bleeding head. "Eduard, say something!"

Dripping upon the priest, Eduard absorbed the pounding of his head. At last, the deacon picked him up and carried him back to the church and down to the basement where he rested and bled on a musty couch.

\*\*\*

After about two hours Eduard opened his eyes. "It's dark. Is it night already?"

"No," said Father Kraus from a nearby chair, "we're in the basement and short on oil. I think you blacked out."

"I've just had my eyes closed. Listening to the music."

"There's no music, Eduard."

Eduard rubbed his eyes. "There's always music."

"Eduard, I'm glad you're alright, but I'm very concerned." Father Kraus put his hand on Eduard's forehead to check his temperature. "You don't look well. You and I have always gotten along, so I don't understand why you struck me."

"I was trying to hit the woman."

"A woman? Is this the woman you told me about?"

"I'm not sure."

"When was the last time you saw her before today?"

Eduard tried to sit up. "Last night on the hill, father, but she wasn't ugly then. She was beautiful and kind. I coveted her. I coveted her more than food or water."

Father Kraus eased Eduard back down. "Stay resting, my son."

"She was evil, Father. A vampire. I saw her in your face. I thought she might steal my snowflake."

"Steal your snowflake?" Father Kraus looked to the ceiling for words of wisdom, then back to his parishioner. "Eduard, I'm going to tell you what I think is going on here."

"Yes, Father."

"Women, snowflakes, vampires... It seems to me that you love your wife dearly; do you not?"

"I do."

"But then you saw this woman, and desired her."

"Yes, Father."

"She's beautiful when you see her, but later in your mind she turns evil, a vampire of sorts, a thief trying to take away a favorite season in your life and all its white purity - represented by a snowflake."

"But, I have a snowflake."

"Yes, Eduard, of course. We all do. It is your conscience. Don't you see, my child, that your defiled conscience is playing tricks with your mind? You enjoy the pleasure of sin for a moment, and then the Lord afflicts you so that you regret your lust. When the lust has fled, the woman becomes abhorrent to you, literally sucking the life from you. I am a reminder of your defiled conscience and so you saw her when you looked at me."

"Then it's the Lord tormenting me?"

"Perhaps he's using a spirit to do so. Spirits can cause a man to go insane, to scratch himself, to run around hillsides breaking the bonds of fidelity to God and man. God sent a tormenting spirit to King Saul, and only the music of David's harp could sooth his madness. Christ is our 'David,' Eduard."

"Is the music I hear from the Lord, then?"

"Perhaps. What does it sound like?"

Eduard closed his eyes and began to hum along with the tune in his head. It was nothing the priest recognized, but it was pleasant. In reality it was a mix of Mozart, Gregorian chant, and the ringing left in his ear from the officer's baton.

"That's very pretty, son. It could easily have been composed by an angel."

"What if it stops?"

"Sing it again, and keep singing it as long as you need to." Father Kraus stood and turned up the lamp wick.

"Father, I understand that bats cannot see except at night. Do you think perhaps I've been bitten by one? Do you think I'm becoming 'undead'?"

Father Kraus poured his third glass of wine. "My child, you're not a bat or any other animal, you are a child of God. But, as all children, you are undergoing discipline. Remember Nebuchadnezzar and how the Lord humbled him until he resembled a beast? But, the Lord restored him, did he not?"

Eduard thought for a moment. "Father, King Saul killed himself. Has he gone to hell?"

Father Kraus picked a gnat out of his glass and continued, "I have to leave for a few moments for a confession upstairs, but I want you to stay here for a while. I'll leave this bottle by the couch in case you get thirsty."

Eduard closed his eyes while Father Kraus left. It was now nearing noon, and Eduard would stay in the basement humming until about six o'clock, receiving frequent visits from Father Kraus.

"Are you sure you want to go home?" Father Kraus asked at the end of the day. "You can stay here as long as you like, I can have someone tell Nadine that you're here."

"Thank you, Father, but I think I'm ready to go now."

Reluctantly, Father Kraus helped Eduard up the basement steps and out to the street. He looked on as Eduard began wobbling down the road. "Are you sure you don't want me to walk you home, Eduard?" The priest called out. "Deacon Alex can assist you if you prefer."

"Thank you, Father," Eduard turned and said, "I'll be alright. Tell Nadine that I loved her... the children too." Eduard then stumbled away, lead by an imaginary woman to the Danube. She sang to him a foreign song. It was a soothing melody that wrapped around his neck like a noose and drew him along into the river side. He then walked in up to his shoulders, dipped his head beneath the cool water, took a deep breath to fill his lungs and to end his earthly torment.

## ❈ Chapter 26 ❈

# TEARING THE HOUSE APART

"Been about four months since the diagnosis, and have maybe three months until the baby comes, but how many left to live? How premature is too premature if I don't make it? Will my baby also die from this? Had a crazy dream last night that my baby was born asleep and couldn't wake up to a mother who was awake and couldn't fall asleep. Although it was stillborn, it sang to me and at that moment I also died and was stillborn in heaven. I can't say that I was unhappy to die but heaven was sad when I arrived too soon." Sara logged out of her web blog, and checked her phone for new text messages.

Between the prenatal care and the failing treatments for her insomnia, Sara spent many of her days with doctors and nurses, and little time with friends. Kyle wanted to join her for these doctor visits, but was reluctant since he was told by Sara's father that he, "had done enough," and to distance himself from Sara for her own sake.

"Sara will not tell you this," her father told him that night outside by the car, "but having you around is only making things more complicated. You know how she feels about you, and we both know you never had any intention of spending your life with her, and frankly, I'm not disappointed by that. You need to get your own act together before you start messing around with other people. I don't want to see you at any more doctor's visits, and the less you contact my daughter the better. You were both very irresponsible, and now Sara's mother and I are the ones who have to pay for your mistake. I know I can't stop you guys from seeing each other, but for her health's sake I hope you realize that you're more of a burden at this point."

Kyle didn't return to Sara's house that night, and after driving around for hours he finally went home and wasted away the night listening to music.

Sara's father told her that Kyle had to leave, but didn't explain why, and since Kyle was too devastated, he thought it best not to reply to her five text-messages until the next day when he wrote back to her, "sorry for everything. lots 2 think about."

Over the next two months, however, Kyle did contact Sara on the phone and occasionally snuck over to see her when her father wasn't home. Her mother knew it, but did not say anything.

"Hey, buddy, what's up?" Kyle whispered, as he climbed through Sara's window one cold March night.

Sara put down her phone. "Just texting back Jen and Darrell. My parents are still up, so be quiet."

"Darrell?"

"He's a nice guy."

Kyle crept over and sat down next to Sara. "He's nice 'cause he wants something."

Sara pulled down the covers for Kyle to get in the bed with her. "Jealous?"

"No," Kyle replied as he lied down. "Just imagine my friend Mark (multiplied by a hundred) and you got Darrell. I know a dirt bag when I see one. Doesn't know the first thing about girls."

"And you do, of course."

"I know enough. What do you know about guys?"

"I know a lot of them are afraid of failure, wedding rings, and crying in front of their friends."

Kyle picked up Sara's phone to look at her texts, but Sara snatched it away. After a moment, Kyle asked, "So, what's with girls and rings? It's only a piece of jewelry. You can love someone without it."

"It is a symbol of commitment, and, there's no such thing as love without commitment."

"How about commitment without love? Lots of married dudes don't love their wives."

"An unhappily married man loves more just by staying married than single men who won't commit."

"See, that's what I'm saying. Commitment is better than love. Chicks don't need rings and all that."

"Well, I don't have anything, so we know who the sucker is in this relationship."

"Aw, come on. I love you in my own kinda way."

Sara lightly patted Kyle's cheek. "No, silly boy, you just like having a friend you can sleep with."

"Well, maybe I'm just confused. I've never been in love, so how should I know what it feels like."

Sara sighed and while shooting back a quick text to Jen, explained, "It feels like you want to talk to that person every day, or just stare at them. They're your first thought in the morning, and your last at night. It's when a day without them feels like years, and when they're always beautiful. It's when you're willing to be a fool just to see them smile. They're your soulmate."

Kyle chuckled. "Or inmate."

Sara plugged in her phone to charge for the night, then rested her head on Kyle's shoulder. "It's not prison, it's freedom."

Kyle sniffed the air. "What's that smell?"

"Burgers. My dad got home late. Want one?"

"No, that's alright. Anyway, love or not, I know I'm glad to be the father."

"It's no problem. I can go get one for you."

Kyle kissed Sara's lips. They were colder than usual. "I also know that you're the prettiest girl I've ever met."

"I look like a skeleton with a bowling ball up my shirt."

Kyle rubbed Sara's belly. "No, you look like Marylyn Monroe's better looking sister (with a bowling ball up your shirt)."

"Oh please!"

"You're so hot that the sun has to put on Sara-screen when you're outside."

"You make me laugh, Kyle."

"Oh, I'll make you laugh." As Kyle began to tickle Sara, he noticed her belly protrude in one area. He stopped and stared. It was an arm! No! An elbow! A leg, maybe? Was that supposed to happen? Did Sara know about this? Before he could ask, a voice came from the hallway.

"Sara, are you ok?"

Sara suddenly sat up and pushed Kyle off the bed. "Get under the bed!"

A moment later Sara's mother opened the door. "Everything alright in here?"

"Sorry, mom, just talking to Darrell from school. Had the speaker phone on. I'll lower it."

Sara's mother smiled. "Darrell, huh? He's such a nice boy -- handsome too. You know, his mother told me he got a full scholarship next year. Well, tell him your father and I said hello next time you talk to him. You can call him back if you want. I won't bother you."

"Thanks mom."

"Can I get you anything while I'm here?"

"Sure, could you bring me up a burger?"

"You're hungry?"

"A little."

"That's great! I'll be right back."

When Sara's mother left the room Kyle came out holding the cat.

Sara giggled. "Aw! You made a new friend."

"Here. I really gotta go now." Kyle tossed the cat to Sara, walked to the window, and straddled the sill. The cat, however, jumped from Sara's arms and walked over to nestle Kyle's leg.

"Kyle?"

Kyle swung his other leg over the sill and began to climb down, but stopped and peaked his head back in the window. "What now? I'm seriously gonna mess my pants, Sara."

"Would you take kitty?"

"What? No! You want me to climb down with this thing on my head or something?"

"I meant, could you take him after I'm...?" Sara stopped. She didn't want to say it.

And, Kyle didn't want to hear it. "Better?" he asked. "Sure, I'll take him after you get better. No problem."

Sara put a kiss in her hand and sent it to Kyle with a wave goodbye. "Thanks, buddy."

# ❄ Chapter 27 ❄

## THE TOWER OF FOOLS

At 6:33 p.m. two fishermen pounded on Eduard's chest until he expelled the water from his mouth. Lying on the river bank, Eduard opened his eyes and saw dark and bristled shapes. They were confused by his rambling, so one of them left to retrieve a police officer, but when the man returned, Eduard was asleep.

"He needs a doctor, officer."

It felt like only a moment to Eduard, but he slept for a good hour and a half through the bumpy carriage ride, and through being wheeled through a hallway, and being verbally assault by strangers, and then tied down to a bed. When at last he opened his eyes, he was greeted by a brawny nurse.

"Don't you dare try to escape," she said.

Eduard lifted his head to survey the dark brick room. "Where am I?"

"The hospital."

"Did... I kill myself?" Eduard laid his head back. "Did you find my wife?"

"Sir, we don't even know your name."

"Eduard. Eduard Strobl."

"Well, Eduard Strobl, I'll tell the doctor, and we'll inform your wife as soon as we can."

When the nurse left the room, Eduard became anxious. Taking the advice of Father Kraus, he began humming a song to himself. The faces on the ceiling left, and moments later a short, stocky doctor entered the room and put his hand on Eduard's panting chest.

"How do you feel, Eduard?"

Eduard attempted to scratch an itch on his nose, but was prevented by the straps. "Tired, doctor. Could you please scratch my nose?"

The doctor motioned with his head for the nurse to come near and scratch Eduard's nose. "You nearly died, it's no wonder you're tired."

"I can't sleep."

"That's common after a trauma and besides, it is almost ten o'clock."

"No doctor, I don't sleep."

"We'll help you." The doctor stuck his ear to Eduard's chest.

"I should've seen you sooner, doctor. Pride has preceded my fall."

"The nurse tells me you're married."

"Nadine. She left me though. I don't know where."

The doctor picked his head up again. "Where do you live?"

"About five minutes from here on the left. Red house—the only red one on the street."

"We'll send someone to tell her, but now I want you to rest."

The doctor checked Eduard's reflexes with a small wooden hammer. The doctor then left the room, but around one o'clock came back to check on him and found him with his eyes open. Moments later he returned again with a glass of clear alcohol.

"Here, Eduard, drink this."

Eduard lifted his head up and drank. He coughed from the fluid and laid back down. The doctor returned an hour later to administer another glass. Eduard coughed again, hummed some more, and an hour later the doctor repeated his treatment. At around five o'clock Monday morning Eduard finally fell asleep. However, at seven o'clock the nurse rushed into the room at the sound of screaming.

"What's wrong?!"

Eduard hummed louder. "Hmmmm, I can't see you, hmmmm, go away, hmmmm..."

Approaching the bedside, the nurse warned, "You stop that, I tell you!"

The alarmed nurse left and immediately recommended to the doctor that her patient be transferred to another section of the hospital for evaluation. Soon afterwards, the doctor arrived. He unfastened the leather straps holding Eduard down.

"Here," the doctor said, "let me help you up."

"Doctor, did you see that ghost that was just here. So large... so pale...so ugly. Dear God, she was dreadful!"

"That was the nurse, Eduard. Now listen, we want to run a few more tests on you just to make sure you've fully recovered from your accident."

"No, doctor, I didn't fall into the river, I walked into it."

"Why would you do that, Mr. Strobl?"

"I was sad. Can't sleep. The wife and vampires, they won't have me."

"Can't sleep? Vampires? Eduard, there's a doctor around here who would like to talk to you about all of this;

his name is Dr. von Croy. We're going to take a walk over to him if you don't mind. He'll aid you well."

Eduard smiled with dreary gratitude and scratched his irritated wrists.

The two walked slowly through the whitewashed stone hallway, passing by miserable nurses and patients. Some patients had been to war and were recovering from amputations or burns, while others had their heads or limbs wrapped in cloth. Through a gate, the two entered a separate wing of the facility. Eduard assumed they were passing through to yet another branch and marveled at the likes of those in the hallways. Some sat and played with toys, others stared out of the barred windows into the small yard, still others engaged in deep conversations with nobody.

"One moment," said the doctor as he stopped Eduard. The doctor walked up to another to speak. The second doctor was tall and wiry, and waving his hands in the air as he spoke.

"Mister, can you show me the way to the food hall?" An old maid in pajamas startled Eduard. She was unkempt, and smelled foul -- missing the front teeth of her pasty mouth.

"Oh, sorry madam, I don't know where it is; I just arrived."

"Seems you've been here for years. Tell me, please."

Eduard looked on at the two doctors still in conversation. "I don't know what to tell you, madam; ask someone else."

"But I asked you, Eduard."

Eduard turned to look at the woman. She was gone. He looked back down the hall and saw the first doctor pointing back at him. The other nodded, then they both approached Eduard.

"Eduard, I would like to introduce you to Dr. von Croy. He's done a lot of work in the area of sleep and the mind."

Eduard extended his hand. "How do you do?"

"Just fine, Eduard. You look familiar. Have we met before?"

"I don't believe so, but yes, you look familiar too."

"Let's take a walk and talk about your situation, shall we?"

"Yes, doctor. This place is haunted."

Dr. von Croy assisted another man up from the ground. The man then scratched his temple as he threw himself to the ground again. "Indeed it is, Eduard. Indeed, it is."

Dr. von Croy led Eduard down the hall and into a room with two other men. One was curled up on a mat, while the other sat silently in a chair. The first man was asleep, and the second would not turn around, but faced the wall with his knees pressed up against it. In front of his face, and wired to the wall, was a pillow.

The doctor sat Eduard down near the entrance of the room. "So tell me about yourself, Eduard."

Eduard hummed and looked over the doctor's shoulder at the wobbling man near the wall. "I'm an accountant."

"How old are you?"

"Can't remember. I think forty-six." The man over the doctor's shoulder slouched, then straightened up.

186

"You're married, I understand. Any children?"

"What? Oh... um, yes, I have two daughters."

Noticing Eduard's humming, the doctor observed, "You enjoy music, I see."

Eduard hummed and fixated upon the wobbling man.

"And," continued Dr. von Croy, "you're having trouble sleeping?"

Eduard turned to the door, but nobody was there. "Trouble, yes."

"And, you see things?"

"Yes Doctor, I..."

"How often do you see them, Eduard?"

"Not as much as before, because the music... so they leave."

The man in the chair slumped forward, and were it not for the pillow would have hit his head against the bricks.

"Doctor," asked Eduard, "what's wrong with him?"

Dr. von Croy laughed and waved away the spectacle. "Lukas? Oh, he's fine. You can't fall asleep, and that's all he does. A tad crabby, but entertaining. And, Boris over there -- well, he's been out for a week now. Never know when he'll wake up. But, let's get back to you. I understand you tried to drown yourself last night. Why would you do that?"

Eduard's eyes brightened as the doctor spoke about the other men. Perhaps they were similar to himself, but had undergone the good doctor's treatment—that's why they were put in the same room. How he would love to be in this other man's condition, falling asleep all the time. Or even the man on the mat, who slept for weeks at a time.

What blessedness! What joy! Thanks be to God Most High! Eduard giggled, and a sudden peace surrounded him.

"Doctor, I was never a good sleeper, but in the past year, especially the past months, it's gotten worse. This past week was the worst of all. Now I only get about two hours of sleep if I'm lucky. I see things. Oh doctor, help me."

"Eduard, I'm glad that you're being honest with me, because I think you may be staying here a while, and we really need to speak the truth to one another. Do you understand this?"

"Yes, Doctor, but please tell my wife. She may worry if I don't return soon."

"We will, Eduard. Now, I brought you here because this room is available for another person, and I wanted you to see it. This is where you'll be staying for now, with Mr. Weber and Mr. Hein. Mr. Weber, well, if he ever gets up again he's a splendid gentleman. Mr. Hein here is harmless, but as I said, a bit grouchy. Perhaps some of your manners will rub off on him. If all goes well, we may have you back home in a week or two. Now make yourself comfortable. There's your bed. We'll find clothes for your dresser. I just need you to empty your pockets for me; we can't have certain items in this unit."

Eduard emptied his pockets, but clung to the snowflake pin. When the doctor asked him to turn his pockets inside out, he hid the pin in the palm of his hand.

The doctor walked to the door. "I'll be back later. In the meantime, maybe Lukas can politely introduce himself."

"Eat dung," said the wobbling man to the wall.

\*\*\*

It was now about 8:30a.m. that same Monday morning. Eduard remained in his chair grasping the snowflake and staring at his new roommate's back. His songs continued, helping to clear his mind, but annoying his roommate.

"Would you please stop that!" asked the man still facing the wall.

"I'm not sure I should."

Eduard stopped when his roommate's head fell forward onto the pillow. Five minutes passed until the man pulled his head off the pillow. Eduard was now sitting on the edge of his straw mat with his hands folded on his lap.

"Hello, friend," Eduard said. "How are you doing? I mean your recovery. Hmmmm... Hmmmm... Hmmmm."

"What's with all the humming?"

"Keeps the demons away. Hmmmm... My name is Eduard... Eduard Strobl."

"I don't care."

"And, you're Lukas? How long have you been here?"

"You're going to keep asking questions, aren't you?"

"I'm just curious how long the treatment takes."

After a huff and a tight squeeze of his eyes, the man replied, "I've been here three years. And, Boris over there has been here even longer."

"Three years!"

"Three years. Thirty years. All the same."

"I only wish to be normal again, then return to my family."

"Great."

"Do you have a family?"

Once again, the man slumped over in the chair, only to wake again five minutes later.

"So," Eduard continued, "you say you have no family?"

"Oh, you're still here?" The man lifted his wobbling head to look at and scold his new roommate, but instead leaned in to get a better look. "I recognize you."

"Possible. I meet many people in my profession. Hmmmm...Hmmmm"

"No, no, no. You're the fellow that passes by all the time. Well, I guess I should at least thank you for sticking up for me."

Eduard now remembered and said, "Ah yes, you're the man on the bench, the one they nearly killed."

"Yeah, well it's a dangerous thing to escape this place. Somehow I knew you'd be joining us one day."

Eduard turned his head to the door, it was the same noise he heard earlier, but no one was there. He closed his eyes and hummed.

"Oh yes," Lukas said. "You'll fit in just fine."

# ❄ Chapter 28 ❄

# AT WAR

The following night Sara's brother Scott called to talk to her. He missed home and told her all about the danger in overseas and also some of the ways he and the others occupied themselves on their downtime. Sara's parents sat at the dinner table finishing a late meal and Sara's mother waited for the phone to be passed.

"Just put it on speaker-phone," Sara's father finally said.

"Hello! Can you guys hear me now?" Scott said.

"Yeah, honey, we're all here," Sara's mother shouted. "How are you doing? Are you safe? What time is it over there? It's about 8:30p.m. here."

"Yeah mom, I'm fine. It's about 6a.m. right now. Already been up for a couple of hours, but we got a tip from so we're relocating to a new area in a couple of hours, so got some rare morning downtime. How's dad?"

"Right here, son," Sara's father said, "Doing great. Where are you now?"

"Can't tell you the exact location, but we're cruising the Arabian Sea. Hey, do you remember Tim Stevens?"

"Yeah, little Timmy Stevens," Scott's father said, "his dad owns the hardware store."

"Yep. Well me, him, and a couple of the guys had to test the life raft the other day, and you should have seen the snapper he pulled out; this thing was a monster."

"You guys were fishing? Where on earth did you get a pole?"

"What was that? Sorry, Hornet taking off."

"I said where'd you get a pole from?" his dad repeated.

"Oh sorry, yeah, they equip the rafts with one, and tackle."

"Did he get in trouble?"

"Nah! He brought it onboard for the captain. Grilled it that night. Even got a plate myself. Man! Beautiful. Took a picture, I'll have to send it to you."

"Well, glad to hear you're enjoying yourself, Scott. And here we were thinking you were fighting a war over there."

"Ha-ha, well there's a few perks I guess. Got a tattoo too. So anyway, how's things there?"

"Your grandmother is getting surgery on her hip," Sara's mom said, "So pray for her."

"Aw, poor Nana. And how's Sara feeling?"

"I feel fine," Sara said, "just tired. The baby says hi too."

"Not even born and it can talk? Got a little genius there."

"Yep, going to be the smartest, most beautiful baby ever. I told Kyle to read to him (or her) every night before bed."

"Can Kyle read?"

Sara's father snickered and said, "He's working on the comics, I think. But don't worry, we'll be taking care of the baby, so it should turn out alright."

Scott chuckled. "Well, hey, I have to go now, but tell Nana I said I hope she feels better, and Sara... you behave yourself alright? Mom, Dad, I miss you, and I'll try to call later in the week."

"Love you too, honey," Sara's mother said, "Stay safe."

Scott hung up the phone, and the Sara's parents recounted the conversation as though it happened years ago. Her father corrected her mother on the geography of the Middle East, and Sara's mother rolled her eyes at the trivia. Sara, however, just glared at them until her mother finally noticed and asked what was wrong.

"Are you feeling alright, honey? Can I get you something?"

Sara shook her head and said, "I feel fine. What did you mean when you said you were going to take care of the baby? When was this decided?"

"Well, you don't expect Kyle is ready to handle a child do you?" Sara's father put the napkin from his lap onto the table. "It takes a lot of money to raise a family, then there's the dirty diapers, and—"

"I know," Sara interrupted. "Kyle can handle that."

"Honey," her father continued, "he couldn't even handle high school. Now he's putting in all those hours at the gas station, and trying to be some sort of rock star. So, who's going to watch the baby? He can't afford a nanny on what he makes. No. Your mother is going to work part time when the baby comes to help you out, and if we need to hire a nanny, then we can get one."

"But I want Kyle to have custody, and I want Kyle to raise it."

"And how does Kyle feel about that, Sara? Have you asked him? I would think he'd be happy to have someone else take responsibility. Have you even asked him?"

"As a matter of fact I did," Sara lied, "and he said he wanted to have the baby. And, I don't care what you say," Sara stood and shoved her chair in, "Kyle is the father, and Kyle's going to take care of it. And, I'm tired of you running him down all the time. This is our baby, not yours."

Sara stormed to the front door. "And he's taking my cat too!" she yelled before walking out.

"Well, he can definitely have the cat!" her father yelled out before the door slammed. Sara's mother got up to chase after her, but her father waved his hand. "Let her cool off, Carol. She's just upset. She'll come to her senses when she thinks more about it. Someone has to stay levelheaded around here."

"Jim, if this is the last year I have with my daughter, I don't want it to be full of fighting."

Sara's mom left the table and went to the kitchen to call her sister, while Sara's father went up to the bathroom, opened the window, and smoked an 'emergency cigarette' he had hidden in back of the towel closet which was now broken near the filter. He pinched the broken part with his fingers to close the hole, inhaled deeply, and talked to himself.

# ❄ Chapter 29 ❄

## NEW FRIENDS

It was around nine o'clock Tuesday morning. Eduard had not slept at all the previous night, but instead spent his night in the summer of 1278 fighting alongside Rudolf I, the first Austrian Emperor, against the Czech king, Otakar. In Eduard's delusion he was naturally Rudolf's right hand man, trusted with leading the troops to the banks of the River March. After long and difficult deliberations, the decision was made.

"To war!"

Eduard donned the armor of a knight and mounted up with the other brave souls. They traced the landscape eagerly searching for the first sign of the Czechs. At last they spotted them in the distance. With his cavalry charging behind, Eduard flew upon the back on his giant wolpertinger—the same one he had met at the Danube. He would swoop down to meet the enemy head on.

"Retreat!" yelled the enemy Otakar when he saw Eduard's amalgamation of horror stalking him. The teeth of Eduard's beast were sharper than swords, and its wingspan cast a mighty shadow below. It had revenge in its eyes for all of the doubts and jokes little Czech children had made about its appearance. There was nothing humorous about a flying rabbit with fangs and deer antlers *now*, was there?

The usurper and his men turned to run, but Eduard's flight was too swift. Faster, faster, the wolpertinger dropped like a hawk, plunging straight downward, cutting the air like an arrow until at last rampaging through the battlefield in a fury. Man and horse were bludgeoned by the beast's antlers, and swept aside like dirt from a broom.

"Over there!" Eduard yelled to his trusty beast, and the wolpertinger swiftly ran his antlers through Otakar's back, bringing his body up to the clouds only to drop it again onto the earth with the thud of defeat. After this, Eduard was made vice-regent of Austria, and ruled with Catholic charity. The wolpertinger was rewarded with the spoils of war—the body of Otakar to feast upon.

It was now around nine o'clock when Eduard's reign was ended by a crash on the floor. Lukas had been drinking a clay mug of tea and pacing the floor when he fell. Eduard's back was stiff from sitting up all night, but he eased himself off the bed enough to push at Lukas' body with his foot until he awoke again. Lukas brushed the clay shards from his shirt and sat back down. Eduard too returned to his position on the bed.

"Tell me Lukas, if it's no imposition, how you came here."

Lukas was not generally warm to strangers, or to anyone for that matter, but since he had realized Eduard was the man he had seen before, and since Eduard had just aided him once again, he felt an odd comfort with him, and perhaps an indebtedness.

"Okay, listen," Lukas said, "I was found on the street, much like yourself."

"I was found floating in a river," Eduard replied.

"A river? How did you end up there?"

"I walked."

"I see. Well, I was on my way to the tavern, when I passed out on the ground. A group of young men who were following me ran over me. Unfortunately they weren't so much interested in helping me, as taking my purse. When they saw that I wouldn't get up or answer them, they taunted me.

"Well anyway, they hit and pinched me, they kicked me and cut me, but I couldn't move. Finally a policeman chased them away, and brought me to the station. I was so flustered that I kept falling asleep and falling over. Even the police got a laugh out of it, kept me there a whole day, waking me up just to show me off. One of them finally stopped it, and brought me here to be evaluated. He thought I might have been on opium, but I've never touched it.

"My life has been fairly ruined, Eduard. I spend my days with bruises and cuts from falling down. I even burned myself once when I fell close to the fireplace and my leg rested too near to the coals." Lukas lifted his pants and showed the scars. "It happens whenever I get excited about something, or scared, or sad, so I've been learning not to feel... anything. Not like Boris over there. He wakes up, and all he cares about is food and women.

"I've concluded that my emotions will be the death of me, so I must be the death of them. It's as simple as that. When I'm asleep I can feel no pain. I probably just care too much, think too much, feel too much, and this is my downfall. I almost died once in here because I fell on my mat into the pillow and nearly suffocated. That was the only time I was happy to see Dr. von Croy—he turned me over so I could breathe."

"So, you've always been like this?" Eduard asked.

"No, it started as a young man. I think a maiden put a curse on me."

"And the treatments? They haven't worked?"

"I was doing a little better until they started more 'extreme measures'. Those just made it worse because it would get me nervous and angry."

"Extreme measures?"

"Yeah, when their cocktails fail, they use fire from the sky. A little machine attached to a rod on the roof that channels the fire through your body. It's painful, but they seem to think it helps."

"My God..." Eduard's humming began in earnest. "I don't want that!"

"Don't matter what you want, you'll get what they think you need."

"Hmmmm..."

"More humming? Well, hum all you want. Just keep it down please."

The two spoke no more for the next two hours, except for Lukas telling Eduard to quiet himself. Eduard lay on the straw mat staring at the ceiling. Finally Dr. von Croy returned around eleven o'clock

"Come on you two, lunch time. Eduard... Here, let me help you up. Boris, you awake? Okay, Lukas come on... No you can't stay here—well, we can talk about that later. Ha! Yes, of course we're having "boiled cat and rotten eggs," nothing but the best for my patients."

The two followed the doctor down the hall into another room where over two dozen patients were sitting in anticipation of the leftover scraps from the main hospital. Eduard and Lukas sat across from each other. Both were drowsy, and neither was hungry. Five other patients sat down beside them, and Lukas introduced his new roommate.

"Eduard... Eduard!" Lukas shook him by the arm to alert him. "This is Franz, Simon, Julian, Karl, and Erwin."

"Nice to meet you," Eduard said.

"Nice meet you," said Erwin.

Eduard wiped the drool from his lip and shook Erwin's hand. He tried not to stare, but he had never seen a man so unique looking. His chin was small for his large round face, his eyes were very deep-set, and his extended arm was shorter than normal. He seemed like a jolly enough fellow, but talked as though his tongue were too big.

"M'm'm'my name is Ffffranz," said the man next to Erwin.

"Lukas?" Eduard turned to his roommate with concern.

"It's alright Eduard, Franz here likes to take his time, puts a lot of thought into what he says."

Simon sat across from Eduard, and scratched his arm nervously in a perfect crisscross pattern, touching his elbow after every five 'x's. Next to Simon was Julian, whose twitching and grunting was making Eduard more nervous, but then he spoke, removing all doubt that he was similarly afflicted by spirits.

"I grrr ate shark once."

"Is that so?" said Eduard

"Yeah, wasn't too bad—SHEISSE!"

"I hmmmm meant no offense," Eduard apologized.

"None grrr taken—SHEISSE!"

"I saw a whale once," said Karl. With great hand motions he continued, "After a visit to Mount Etna I boarded a Dutchman. We sailed far and wide, and landed on an island made of cheese surrounded by an ocean of milk. When we left, our ship encountered the largest fish ever created. Luckily it spit us out and we all survived."

"You're funny, I like you story" said Erwin.

"Lukas," Eduard said, "did you see that?"

"See what?"

"The man with the big head, I think he was looking for me, but now he's... hmmmm...he's gone."

"Probably just von Croy trolling about."

"Ah, looks like he may have found a victim," Karl said. "That reminds me of the time I lost my horse and had to have a wolf tow my carriage. Dangerous creatures, they..."

As Karl launched into another fantastic tale, Eduard was startled by the screaming of one of the diners. The man was not allowed to finish his lunch, and was instead removed from the dining hall. The others at the table didn't seem bothered by this.

"Fire... for... him," said Erwin to Eduard.

"You're right, Erwin," returned Lukas, "and for all of us if we don't behave."

Eduard's eyes grew heavy as he sat listening to the chewing of food, the clanking of silverware and plates, and murmur of conversations. He leaned his head back and closed his eyes, but it hurt to shut them. He opened them again and stared at the white pealed ceiling. He hummed a tune which upset Lukas, but before Lukas could reach over and slap Eduard out of his trance, Lukas fell onto the table hitting his chin on a plate, sending the food flying onto the floor. A nurse came over, picked up the food, and put it back in the bowl. When at last Lukas awoke, Eduard was silent, humming only in his head towards the same spot on the ceiling.

"Nadine," Eduard then said.

"W'w'what did he ssssay?" Franz said.

"He misses his wife," Lukas said.

"Nadine!" Eduard yelled.

Lukas hit Eduard on the arm. "Silence! Do you want to be next?"

"Nadine!"

The same nurse that had visited the table only moments ago returned with two others.

"Hey beautiful," Karl said as Eduard was pulled from the table.

"How dare you!" The nurse slapped his face.

"SHEISSE!" Julian yelled. The nurse raised her hand again, but the two orderlies told her to ignore him. The three then left with Eduard.

"Well, it was just a matter of time, I guess," Karl said. "Nice fellow, but you can see the crazy in his eyes. Crazy people got a look about them."

"I like Eduard. Please, God bless him." Erwin said.

Wagging his spoon at the others, Lukas said, "I don't know about the rest of you, but I've had it. First chance I get, I'm breaking out."

"Where you going to go?" Simon said. "Come on, we won't tell."

"Oh certainly, Simon, like the last time you weren't going to tell, and I ended up in confinement for a week. And the time Harold, God rest his pathetic soul, told you he was the one that killed Dr. Berger. Or the time—"

"Alright, alright," Simon said, "I just can't help it, I get nervous, it's like I have to, you know... Listen, I promise, this time I won't say anything, I swear it, I swear."

"You know where I'm going when I get out of here." Karl stood on his chair. "Back to Bodenwerder, back to my Jacobine, my greatest adventure yet."

"Sit down," Lukas said. "Your hearing isn't for another two weeks, and if you keep up your stories, you can kiss your Jacobine goodbye for good."

"I don't have no one."

"Really Erw'w'win? D'd'd'don't you have any rrrrelatives t't'to t't'take c'c'care of yyyou?"

"No, left here as baby, Dr. von Croy my poppy now. Wish I had family. Hey Lukas, Eduard really want go with you, you should take him, and be nice person."

"Eduard's a grown man, Erwin, like the rest of us. If he really wants to leave, he'll have to find his own way out. I'm no friend of charity, and charity is obviously no friend of mine. And, that goes for all of you. Don't expect to ride my coattails. Find your own way out."

# ❄ Chapter 30 ❄

## THE MOST IMPORTANT THING

When Sara got out to the driveway she realized she had no keys to take the car, and little energy to walk very far. She noticed her neighbor's light on, walked over, and knocked on the door.

"Sara!" Mrs. Cohen said when she opened the door, "What a surprise. How are you, dear? What can I help you with?"

"Can I come in?"

"Um... of course... of course, come right in. Can I get you something? I just made a nut bread. It's still warm. Why don't I cut you a slice?"

"No thanks, Mrs. Cohen, I just needed to get out of the house. My parents are being jerks."

"Now, now, Sara, come on into the family room."

Mrs. Cohen and Sara walked into the living room where Mr. Cohen was sleeping soundly in his recliner. He didn't budge as the two sat on the plastic covered couch. Mrs. Cohen lowered the television with the remote control, and then folded her hands in her lap preparing to listen. The concerned look on her face showed she had done this many times before with her own children and grandchildren. This was her territory, her life's work.

"Now, tell me what happened with your parents, dear? Is it about a boy? Your friend Kyle?"

Sara sighed. "Yeah, I guess. It's just everything."

"Parents don't ever seem to understand, do they?"

"No, they don't. They treat me like I'm a kid, but I'm not. They talk like I'm not even there, like I'm already dead and it doesn't even matter. You know my situation, Mrs. Cohen, I'm going to be a mother soon, but I'm... I'm not going to be here to raise it."

"You're concerned what will happen when you're not here?"

"Well, yeah. I mean, I have the right to decide what's right for my baby, but they think they're in charge or something. Tonight they said they wanted to raise the baby, but I want Kyle to raise the baby."

"Kyle seems like a nice young man, at least from the couple times I've met him. Your parents don't like him?"

"They think he's irresponsible and not going anywhere in life. They think this whole thing is his fault, but it's not. If he's not a responsible person, then neither am I, which means they don't think I'd make a good mother either. And that hurts, Mrs. Cohen, that really hurts. So we made a mistake... big deal! I don't think of my baby as a mistake, and I don't think they should have the right to tell me or Kyle how to live."

"You're a big girl now, Sara, but I remember you when you were just a child yourself, riding your bike up and down the street, scaring my dogs half to death. It's hard for parents to let go."

"But, you have to let go. At some point you just have to let go. It's insulting, disrespectful, and uncaring not to."

"Sara, at my age I'd give just about anything to relive even one of those days when my boys were still at home, when I could fuss all over them, fix them supper, and tuck them in. It was hard at times, but it was good. No one wants to get old and lose the things that mean the most to them. Yes, you have to let go eventually, but not of your love for them. And, love is always protective."

"I guess, maybe."

"Definitely, my dear. Be patient, Sara. Parents may not always understand, or always do the right things, but they love you, and only want what's best for their child as you want what's best for yours. Be happy that your baby has the love and concern of so many people already. There are so many children in this world who have no one to fight over them, and that would be worse, wouldn't you agree?"

"Well, when you put it that way, yeah, I guess it's better than having a baby no one cared about."

"See that. And, you'll figure out the details in time. But, right now your baby has the most important thing anyone needs: love."

"Thanks, Mrs. Cohen."

"You're welcome, dear."

"Well, I guess I should get back home before my parents flip out."

"Probably a good idea. Come now, I'll walk you out."

When Sara returned home, she didn't say a word to her parents, but went to her room, locked the door, and called Kyle.

"I'm just hanging out," Kyle said, "just practicing some arpeggios and stuff. You sound mad. What's up?"

"Ugh, it's just my stupid parents again. I know they're trying to be helpful, but..."

"But what?" Kyle turned the volume off on his practice amplifier, but continued to practice.

"But... tonight they were talking as if they were going to raise the baby, and I'm like 'No way! You're not. Kyle is,' and my dad was like, 'Kyle's irresponsible,' and I was like, 'What on earth! It's our kid, it's not your kid, you're not the ones having it, and you're not the ones who get to raise it.' And then I started thinking and getting even more mad because I know you don't want this baby and so you probably wouldn't even care if someone else raised it, so my parents are right.'"

"Whoa! Sara," Kyle put the guitar down on his bed. "Who said I don't want the baby?"

"Kyle, be serious. You know it's the last thing in the world you wanted. Are you really going to change diapers, spend money, give up your free time, and all that sort of stuff? You're honestly going to sit there and tell me you want all of that?"

"Chill out, Sara. What the heck? You call here all upset about your parents and now I'm the bad guy... telling me what I want and don't want. Well, yeah! I didn't want a baby, and I sure didn't want to raise one on my own, and I didn't want to be—oh forget it! Why don't you just tell me what I want, Sara, or better yet, get your dad on the phone since he knows so much about everything."

Kyle hung up the phone and threw it across the room, then cranked his amplifier up and went back to practicing the guitar. Up and down the fret board, scales rising and descending, faster and faster, until twenty minutes later the calluses on his fingers gave way to blood-raw skin sliding painfully across the tightly wound steel strings.

"Kyle! Kyle!" Kyle's aunt opened the door. "We're trying to watch TV., could you turn that down. Oh my goodness! Is that blood?"

"Um, yeah. I guess." Kyle's fret board was smeared with red fingerprints.

"Honey, I think you've practiced enough for one night. Why don't you come downstairs and watch some TV with us?"

"I can't. I gotta call Sara."

"Alright, but just keep the volume down. Better yet, put something on those fingers and do something else."

"Sure, Gina."

After his aunt left, Kyle found his phone behind a pile of clothes on the floor and called Sara's cell phone.

"Hello..." Sara said.

"Sara, it's Kyle, I—"

"... This is Sara, sorry I missed your call. Leave a message at the beep. *Ciao!*"

Oh, how he hated her voicemail message with its long pause after the greeting. "Sara," Kyle said, "it's me. Call me back."

Over the next hour Kyle left three more messages. As he took his phone to call one last time, his phone buzzed. "It's about time!" he said before answering. "Sara, hi, it's Kyle."

"Yeah, no kidding," Sara said, "I just called you, remember?"

"I know you're mad at me, but I'm mad at you too."

"Then why did you call?"

"Because, you owe me an apology."

"I owe you an apology? You owe me an apology!"

"What? I'm just sitting here minding my own business and you called to bite my head off, saying I'm going to be a bad father and all."

"I didn't say that, Kyle. If you'd listen, you'd know that."

"So that's not what you said? I think that's what you said, Sara. You said I didn't want my own kid, and basically called me a loser."

"I didn't call you that, my parents did."

"Oh! But you agree with them, don't you?"

"No! I don't. I think *you* think you're a loser, and I think you think what my parents think is true, and so you don't think you can handle a baby."

"I can handle a baby, for crying out loud!"

"Don't yell at me again, Kyle, I'll hang this phone up right now."

"I'm not yelling! I'm... oh my goodness, this is..." Kyle paused and began again, "Sara, I'm...not...yelling at you. I'm just telling you that despite what your wonderful parents think, I'm not a complete idiot. I've changed diapers before."

Sara laughed, "Bull! What diapers have you changed?"

"My little nephew. A couple of years ago. I helped my aunt when we were watching him."

"Oh wow! You changed a diaper once. Call the President and get this guy a medal."

Kyle put the phone down near his leg and took a deep breath then put it back to his ear and said, "I don't know why I even bother. Maybe your parents are right; you should just let them raise the baby. You all obviously don't think I can. Oh well, I guess you should have thought about that before you let such a dumb loser have sex with you."

"Kyle," Sara spoke deliberately, "I'm about two seconds from getting in the car and coming over there to slap you. How dare you —"

"Oh, give it a rest," Kyle interrupted. "Listen, I don't care what you or your parents want anymore, it's my kid and I'm going to raise him, and if I have to go to court or to jail to do it, I will. So your parents can stuff it, your brother can too, and if you feel the same as them then you can too. I'm tired of getting dumped on by people. I know you're going through a lot of crap, but so am I, and what the heck is wrong with everyone? Everyone's got something to complain about, and I'm to blame for it. Sorry I'm not perfect, folks, sorry I'm just a loser. Someone just shoot me already."

Kyle waited for Sara's retaliation, but he heard nothing. She was definitely still on the line, but quiet.

"You know what I mean?" Kyle said, and waited...

"It's just screwed, up," he said, and waited some more...

"Sara, are you there, or what? I know you're there, for crying out loud."

"Sorry, Kyle, I was just using the bathroom, what were you saying again? The last thing I heard was something about letting some jerk have sex with me."

"Are you kidding me?!"

Sara waited to let Kyle stew. "Yeah," she finally said. "Just giving you a dose of your own medicine. You don't listen to me when I talk, so why should I listen to you?"

"Alright, Sara, this is getting really stupid. Why did you call in the first place?"

"You called me, remember?"

"No, I called you back. Why did you call before?"

"I told you. I was mad at my parents for wanting to take the baby. And mad at you because I didn't think you'd care if they did."

"Well, I do care, Sara. Your parents aren't taking the baby. I'm going to take care of it. How much clearer can I say it?"

"You don't mind?"

"Listen to yourself! It's my kid! No, I don't 'mind'. I want to do it. I *will* do it. And, I'm sorry about what I said about your parents, and you, and your brother, and everything and everyone. I'm not dumb, I know it'll be hard, but I need you to believe in me."

"I do, Kyle, I do." Sara began to cry. "I've always believed in you. Believe in yourself!... In us!"

Kyle listened as Sara wept on the other end. It wasn't the first time he made her cry, so why did he feel so much worse about it now? They had more arguments over the years than he could remember, but they somehow always ended up working it out. Why? He didn't know. A lot of people he would have just written out of his life without a second thought, but Sara was... well, she was Sara.

"C'mon, don't cry. I know you believe in me. I'm sorry." Kyle waited.

"I'm fine," Sara answered. "You're fine. Everything's... just... fine."

# ❄ Chapter 31 ❄

# THE CHAIR

When Eduard left the lunch room, he was taken to a room with a large wooden chair. The nurse helped him into it and strapped his arms and legs down.

"Nadine!" he yelled, thinking he had heard her singing in the courtyard. "Nadine, I'm here!"

Eduard was cuffed with metal clamps that were hooked up to wire. A bit was placed in his mouth as though he were about to have his arm amputated.

Dr. von Croy entered with his worn leather boots. "Eduard, my friend, this will only hurt a little," he said, "but it will help you in the end. You do want to be helped, don't you?"

Eduard remembered those boots and now remembered where he had seen Dr. von Croy before; it was that same day he had seen Lukas beaten not very long ago. Eduard stopped screaming and began humming, "Yes doctor, I do. Please help me!"

"Nurse, turn it on."

The nurse turned a large knob on the side of the device and a current began to flow into Eduard's body.

"A little more," said the doctor.

The nurse turned the dial.

Eduard moaned at the top of his lungs.

The nurse turned the dial.

Eduard stopped, and cringed, and looked blankly at Dr. von Croy. He remembered how those pupils stared him down in the snow like two musket barrels. Dr. von Croy returned with a grin, and Eduard's thoughts emptied like a dropped mug upon the floor.

Nearly ten minutes had passed when Eduard was unstrapped and led back to his room. His steps were short and deliberate, delicate and timid, like a man twice his age. When he arrived in his room, Lukas was sitting with his forehead pressed against the pillow. Eduard was led to his bed, his music soft now, as soft as his prayers. He prayed to Jesus, and Mary, and the merciful angels. Like the great heavenly silence of the seventh seal, Eduard's world was quiet, except for a harp in the distance destined to be thrown down with the Luciferian stars upon a scorched earth.

Around 12:30p.m., Lukas sat by Eduard on the bed. He wanted not to feel sorry for him but collapsed over him anyway. Eduard did not notice, and after five minutes it did not matter, for Lukas was again sitting by the side of the bed. He turned away from Eduard to keep himself awake, then said with determination, "Don't make me feel sorry for you." With that he sat back in his chair, meditating upon the stone. Six hours passed like that, only interrupted by a nurse checking up on Boris.

Dinnertime came and went, as did Lukas. Like Boris, Eduard did not respond to the order to eat, so after consulting Dr. von Croy the nurse let him stay in the room. When dinner was done, Lukas returned to the room. Around eleven o'clock at night Eduard finally spoke.

"Lukas, are you there?"

"I'm trying to sleep."

"I want to go home."

"Don't we all?"

"If I die before I sleep," Eduard said, "I pray the Lord my soul to keep."

***

"Still fighting those demons today, eh?" asked Karl the next day at breakfast.

"Yes," whispered Eduard as his eyelids fluttered and his pupils dilated without reason.

Throughout breakfast, the men at the table ignored Eduard's disconnection and humming, and Eduard took little notice of them. Their conversation was most of the same nonsense as usual, but one thing aroused Eduard's attention.

After witnessing an orderly yell at a patient, Lukas said with a full mouth, "I swear to God I'm getting out of this place. I'm no animal, one of those damn feral cats, and I sure am not to become one. That's what happens when you die in here, understand?"

"I'll believe it grrr when I see it." Julian said with a twitch.

"Oh, you'll see it soon enough."

"C'mon Lukas, tell us, when are you going? Where to? How do you propose to do it? How?"

"Alright Simon," Lukas said, then leaned in to whisper, "I got it all worked out. It's taken me years to learn to control my condition, but I think last night helped. I'm as callous as I need to be to make it past the gate and over the border to Hungary. Should only take about an hour or two, and I'll be safe there. Spent a lot of time as a child in

Pressburg, and the Slovaks have it in for the Emperor. Can't blame them. Good people. Pressburg, that's when my condition first showed. Funny really, actually." Lukas then paused and thought.

"Well, you can't stop there," Karl said, "go on, for pity's sake."

"I shouldn't."

"Then," Karl said, "let me tell you about this girl I met down in—"

"Alright," Lukas interrupted Karl's tale, "I'll continue. Where was I? Ah yes, I met a girl. We crept out and met behind a tree in the yard. When she leaned in to kiss me, I just flopped over. She thought I died, ran away screaming for her parents and confessed the whole thing. Well, I was awake by the time they got to me, so I got in trouble for sneaking out, and for 'playing a trick' on everyone."

"You gonna grrr look for her grrr—SHEISSE!"

"Well, I doubt she's still there, but I suppose I could look, finally get that kiss... though I don't suppose I could enjoy it much now. Hey, maybe it would reverse this spell she placed on me."

"Take me," Eduard whispered.

"Not a chance." Lukas swatted the air around his face as though Eduard was a fly. The others laughed.

"You guys shouldn't laugh at that," Erwin said, "Shame on you, Lukas."

Lukas ignored Erwin and continued, "So anyway, here's the plan..."

Eduard was about to repeat his request when he was asked to leave by a nurse.

"You have a guest, Mr. Strobl. Come with me."

It was now around noon on Wednesday when the nurse brought Eduard to a room where Nadine was sitting with Dr. von Croy. When he stumbled into the room, Nadine ran up to him and kissed his face.

"Oh honey, I'm so sorry," Nadine said, "I was scared, I didn't know what to do, I thought you would be there when I returned, I know you wouldn't hurt me, I just... I just..."

Eduard's serenity told Nadine that it didn't matter, that there was nothing to apologize for. The sight of her erased any transgression, real or imaginary, he or she could ever commit. The woman on the hill was nowhere in the room, nowhere in his mind, and nowhere in the world. He had trouble speaking, but her coming to see him mustered an energy and awareness that had abandoned him over the last few days.

"I love you, Nadine."

"I love you too."

"I'm sorry."

"Dear, it'll be alright," replied Nadine, "You'll be home soon, and everything will be back to normal."

Eduard peered into her eyes, and as a soft glow of sun beamed through the window he tried to recite the poem he had been composing in his journal, but just muttered something unintelligible.

"Oh Eduard." Nadine peered into Eduard's eyes and held back tears, "What's happened to you? I can't understand what you're trying to tell me."

"Latin... 'queen of the flowers'," Eduard answered. "Floarea... Regin..."

"When will he be better, doctor?" Nadine asked, still looking into Eduard's blank, unshaven face.

"It is hard to say, Mrs. Strobl, but by law we need to keep him here as long as necessary. However, we have very advanced treatments here, and you should have him back in no time."

"Thank you doctor, thank you so much," Nadine then turned her head to the doctor. "Can I spend some time alone with him, please?"

After the doctor and the nurse left the room, Nadine led Eduard to a chair for him to sit, then she knelt down and took hold of his hands, "Eduard, I want you to listen to me. You need to get better now, you really need to try. These people will never let you leave if you don't and... and, I can't live without you. Julia came back from Pressburg and was asking about you. I didn't know what to tell her. Then I found out you were here, but I didn't want to bring the children. I don't know that they could handle it. I need you to try for me; I need you to... Oh Eduard, please don't leave me like this!"

Eduard gripped Nadine's hands tighter, and closed his eyes in delight. "Nadine," he said, and said over and over for the mere joy of hearing it. "I'll come home... I promise... lie next to you and wake up... brand new... love you better."

Eduard's voice was dry like chalk. He did not hum or sing during this time, but soon the doctor and nurse walked in and he began again.

"Alright, Mrs. Strobl," said Dr. von Croy, "it's time to bid farewell. That humming is an indication of anxiety. Your presence may be counterproductive. We need to bring Mr. Strobl to another room for treatment."

"Can I stay with him?"

"I'm sorry, Mrs. Strobl," answered the doctor, "but, I think Eduard would do better without any distractions."

"I'd really like to stay if you don't mind."

"I'm sorry, but you don't have that option, Mrs. Strobl."

"Well, shouldn't I?"

"Nurse," the doctor addressed his assistant, "could you please escort Mrs. Strobl to the door?"

"Get your hands off of me," Nadine said as the nurse attempted to grab her arm. The nurse shrunk back. Nadine rose to her feet, then gave Eduard (now humming louder) one last kiss on the forehead before she left the room.

Eduard was then led to the room again with the chair and the machine. He underwent his treatment, and then left again virtually immobile. When he returned to his room, Father Kraus was there in holy garb and crucifix in hand. Lukas ignored him from his chair.

"Here he is, Father."

"Thank you, Doctor, I'll try not to keep him long."

Dr. von Croy left the room, and Eduard sat upon his mattress with his hands clenched beneath his legs. The priest pulled up the desk chair and sat beside him welling up with tears.

"I'm very sorry that it's come to this, Eduard; but alas, it seems that it is for your own good. The Lord sometimes works through the hands of doctors and medicine, and perhaps that's what you truly need. I fear I led you astray when I suggested this was a spirit or demon. Like Job's companions, I was quick to blame you, when the truth is that no one but the Lord knows and we must simply trust that He is good and knows what He is doing. Where were we when He created the world? Can we bind the chains of the Pleiades? No! Nor can we loosen the belt of Orion. Job was righteous but suffered. He longed for an explanation, but none was given except to trust in a Father who wants what's best for our eternal souls. The Lord stripped King Saul of his crown to give it to a man after his own heart. You too are a man after God's own heart, and for you a crown verily awaits."

"Yes, Father."

"However, I want you to continue to say your prayers and supplicate the Lord's favor. Although, it may not seem like it, His grace already rests upon you in great measure. May the Lord restore your fortunes like Job and give to you twice what you had before - whether in this life, or the life to come."

"Yes, Father."

"I'm very sorry, Eduard. God has a plan in all of this, and..." Father Kraus stopped when interrupted by laughter from Lukas. "Is there something wrong, sir?"

"No," Lukas said.

"Have I offended you?"

"Never mind!" Lukas's forehead plunged against the pillow.

"Eduard," Father Kraus continued as he gave to Eduard a bite of bread and a sip of wine, "don't give up faith. The saints and angels have seen more trying times than these, but they have persevered. You will too."

"Father," Eduard said, "Does God want me to die?"

"Eduard, the Lord wants you to live forever, and you shall. Christ has declared that those who believe in him, though they die, yet shall they live. Your passing, as with all the righteous will not go unnoticed, but as the Psalmist has said, 'precious in the sight of the Lord is the death of his saints.'"

"When?"

"In his time. You only need to believe."

"Yes, Father."

"I've much to do today, so I cannot stay, but I shall return again." Father Kraus blessed Eduard with the sign of the cross, and left.

Eduard sat on the bed trying to pray, and Lukas awoke again. Turning to Eduard, he said, "Those guys get me worked up! If God speaks through men, he certainly chose a fine bunch to do it... What's so funny?"

"My hands...," Eduard wore a delirious smile. He slowly removed his hands from under his lap.

"Yes," Lukas continued, "and what's so funny about them?"

Eduard held his hands up to his face. "They're asleep."

# ❄ Chapter 32 ❄

## VIEW FROM AN ASYLUM

Although the school year was halfway over, Sara still did not regret not going. She was what the others called an "art geek" with only a few friends, and spent most of her study-halls and lunch breaks in the art room with Mrs. Donahue. It was not as though she were unpopular, but she just found many of her peers boring, except of course for her musician friend Kyle. Although he was bad at dealing with issues, he was more emotional than most guys she knew.

"Ignore those jerks," Sara said noticing some boys laughing at Kyle eating alone in the cafeteria. That was the first day they ever talked. It was sometime around the middle of October in the eighth grade. They had been in a couple of classes together, but Kyle was painfully shy and ignored the few times he noticed her looking at him.

"They don't bother me," Kyle said. "Bunch of losers."

"You mind if I join you?" Sara had already put down her tray and sat across from him.

"I don't mind."

"Good. My table is so boring. Makeup and clothes, that's all they ever talk about."

"You don't like makeup?"

"Eh, I wear it, but I don't want to talk about it all the time. I like art and stuff. What do you like?"

"Um, music, I guess."

"Cool. Do you, like, play in the school band?"

"No, I play guitar... well, I will soon. My aunt and uncle are buying me one for Christmas."

"Wow! That's neat. My aunt and uncle always get me stupid stuff. My parents do okay though. How about yours?"

"No. I don't have parents."

"What happened to them?"

"They died."

"Oh, sorry. Yeah, my cat just died, but I'm getting another one soon. My dad hates cats, but my mom said it's okay. Do you have any pets?"

"Nope."

"Not even a bird?"

"Nope. Had a hamster, but it died... I think your friends are looking for you."

Sara turned around and noticed her friend Jen and the others waving and giggling from their table. They blew kisses and made other gestures designed to embarrass the two. Sara smiled and blushed, and said "I guess I should go back. Well, it was nice talking to you. Good luck with the guitar."

"Thanks."

\*\*\*

As Sara grew sicker, she stayed in contact with a few other friends, especially her fellow "art geek" Jen, but didn't care to see anyone else, nor wish for the drudgery of irrelevant classes, class clowns, note-passers, and other 'cogs in the system' (as Kyle called them). It was a relief to be left alone with her brushes. They were the tools by which to exercise demons, construct cities and landscapes, and amuse her senses with color.

Her paintings where becoming more abstract and intense—much too bizarre for a girl her age, or anyone of any age. But she was old now—older than her parents, her teachers, even her own lethargic hands that became more skilled by the hour despite the porous holes slowly being carved into her brain. These destructive prions brought to her strange thoughts and created a sponge in her skull that wrung itself out onto the canvass whenever she unscrewed the caps of her depleting oils. In fact, it wasn't until she was low on linseed oil that she returned to school for the first time.

"Are you sure you don't want to come in?" Sara's mom asked in the parking lot of her high school.

"That's alright. I look awful."

"You look fine. All the kids have left for the day and I'm sure your teachers would love to see you."

"I'll just stay here. Oh, and make sure you grab my linseed oil; it should be in a drawer near my other stuff. It has my name on it."

"Okay, honey," Sara's mom said as she opened the car door, "I'll be right back, then."

Sara's mom had taken the day off from work at the real estate office where she worked as an office manager. She spent the cool March day with Sara going to both breakfast and lunch together and shopping in between. This was their last stop of the day, to pick up things Sara had left in her locker and in the art room.

It felt odd to Sara to be back at school. How many times she had parked in this same parking lot, walked up to those front doors with books in hand, and hurried to homeroom before the bell rang. Like the mall, it felt surreal, or unreal, like she could wave her hand through the entire scene and it would disperse like a vapor. Then she spotted some classmates leaving from an after-school activity and the realism returned. She ducked down.

Yes, she had lost weight, and wasn't wearing make-up, but she was not a particularly vain girl. No, she was more afraid that if they saw her they would come to the car and make conversation about how she was feeling, where she had been etc. etc. blah, blah, blah—a time and energy consuming exercise she was not in the mood to go through for the millionth time. Doctors, friends, parents, relatives, church people, everyone wanted to know 'how she's doing'. Although she appreciated it, it was getting on her nerves.

Fifteen minutes later, however, her head picked back up when her mother returned outside accompanied by Mrs. Donahue. The two were talking pleasantly on their way to the car, their hands full of art projects Sara had left: paintings, sketches, doodles, a clay mug, a paper maché head, and even an ugly pastel drawing she had thrown out but was apparently rescued.

As her mother opened the backdoor for the art work, Sara rolled down the window for her bubbly mentor.

"I thought I threw that out," Sara joked.

"Sara, my little protégé, you look beautiful as always. How are you? My room seems so empty this year without you."

"I'm okay, just a little under the weather most days... tired and stuff. But, I've been painting a lot."

"Is that so? Well, I would love to see sometime."

"You should stop by the house one night," Sara's mother said.

"Well, I was actually planning to call Sara. I'm going to the Metropolitan Museum of Art. to see the new Van Gogh exhibit they have this month and wanted to know if she would like to join me. I can come by and pick you up, and maybe then you can show me some of the things you've been working on."

"The Met? Sounds good to me!"

"Well, what is it, Tuesday?" Mrs. Donahue quickly got her bearings and went through the calendar in her mind. "This Saturday is no good—my son's finally tying the knot, but the following Saturday would be fine."

For the next two weeks Sara worked hard at finishing various projects she had begun, and even started a few others for when Mrs. Donahue visited. Her parents let her take over the enclosed porch and turn it into a makeshift studio. It was bright, and compelled her to leave her small dark bedroom upstairs; moreover, her parents could see her from the living room and enjoy her enthusiasm.

"What is that?" her father said when stopping in to notify her of dinner, "Some abstract modern art thing?"

"It's God," Sara answered stepping back from the canvass.

"I thought God was an old man with a long white beard."

"That's Santa, dad. God is a light surrounded by a rainbow, kind of like the opposite of a black hole."

"Well, keep up the good work." Sara's father pulled the glass doors closed again as Sara stepped back toward the canvass.

When on the following Saturday Mrs. Donahue stopped in to pick Sara up for the museum, she walked into the studio where Sara was again hard at work.

"Wow! Look at all of this. This is really amazing, Sara. Truly mesmerizing."

"You really like it?"

"Like it? These are absolutely gorgeous. Where did you learn to paint like this?"

"From you, of course."

"Oh no," Mrs. Donahue said, "I can't take credit for this, although I'd love to. You've really come into your own. Very impressive."

Sara smiled at the flattery, not being sure how sincere her mentor was. "Let me get changed, and we'll get going."

After twenty minutes, Sara and Mrs. Donahue drove to the Metropolitan Museum of Art in Manhattan which took about another forty minutes. When they arrived and paid the suggested donation, they headed straight for the new Van Gogh exhibit where five new paintings were on loan from the Van Gogh Museum in Amsterdam, including Mrs. Donahue's favorite, *Boulevard de Clichy*.

"It's just so gentle and bright," Mrs. Donahue explained, "The lines actually draw you through the city streets. Reminds me of my trip to Paris in college."

"You went to Paris...? Lucky."

After admiring this and the four others, they came upon Sara's (and everyone else's) favorite, *Starry Night*, or rather it came upon them—catching up the spectators in the swirling winds, and the yellow stars glistening in the deep blue night above the town outside the artist's asylum.

"I see a lot more of the night these days." Sara said, mesmerized by the painting.

"Does it look like this when you see it?" asked Mrs. Donahue.

"When I take out my contact lenses," Sara joked.

The two journeyed into another room where scruffy students from a nearby college were sketching in pads and writing notes. Mrs. Donahue walked around to each painting while Sara sat on a bench in the middle of the room. The paintings came alive to her. The subjects of portraits looked at her, even talked. She felt herself becoming a part of the works until paint flooded the floor to her knees, her flesh turned to taut canvass covered in crackled varnish. The walls framed her in, the light—

"You've got the right idea," Mrs. Donahue said as she sat down next to Sara, "These heels are killing me."

"I think I could spend the rest of my life here," Sara said.

"It'd take two lifetimes just to see everything. Gosh, this place is huge. I should have worn my flats."

"So why do we do it?"

"Wear heels?"

"No, I mean, why do people paint? What is it about painting?"

Mrs. Donahue paused and said, "Well, I suppose it's the same reason why some write or compose music—fascination with the world around us, the need to create. Some use words, some notes, and some paint. Maybe painters are more visual; our music is on canvass."

Still staring at the wall before her, Sara asked, "When did you start painting, Mrs. Donahue?"

"Oh dear," Mrs. Donahue searched her mind, "Let's see... I think I got my first water-color set in elementary school, and was hooked ever since. I still prefer water to be honest; it just has a unique, soft aura about it. It's easy to do a bad water-color, but a good one can be as challenging as oil. It's really not what you're using, but how you're using it."

"Did you want to be a professional painter?"

"Well, yes. But that's different than being a 'famous' painter. I make a living teaching art and selling my works at fairs and such, so I suppose I achieved my dream." Mrs. Donahue paused. "And, what's your dream, Sara?"

Sara stood with her arms stretched and turned to Mrs. Donahue with a voice too loud for the museum. "I want to travel the world: Paris, Venice, and Vienna! Paint everything I see—everything! Just capture life, freeze it, and frame it so it can last forever, so everyone can enjoy it like me." Sara sat back down, now staring at her own sneakers. "I don't want to die, Mrs. Donahue. That's my dream."

Mrs. Donahue patted Sara's knee. "Sara, no one wants to die. It's the unknown, and of course that's scary. It's like walking into your first day at a new school. It's sad to think about leaving everything you're familiar with behind."

"If you don't mind me asking, Mrs. Donahue, do you believe in God or the afterlife and stuff?"

Mrs. Donahue chuckled. "Well, I'm honestly not the most religious person, but my father certainly was. I remember he once said that death was like a quick catnap before the resurrection. I'm not so sure about all of that, but I certainly think about it—I'm not getting any younger, you know."

"So what do you believe?"

Mrs. Donahue thought for a moment while she glanced around the room. "Actually, I guess I believe that dying is like a change of perspective, a stepping back from the canvass to see the big picture. Heaven? Sure. Why not? I think we're going to see things no artist here could ever dream of, and who knows, maybe they'll even have oils and watercolors there. Heck, you may even get Van Gogh, Monet, or Picasso as a tutor. And if you get there before me then you can be mine. Deal?"

Sara smiled. "Deal." She didn't like to talk too much about death, but she was glad she let it slip out to Mrs. Donahue. She felt more comfortable talking to her. The two then got up, hugged, and finished out a day together in the closest place to heaven they could find.

# ❄ Chapter 33 ❄

## BLOOD SUCKERS

"So what is it?" Lukas said from his chair, now with his back to the wall. It had only been a week since Eduard arrived, but his presence lifted Lukas' mood like nothing before. Eduard was an amicable gentleman, even if a bit deranged. He had an innocence to his soul in spite of (or perhaps because of) his demons. The degree to which Lukas almost cared for Eduard was greater than the degree he had almost cared about anyone in awhile, which helped when Lukas lacked things to harden himself against. In some ways he needed to care for someone again if only for pragmatic reasons. Eduard was easy to like, so the challenge to dislike him was fortifying, and a helpful step in his recovery.

"What?" asked Eduard.

"The thing in your pocket? I see you playing with something."

Eduard removed the object from his pocket, and without looking over, stretched out his hand for Lukas to see.

"For a girl I assume. It's nice. I think she'll like it."

Just then, Dr. von Croy opened the door. His clunking boots were usually enough to excite Lukas, but not today. Lukas did not nod his head once, even when the good doctor playfully messed up his hair.

"Ah Lukas, I see you left your usual position, perhaps the treatments are effective after all. Now if we could just get poor Boris there to budge, we'd have a most progressive day. It's about time for your friend here to be treated." The doctor approached Eduard's bedside and examined his countenance. "Are you ready to go, Eduard?"

Eduard hummed and said, "May I see her?"

"Your wife? Of course you may, just as soon as your health improves."

"She'd make me better."

"Well, my friend, I've something else in mind."

Lukas caught a glimpse of Eduard, and the fear in his eyes, but then turned away before sympathy could arise.

"Come now Eduard, let's get you down the hall."

The doctor grabbed Eduard's arm to help, and the silver pin dropped to the floor. He picked up the pin. "Ah, what's this? I don't think you should have this right now. I'll hang onto it. We wouldn't want you to injure yourself with it." He pocketed the pin. "Can you walk with me?"

Eduard made no reply.

"Alright then, I'll have one of the nurses bring you a wheelchair."

Dr. von Croy left the room and shorty returned with a nurse and a wheelchair. They helped Eduard into it and then wheeled him down the hall.

Lukas rose to his feet and to the door to watch the three disappear. He felt drowsy but with a deep breath he walked back to his chair, sat down, removed the pillow from the wall and placed it behind his back. "Good luck, Eduard."

Meanwhile, the nurse rolled Eduard into the room in which the chair resided amidst other various instruments, pointed, blunt, hinged, leather, and glass.

Eduard's hands gripped the arms of the wheelchair. "Don't," he begged.

Eduard was helped from the wheelchair into the other chair, and strapped down. After five minutes the current began to flow afresh into his body. This time they increased the voltage, and the duration from five minutes to ten. His teeth grit against the bit. His vocal chords strained to scream, but they were hindered in his throat. When at last they were through, Eduard's eyes were wide open and his mouth clenched. After ten minutes, he was unstrapped. However, when the nurse reached out to help him, he began to swing his arms, hitting her in the chest. Dr. von Croy rushed over to assist her, put his knee into Eduard's chest, and strapped his arms back into the chair.

"I don't think it is a good idea to let him around others," said the nurse,

Eduard knew better than to protest. It had been a week since he saw his wife and he shuddered at the idea of missing her for longer. Instead, he took the cure peacefully.

"Now Eduard," Dr. von Croy said, "we're going to try a new treatment today that has worked with some success on our veterans." He went to a cabinet and pulled out a glass jar, unscrewed the top, and pulled out something long and brown. It wiggled in his hand as he brought it over. The nurse lifted Eduard's shirt and the doctor placed it on his stomach, then another, and another, until over a dozen were attached. "*Hirudo Medicinalis*," he said, "or what we like to call, 'Leech Therapy'. These will take the poison out of you."

## ❄ Chapter 34 ❄

# EMBRACING THE HORRIFIC BEAUTY

Maybe it was the warm April air or the flower buds in the dusk, or perhaps it was shopping for prom tuxedoes earlier that day, or maybe even fatherhood being only two months away or the nerves about life in general stemming from the show Sticky Wicket was playing that night at The Pulse. Whatever is was, after dinner that evening Kyle asked his aunt about love, and her opinion of his situation.

"When you love someone, Kyle, you want to be with them. It's not a burden, but a pleasure. And if you never want to be without them, you do what you can to make that possible... Usually people get married. It's really not much more complicated than that."

Kyle also asked about his parents, and they spent about an hour of that evening looking through old pictures and mementos brought down from the basement.

"This is a picture of your dad and I when your grandparents brought us to Disney World in Florida." Kyle's aunt held up a photo. "Your father tormented me on the Magic Mountain ride so much that I refused to go on any more rides with him. The picture is so faded, but the memory is as clear as day. Oh, and this is later that night at the hotel."

"What's that pink thing on the floor?"

"That, Kyle, is what was left of a stuffed animal I won after your father got through with it."

"Dad was a little punk when he was a kid, huh?"

"No, just a boy."

Kyle laughed. "I never had a sister to torment."

"Well, actually we got along pretty well, but at that age... well, I suppose we both could have been a little nicer. It's like that with siblings. Oh, and what is this?"

"Is that mom?" Kyle took the picture from his aunt and held it closer to his face.

"That was, I believe, the day after the prom. We didn't return our dresses until later, so we decided to wear them to breakfast at the diner. Quite a looker, huh?"

"She was... yeah, she was pretty. You both were... are." Kyle quickly changed the subject. "What's this?" he said as he pulled a newspaper clipping from a shoe box. He then read through the obituary intently. "I never knew my dad was in the Reserves."

"For all the sibling rivalry growing up, I can say this, Kyle: Your dad was a good, and honorable man. He loved his family, and went out of his way to help people. I can still see his funny smile and hear his laugh. One of a kind."

"Who wrote this?"

"I did. Wasn't easy. Haven't read it in years. It was hard on us all, Kyle. You spend so much time with someone, invest so much of your heart into them, and then suddenly they're gone. Doesn't seem fair, but you have to be grateful for the time you did have together, and hang on to the good stuff. You know what I mean?"

"I think so."

"Here," his aunt said, "I want you to have something," Kyle's aunt opened one of the larger boxes they had taken down and pushed some of its contents aside. At the bottom of the cardboard box was a smaller black box.

"This was your mother's engagement ring. She wanted it to be handed down to you. It means there's a past that's worth remembering and a future worth having. It's been in our family for a long time."

"It's kind of different," Kyle said, "but it's nice."

"Look," his aunt continued, "I want you to hold onto this from now on, and you'll know when the time is right, okay?"

"Thanks, that means a lot." Kyle hugged his aunt, put the ring case in the box and put the other contents back in. Kyle then went to his room to gaze at the ring in silence. Mingled in his mind were thoughts of his mother and Sara. He thought about the smile on his mother's face in her wedding pictures. It resembled so much Sara's smile when they were together. He too began to smile, and when he looked up into the mirror hanging on his closet door, he saw the same look of contentment. He had been afraid of that smile, but now it made him laugh. These mingled thoughts, however, soon unraveled and left only one woman in his mind.

"I'm such an idiot," he said to the mirror. "Kyle, what on earth are you doing?"

Kyle's aunt knocked on the door when she heard some strange noises. When she opened it she found him laying face down on the bed crying.

"Hey, come here." Kyle's aunt helped him sit up and wrapped her arms around him. For nearly ten minutes Kyle poured out his soul with his tears. He confessed the ugly truth that he had almost been relieved Sara was going to die, because it freed him of obligation to her, of responsibility, of having to face adult problems and adult feelings. But now, with his heart revealed, he saw the scared boy Sara spoke of and wanted nothing more to do with him.

"I have to see her."

"Kyle, it's getting late. And you have a show to play. Tomorrow's a new day."

"Oh crap!" Kyle looked at the clock on his nightstand. "Sorry, aunt Gina, I have to go." Kyle shot up to his feet, grabbed his keys and wallet from the dresser, and hurried out of the house, running into his uncle at the door who was just getting home from work.

"Whoa! What's your hurry?"

"Sorry, Pat, can't talk now. Got a show to play. Already late."

Thankfully, Steve and Jay were bringing Kyle's stuff to the club, so he didn't need to worry about that, but the band was supposed to meet with Brian and Bruce beforehand to discuss business with their record label. The last thing Kyle wanted was to appear unprofessional or disinterested on the most important day of his budding musical career.

"I don't know," Kyle's aunt said to herself still on the bed, "maybe I should have waited to show him this stuff."

"What was that all about?" Pat came to the doorway of the room.

"He's late for his big show."

"Oh, okay. So what's wrong? You alright?"

"Well, I gave Kyle his mother's ring. I don't know. I hope it was the right thing to do."

Pat came in and sat down. "Well, it's out of our

hands now. Did you tell him to put it somewhere safe?"

"Yes, I told him. But, I don't see it anywhere."

# ❄ Chapter 35 ❄

## MAYBE EVERYONE IS CRAZY

Another week had passed when Nadine came back to visit Eduard the following Sunday.

"I'm sorry, but you can't see him," said the orderly at the desk. "he's been misbehaving."

"You can't be serious," Nadine said. Anna and Julia looked on from behind. "Surely, not my husband."

"He struck a nurse this past week, Mrs. Strobl. We would not trust him around the little ones right now."

Nadine grabbed Anna and Julia by the hand, and stormed out of the hospital. When she returned home, she fumed with her friend Regina whom she invited over.

"It's not right!" Nadine sat on her front step as Regina stood near.

"Why don't you write a letter of appeal?" Regina said.

"To who, the doctors? They don't care, they're the ones in charge of it. No, I just have to wait this out. I was not proper with the orderly today, and I fear I may have caused Eduard more trouble."

"Nadine," Regina pulled Nadine up by her hands and held her face, "you have never been a quitter. I know you, you'll think of something. Do you want me to have Diederich go down there and talk to them?"

"That's not necessary, and I don't think it would help." Nadine sighed. "I've got children to worry about.

What am I supposed to do if Eduard is gone for another few weeks, or even months?"

"You'll never be out on the street, Nadine, even if you have to come settle with us. The children get along famously."

Anna and Julia were very quiet around the house, and didn't dare upset their mother more, instead they half-heartedly played with puppets upstairs with the Trommler's four-year-olds, Dirk and Doris.

"Daddy's never coming home, and it's my fault, I shouldn't have gone to Pressburg."

"That's foolish Julia. How's it your fault?"

"I should've been here to help."

"How?"

"I don't know, maybe we could have gone fishing together, talked about things. I think dad needs a friend." Julia pulled her doll away from Dirk, who was grabbing at it. "Play with your own, Dirk, it's not nice to grab." Dirk sulked.

"He's sick is all," Anna continued, "Fishing can't cure sickness."

"When people are sick they cough or throw up, but they put dad with all the crazies. He has sickness in the head, and talking helps that."

"Daddy's not crazy, Julia."

"The doctors think so."

"Maybe they're crazy."

"Maybe you're crazy."

Anna put her hands on her hips. "Well, why are you playing with a crazy person then?"

"I don't know, maybe I won't." Julia stuck out her tongue.

"... Or maybe you're crazy."

Exasperated, Julia put down her puppet and lay back on the floor with a sigh. "Maybe everyone's crazy."

Dirk snatched Julia's puppet from the ground and began beating it on the floor. Julia quickly reprimanded him with a slap on the wrist, sending the child running downstairs crying for his mother.

"Now you've done it," Anna scolded.

"Keep quiet!" Julia returned, "Or play in your own damned room."

Anna's mouth was agape at her little sister's foul mouth. She got up from the floor and punched Julia in the shoulder, sending her crying downstairs too. "I'm telling mother what you said!" she yelled out as Julia fled.

All three children would go to bed that night without dinner or dessert, but little Doris was given an extra piece of cake. The sweet four-year-old twin didn't speak or cry much, being born mostly deaf and aware of the trouble talking seemed to cause for her brother Dirk.

\*\*\*

"What did you say?" asked Lukas from his chair.

Sitting on his bed, Eduard repeated softly what he had unconsciously whispered. His words were few and slow. Not all of the conversations between the two made sense, but the shock therapy seemed to jolt Eduard's mind enough in the hours following it that some conversation could be had.

"And the Lord..." Eduard whispered, "... blessed the latter end of Job more than his beginning."

"Oh, more of that? Okay, Eduard, let me tell you something." Lukas shifted his seat to face Eduard. "There was a time when I believed in the Church. I have no problem with God—used to talk to him all the time—but the Church could make a heathen out of the truest saint. I've learned to let it all roll off my shoulders, had to get over all that religious affection nonsense."

Eduard whispered. "I'd rather feel everything in sleep... then nothing awake."

"You see that," Lukas said, "not too long ago that kind of judgmentalism would have got me riled up, but not today. There's nothing you could say, Eduard, that would make me upset. I'm done with the doctor's chair, and I'm done with this place. You can stay as long as you'd like, but I'm gone." Lukas shifted his seat back again, back against the wall. My purgatory is done."

"They won't... let you."

"Well, now who lacks faith? See Eduard, someday I'll be the one passing by on the street, and you'll be the one on the bench. Oh, sweet freedom."

"I... don't... have long," Eduard said, "without her."

Lukas scoffed, "I've survived for years without a wife. And now, well now I can't even afford to love anymore, not if I want to be free. It's one or the other."

"Love is... freedom," said Eduard.

Lukas sat on the end of Eduard's bed and leaned in. "No. Love is a tower of fools; Hungary is freedom. The asinine things men have done for the hankering of women, country, and friend could fill the royal library... By the way, what is that on your neck?" Lukas leaned over to Eduard and pulled off a leech, leaving a trail of blood on Eduard's shirt. "Looks like the doctor forgot one of his comrades."

Eduard said no more. It was Sunday, but Father Kraus was busy that day, so Eduard was without visitors. He was happy, however, that Lukas had warmed up to him. Over the next few days they (mostly Lukas) would talk more about their lives outside of the Tower. It was more an exercise, thought Lukas, to prepare himself.

"Well, my father was a harvester," Lukas rambled on, "...liked to move around a lot. My family was pretty poor, but we were friendly; we took whatever help we could get, and that included used books. I love to read, it's how I received my education, but books are hard to come by in here. Good literature never killed a man, Eduard. On the contrary, it's those who fill their heads with sanitized, State-commissioned literature, who are as void of life as the grave. Don't let that Maria Theresa tell you what to read. *The Sorrows of Young Werther* is no different than the gospel. A man in love cannot be with the beloved and so kills himself.

"Goethe is doing what a good writer ought: portraying life in all its callous realities. He doesn't piss in a bowl and call it soup." Lukas began to recall his books, "'life is but a dream,' 'prison walls.' See! Old-bag Maria wants to hide that from us. Tell us we're walking on streets of gold - that the dung on our shoes is angel dust. Life is raw and rude, and possibly unreal, but it's all we have, and why kid ourselves about it? Life is a prude maiden's slap in the face, but fools like me are willing to risk it to break out of our prison for it, if only to be left with an unsatisfied ache in the groin. The maiden? She just laughs and walks away swinging her hips."

"I know, son," Eduard mumbled, "I'm... sorry I ran from you. Don't... kill me."

"But I suppose—Hey! Snap out of it, Eduard!" Lukas slapped Eduard's face causing his delusion to cease momentarily, then he continued to himself, "If Goethe is right about life being a dream, then I'm more alive than anyone? Although, I guess that's not very good news for you, Eduard. Maybe Boris, however. Hey, you alright there, Eduard? You look like you're in pain."

"I'm... dying, Nadine."

Lukas stood to call for a nurse.

Eduard took a deep breath and with his eyes glued to the wall said, "No."

By the end of the week Eduard was barely able to speak, though sometimes he wrote short notes. The next Saturday, nearing midnight, Eduard and Lukas would share their final words.

# ❋ Chapter 36 ❋

## TAKING AND LEAVING THE PULSE

"Well, it's about time," Steve said as Kyle hurried over to their table at The Pulse and sat down amidst the black lights, blaring music, and cheap beer.

"Sorry guys, got caught up with stuff at home. Where's Brian and Bruce?"

"They're late too," Steve said.

"Awesome! Then I didn't miss anything."

"Only the chance to see Mark get carded at the bar," Jay said and laughed.

"You guys brought my stuff, right?"

"Yup," Steve said, "it's backstage. Oh man, you should see it back there. Jay and I even got to talk with the drummer of Lunar Unit... coolest guy ever! His roadie was sick or something, so he was tuning his drums and stuff. Jay got to help."

"Oh yeah!" Jay gave everyone at the table a high five except Kyle who took out his phone, began texting someone, but then put it away before he was done.

The band was scheduled to play at 10:30p.m. for half-an-hour. They wanted to go on earlier and play longer, but the club was hosting a contest for a radio station which wouldn't be over until late. The manager was not even going to let them play since 11:00p.m. was fairly late to expect the headlining band to start. However, Mark's girlfriend, Angela, was able to pull some strings, being a friend of the family. With time to kill, they passed a couple hours soaking up the moment at one of the booths near the bar, and waited for Brian and Bruce. Now around 10p.m., *Sticky Wicket* was itching to get on stage.

"Oops, hold on," Kyle interrupted his conversation with Jay to read an incoming text message from Sara:

"Good luck tonite... wish i could b there. baby kicking... "

"ur sweet," Kyle texted back, "wish u were here too... ttyl"

Kyle put the phone back in his pocket. He wanted to say so much more to Sara, but wanted to say it in person. He must have looked distraught because even Mark (who was never the most sensitive person) picked up on it.

"Who was that?" Mark said with his ex-girlfriend Angela hanging all over him.

"Oh, just Sara."

"Everything cool?"

"Hey," Steve interrupted the table "can you guys believe we're actually here? I mean, we're actually playing tonight, opening for Lunar Unit, and could quite possibly be signed. What a night!"

"It's a bummer more of our friends couldn't be here," Jay lamented, "stupid eighteen-or-older rule. For crying out loud, we're in the band and they won't even serve us beer."

"Angela," Steve leaned over Mark and said, "thanks for hooking us up with the show. You're awesome."

"Whatever..." she dismissed Steve, then burst out with a sudden change of mood, "Oh wow! I love this song!" While the guys talked together, Angela bobbed her head and sang along.

"Oh boy," Jay said looking over to Kyle spacey face, "Kyle's off in no-man's land again." He then snapped his fingers in front of Kyle's face.

"What?" Kyle said as his attention to a florescent sign in the distance was broken.

"Stay focused, man, we need you on your A-game tonight."

"Sorry, just thinking about stuff."

"Yo!" Steve encouraged Kyle, "Deal with that garbage tomorrow. Enjoy yourself. We got another half-an-hour or so before we're big-time. About ten more minutes before we go backstage and get our gear ready. After that our lives will be trouble-free. All that nonsense won't mean a thing."

Kyle knew Steve was trying to be helpful, nevertheless it was wearing on him, especially hearing his feelings for Sara and his child referred to as 'garbage'. Kyle took a sip of his Coke and said, "You really think making it big is going to solve all your problems or something?"

"Money, women, fame..." Steve said and backhanded Mark's shoulder with a laugh, "Yeah, I think that about covers all my problems. How 'bout you, Mark?"

Mark nodded. "Works for me."

"Well, it doesn't solve mine." Kyle said and took another sip from his straw.

"Give me a break already," Steve said and shook his head. "I mean, life will go on. But, what kind of life do you want, man? Working at a dumpy gas station or playing music. Her whole family hates your guts anyways; let them worry about it. Choice is yours, dude, but don't rain on *our* parade... not tonight."

"Hey! Would you stop singing in my ear already!" Mark yelled over the music to Angela.

"I have to go, guys. I'm sorry." Kyle shot up from the table and hurried out of the club, and into his car. Speeding out of the parking lot he left his friends confused—and then horrified when he didn't return.

# ❄ Chapter 37 ❄

## ANGEL'S SONG

Another week had passed for Eduard in the Tower. Father Kraus had stopped by on Wednesday to pray for him, but Nadine was refused entrance to his room when she came on Monday and Friday. Now Saturday, Vienna was covered in a blanket of midnight. One dim candle burned in a room at the Tower of Fools—the last stubborn radiance of the past horrific week, refusing to be extinguished.

"You still awake...?" Lukas hovered over Eduard in fascination and peered deep into his distant eyes. He stood back again and said, "I'm just teasing you, Eduard."

Eduard was propped up in his bed. Though his eyes were wide, he barely acknowledged his roommate's suspicious behavior in the dark, except to motion with shaky hand for the pen and paper.

"You want this?" Lukas put the pen in Eduard's hand, and directed it to the paper

"Take me. Pin." Eduard scribbled.

"Sorry friend, too risky. Besides, you're in no condition to go anywhere."

Eduard was unresponsive, not even a hushed melody passed his lips as the music in his head finally ceased for good. Now defenseless, imaginary eyes peaked into the door. He sat for a half an hour unable to wipe the beading sweat from his forehead. His torment was interrupted only once, when Lukas slapped him hard on the back.

"Take care of yourself, Eduard, and thanks again for... ah, never mind, you haven't clue what I'm talking about, have you?" Lukas blew out the candle and snuck out of the room.

For another twenty minutes, Eduard struggled motionless as his imaginary tormentors enclosed his bed. He was awake but dreaming. A ladder descended from the ceiling, and the melon head began to climb up. In his mind, Eduard arose and followed him.

"Sorry, you can't come up here." The man nudged Eduard away from the glowing steps, and continued up the stairs into purgatory. The ceiling was low. He ducked his head so as not to hit it on the exposed nails protruding from Heaven's floor. He made his way to the back of the realm where a hefty box lay.

"Eduard, what did I tell you?" The man said noticing Eduard had followed anyway. "I'm not carrying you back down."

The man opened up the top of the box and sighed. He carefully placed his items inside. After nailing the box closed, the man walked back to the ladder. "I said get down!" The man yelled and pushed Eduard off the ladder.

After struggling to get up, Eduard crawled back onto the bed again.

Following the man on the ladder back down were twelve demons wearing masks as though they were about to perform at the opera. Each of them surrounded Eduard's bed, taunting and prodding him with pitchforks and spears, except one who played a harpsichord in the corner with his bone fingers.

"Why are you here?" Eduard imagined himself saying.

"Don't you remember?" spoke one with a leopard mask. "You called for us on the hill. You called for any angel or demon that would take you, and well, our master's not picky, just a bit busy. We're here to open your mind; to perform a surgery of sorts. It is a simple procedure really. First, we must drill a hole in your skull, and then we cut your brain. You're a sick man, Eduard Strobl, but this will help."

"Cut my brain?" Eduard thought "Who's heard of such a thing?"

"No one... not yet. Perfectly safe though."

"Will it hurt?"

"Oh yes," the demon said. "A lot."

"Please be quick."

The melon head sat next to Boris's sleeping body and tried to watch. He did not seem to enjoy the torture or the splintering bone and splashing blood. He turned his eyes to the floor as one of the demons rubbed his spear in his hands against Eduard's skull like one trying to start a fire with a bow drill. At last, the melon head stood up and tried to move one of the demons aside.

"It's not his fault," the melon head said. "He did not mean to abandon me in the vineyard. He was afraid because I was angry and filled with hate, but no more. Leave him be, please."

The demon who had been nudged aside smacked the melon head down to the ground.

Finally, a muscular angel, standing six-feet seven inches opened the door and stood in their midst like a mighty giant. The demons fled as the angel grabbed

Eduard's hand and lifted him out of the bed and onto his shoulder. He then carried him quietly down the hall, passing by three orderlies, who were knocked out near the front door, and a nurse gagged and bound to a table top.

The mighty angel opened the door and ran to the front gate with keys in his hand from one of the orderlies. On the ground unconscious lay two guards—more victims of the liberator's zealous rampage on his first pass through the area. He undid the latch and carried Eduard as through the Red Sea. He then jogged down the road humming a heavenly song to keep the demons and the hissing cats at bay.

# ❊ Chapter 38 ❊

## HEAVEN CAN'T WAIT

The evening was quiet. Sara lay on the sofa in the living room with a bag of corn chips. She had been very nauseous that day and suffering cramps, so the bag remained untouched despite her best intentions. Her parents had called the doctor earlier in the day. He told them to keep an eye on things and to call if they got worse. But nothing changed. Nevertheless, her parents made an appointment for the following day just to ensure everything was normal. It was now around 10p.m. and her parents were about to go to bed. Since Sara was having trouble sleeping, she occupied herself downstairs on the couch.

"miss u," she texted to her brother Scott, "stay safe... 1 month til baby, so excited :)

Just then her phone buzzed and she checked the new message. It was Kyle at the show:

""ur sweet," said the text message, "wish u were here too... ttyl"

Sara lifted the sun glasses she had begun wearing in the house and rubbed her pink and vein-filled eyes. She rubbed her bulging belly. She felt a kick. She talked to her belly.

"Hey there, little one. How are you? Are you upset? Me too. Why? Well, you know how it is. I guess I'm just sorry I won't see your first birthday, or your first steps. But who knows, maybe God will let me watch from Heaven. Wouldn't that be great?"

Reality did not matter at that moment, Sara would be there with her baby somehow, if only in memories never made, and stories told by others of what a proud mother she would have been.

"Tell me," she whispered, "what will be your first words? I wonder what you'll say. I hope it's 'mamma', but I'll understand if it's 'dadda'. Daddy's a nice guy. You two will be okay without me. Just make sure he doesn't marry someone else that doesn't love you, okay? No, of course not! No one will ever love you like me. I'm your mommy, and I'll always be your mommy. I can't be there for you, so listen to me now if you can." Sara continued counseling her baby about a myriad of topics.

"And remember," she said, "if you're a girl, boys may sweet talk, but wait for the right one. And, when you put on makeup, don't overdo it. And, on your wedding remember—"

"I'll miss you too, mommy," Sara suddenly heard the baby say. She was surprised it could speak already, but she could hear it as clear as if it was cradled in her arms. She got excited when it continued, "Mommy, is it cold out there? Is it bright? Do I ever have to leave this place? I want to stay with you."

Then Sara heard another voice.

"Isn't she gorgeous?"

She looked to see if Kyle was already there. "Kyle is that you?" Was he in the other room? "I'm in the living room. Come here."

Sara felt a release of moisture beneath her and thought she might have lost bladder control. Embarrassed that Kyle would walk in from the kitchen and notice, she grabbed tissues from a box on the coffee table and began to dab her pants. Kyle never came, but a bitter chill entered her. Then a pain shot through her side and up her spine. She crunched over and held her stomach, then threw up on her pajamas. Short of breath she began to yell for Kyle. Hearing her cries, her parents ran down the stairs and into the living room.

"Are you alright, honey?" Sara's mother rushed to her side. "What's wrong, tell me what you need."

"The baby, I think it's... it's coming." Sara grimaced and whined, "Oh God, help me!" The pain amplified with deeper affliction, she slumped over on her side and curled up her legs.

"We'll get your things and take you to the hospital."

"No, I... I can't move. Something's wrong."

"Honey," Sara's father said, "Let me help you up."

Sara screamed in pain when her father tried to assist her, then curled back up on the couch.

"Honey," her mother said, "I know it hurts, but you have to try and stand for me. We'll go real slowly, okay, sweetie?"

"I can't," Sara said, "Something's wrong. My baby. God, please help my baby."

"I'll call for an ambulance." Sara's father rushed to call 911.

"Help please," he pleaded to the dispatcher on the other end, "my daughter is having a baby... No, I can't move her... No, she's in a lot of pain... Please, just send someone! We need an ambulance. Hurry!"

The dispatcher took the address and tried to calm down Sara's father down. After rushing through his information, he ran back to Sara.

"Honey, it's going to be alright, someone's on their way. Hang in there, angel."

Sara remained curled up for the next fifteen minutes when at last the E.M.S. arrived and carried her out into the red and white flashing night. Silhouettes appeared in the windows of neighbors as they looked on in the disturbed peace of their suburban homes. Sara's mother climbed into the back of the ambulance and held Sara's hand, while her father pulled the car out of the driveway to follow.

"Everything's going to be alright, honey," Sara's mother said. "You're going to have a baby, isn't that wonderful?"

Sara forced a smile, soon replaced by wincing eyes and breathless moaning.

"She isn't due for another month," Sara's mother explained to one of the E.M.S. volunteers in the back. "But, she's not well."

"We'll do everything we can," the man assured, "We'll be at the hospital in about five minutes."

# ❄ Chapter 39 ❄

## SLEEP AT LAST

"I hope you like this one," Lukas said, "I remember you singing it one time, but I get the ending mixed up."

Eduard heard a melody, then felt himself drop to the ground. He could see Lukas lying next to him in the middle of the road with his top lip cut, and front teeth broken.

It was late so no one was on the road, but in the distance a police officer strolled down the foggy road. Before the officer noticed them, Eduard was once again lifted and whisked away off of the main road and into an ally. He moaned when set on the ground.

Lukas shushed him. "You're not going to make me feel sorry for you, Eduard, I only came back because... well, I wanted to irritate von Croy... wish I could see his face in the morning."

Lukas took a seat on the ground. He turned and saw the police officer pass by the entrance of the ally.

Lukas scorned the officer under his breath. "No Lukas, don't get upset... no big deal... And you stop moaning! What is it now, Eduard?" After a moment Lukas huffed, "Fine! Don't move; I'll be right back."

Eduard noticed Lukas at the edge of the ally. He scouted around, then finding the officer gone, he ran off out of view. Fifteen minutes passed before he returned with some ripped pieces of paper, and a quill.

"That's the best I could do, I cut my elbow on the glass, so I hope you appreciate it. I just pray no one heard me. Took a little something for myself while I was at it. Could use something to barter with on the way home." Lukas held out a necklace and smiled.

Eduard felt the pen placed in his hand and the tip touch the paper. In one of his last moments of awareness he scribbled two words: "good night nadine"

The paper and pen dropped to the ground.

Lukas picked it up. He looked at the words and clenched his lips, then placed the note in his pocket. He carried Eduard back out of the ally and down the main road where he hoped to find the lone red house of which Eduard spoke.

"Nothing to worry about," Eduard heard Lukas respond to a man out for a midnight stroll, "My friend here just partook of too much wine. Found out his wife is pregnant again. Big celebration."

The pedestrian laughed and wished Lukas well.

At last, Lukas found the house. He placed Eduard on the front step and began to walk away, but stopped and turned back.

"You're going to get me caught," he said as he picked Eduard's slumped body up again and opened the door, which Anna had forgotten to lock. Through the darkened living room, Lukas barely avoided knocking over an oil lamp on the table near the stairway. He carefully took the first step up the stairs hoping to avoid the inevitable creaking of the old house, but it was quiet. He took another step, and then another, until he was at last at the top. Walking slowly, he passed by the rooms on the right and saw the sleeping children. Turning around he opened the last remaining door and saw a woman fast asleep. She stirred only once as Lukas approached the bedside and gingerly laid Eduard down beside her.

Though his illness had reduced his pupils to the size of pin holes, a look of peace came over Eduard's face. Lukas placed the note in his right hand, and the silver snowflake in his left. He looked on as Eduard breathed deeply and closed his eyes. Now backing away from the bed, he left down the stairs and out through the door. His own freedom would not come so easily, and no one would carry him to it.

Lukas walked quickly down the road again, and planned on taking his first left to avoid passing the Tower, but as he walked, he reached into his pocket to feel for the necklace he had stolen and noticed it missing. He could not remember from this vantage point where the jewelry store was, or he might have gone back and taken something else, so instead he decided to retrace his steps to see if it had fallen out along the way.

By the time Lukas backtracked three blocks, it was now faster to scoot past the Tower and take the next road down through the heart of the city and then further on to the Danube. He maintained his composure the best he could as he passed, but with only a few more yards to the next street, he succumbed to his fear and crashed to the ground, knocking himself unconscious for hours.

In the early morning hours, Dr. von Croy was informed by the orderly who had been punched out that Lukas had fled. The doctor quickly checked the room and noticed Eduard was gone as well.

"Dr. von Croy?"

"Boris, you're awake." Dr. von Croy was pleasantly surprised, but still in a hurry. "Boris, do you know where Lukas or Eduard went to?"

"Who's Eduard?"

"Never mind!"

"Food!" Boris yelled out to the doctor who jogged down to a room where he was sure to get information.

The doctor flung open the next door, and was greeted by Simon. "Oh! Greetings, Doctor. Lovely morning isn't it? Yes, yes, lovely. I heard the news about Lukas. That's a shame, was fond of the fellow, when he was in a good mood at least, which I suppose was not very often, but then—"

"Shut up, Simon!" yelled Dr. von Croy. "Tell me what you know about this."

"Sorry, Doctor," Simon said as he picked the scabs on his arm, "I don't know a thing. Does my arm look alright to you, doctor? What's for breakfast this morning?"

"Doctor," a nurse at the door interrupted, "we've recovered one of them."

As news of the patients' escape broke, two orderlies had been sent out to search for them. They did not need to travel far before they noticed a man on the ground near the facility. They turned him over and slapped him in the face, causing him to wake.

\*\*\*

"I think we found him!" were the first words Lukas heard in the early dusk. "Yeah, that's him, but the other one isn't here."

"We'll send some men to retrieve him," said another, "let's just get this one back inside. Here comes the doctor."

Lukas felt himself being pulled up by the arms and dragged backwards toward the Tower by two large orderlies. His eyes opened and his heart raced, but he spoke to himself and calmed down enough to pull free from them. The orderlies began the chase, and yelled to a nearby police officer for help.

Dr. von Croy, who had been approaching, also followed close behind.

Lukas, being a large man with quick feet, was able to out run them through the back streets now filled with church-goers and carriages.

"Stop that man!" yelled the officer to pedestrians ahead.

Lukas barely escaped the grasp of two men ahead. They grabbed at his shirt. He struck one's stomach, and pushed the other's head away before the man lunged back at him. With his strong arms Lukas threw the man to the floor. Others who had heard the officer and saw Lukas fleeing joined the pursuit. Lukas filled his mind with benign thoughts and continued his flight toward the inner city, knocking over things in his path to thwart his captors.

Having forgotten his way around, Lukas ran down various roads hoping to slip away into a store or stable, but found nothing to afford him a discreet getaway, and so he ran, and ran, and ran. He thought about the brick wall he had stared at for so long, he thought about sitting by the river with a pipe in hands, about the feel of horse mane, the scent of edelweiss, anything to distract his mind from being hunted. At last, he resorted to counting his steps until he reached the river shore, where he could at last collapse on a boat.

"Fifty-three, fifty-four, fifty-five... eighty-seven, eighty-eight, eighty-nine... one hundred and one, two, three..." And on he went. His breathing steadied with his pace, his body filled with energy, his blank mind encouraged him onward. "Life is but a dream, Mr. Goethe," he said to himself. No one was chasing him, he was not fleeing, he had not just punched a man. And when he ran through a house, he did not steal a fireplace poker and threaten to stab the owner if he yelled. When police broke down the front door, he surely did not run up the stairs, nor hurl himself out of a frightened child's window only to roll off an awning, fall one story, and fracture his shoulder and ribs.

"My God! Are you alright, sir?" said a helpful gentleman unaware of the chase.

"Two hundred and ten, eleven, twelve..." Lukas continued down the road.

Scraping the sky in the distance was St. Stephen's Cathedral, and one of the only signs of direction Lukas remembered. He ran toward it, knowing that was the way to the Danube. The police and volunteers were not far behind, and as he neared the church he made the mistake of looking back.

His head nodded, and he slid to the ground. It was only a short episode and he was back on his feet soon enough to evade the nearing officers. He must have hit his head hard during this or the previous fall from the window, because his vision was blurry. His side hurt also, which made every step excruciating. His pace had slowed considerably, and his pursuers were nearly upon him. He would not make it to the Danube without resting and rethinking his plan.

Quickly, he ducked into St. Stephen's, where he thought he might find sanctuary amidst the gargoyles and saints. His pursuers stopped at the door. They had their man trapped and would wait him out rather than defile God's house with brutality.

The Stephansdom's spacious interior was empty, the priests and cantors having yet to arrive. Lukas's steps echoed as he ran to the front and found a door to a long spiral stairway leading up to the north bell tower.

"Can I help you, sir?" the bell-ringer at the bottom asked. "It's not safe here, you know."

It was believed that the north tower was protected by zealous angels eager to punish intruders. In fact, the original constructor, Hans Puschbaum, was not permitted to fully complete it, for having made a hasty pact with the devil and uttering a holy name, he was cast down from the tower into the fiery abyss of hell itself. Lukas determined not to suffer a similar fate. He latched the door behind him and yelled back, "Sanctuary! By God, don't let them in!"

Lukas ran up the stone steps, counting each one along the way. "...three hundred and forty-three" he huffed as he counted the last step and slid onto the floor. He sat breathless near the wooden base of the holy Pummerin bell. This bell, once cast from two-hundred and eight confiscated Muslim canons, would soon toll a sonorous "B" for the Holy Mother, as it had since its erection in 1711. In the meantime, Lukas could hear a growing commotion outside the church, as well as a beating on the latched door.

"Sanctuary!" he again shouted back down to the bell-ringer.

"Sanctuary!" the bell-ringer yelled to those beating at the door.

"We merely want to talk to him," a voice said from the other side.

Lukas slowly stood up, and peered down over the edge of the tower. He saw Dr. von Croy and the crowd over four-hundred feet below looking up and pointing. It was no use. There was no escape to be found.

"Come down from there," Dr. von Croy yelled up. "Come down, and you'll suffer no harm."

In an act of defiance, Lukas hoisted himself up to stand on the ledge. The crowd shuddered and decried his sacrilege. He gloried in his callousness and ability to withstand the growing taunts. He determined to stay until he was deaf, or starved, to show the world below him that he was cured, and as sturdy as the saints and statues encompassing him.

"You're going to fall!" yelled Dr. von Croy, "Now, get down from that ledge!"

"You can no more harm me, than heal me, Doctor!" Lukas yelled. His balance wavered. Lukas thought about Eduard's words from the night before, about love and freedom. He swayed on the ledge of the church and stared at the distant Kahlenberg Mountain rising above the eastern plain of the Danube. He thought of the long chase he had just lost, and of the risky escape with Eduard. He imagined Nadine's dismay when she would find Eduard beside her this morning.

"We beat them, Eduard. And, I'm free."

With crusted, bloodied lips, Lukas smiled wildly into the rising sun—displaying his broken teeth as trophies. He imagined himself as a child again, receiving a gentle kiss from the girl who first revealed his condition. He imagined her in a wedding dress at a finely decorated alter. A priest pronounced them husband and wife, and the two collapsed into each other to become one.

As wedding bells tolled in his imagination, the Pummerin behind Lukas swung back and forth until, at last, the clapper within it hammered the iron bell, sending a wave of sound through Lukas and across the city beneath.

"Dear God," Lukas prayed quietly, "if I die before I wake..."

The blasting wave of the bell and of his own emotions swept him up. His head swung low, his knees gave way. The crowd below gasped and cheered as Lukas tumbled headlong out of the tower onto the unforgiving street beneath.

# ❄ Chapter 40 ❄

## KEEP BREATHING

When Kyle arrived at Sara's house he knocked on the front door. He knew Sara's father would tell him to leave, but he didn't care anymore. With confidence he knocked again with the door knocker. Now getting angrier, he assaulted the doorbell with his finger and yelled, "Hello! I know you're home. I just need to talk to Sara for a minute! Helloooo!"

Kyle backed away from the door. "Great," he murmured to himself, "I missed the show for *this*." He stood in the front yard and looked up to Sara's window. The light was on in her room. "Sara!" he shouted, "Let me in!" and again, "Hey, Sara! Open the door!" He then began dialing her number on his cell phone.

"They're not home." Mrs. Cohen called out. She had heard Kyle's shouting and had come out of her home in slippers and a bathrobe.

"Oh! Sorry for the noise, Mrs. Cohen. I hope I didn't wake you."

"No, I was up. The E.M.S. was here, they took Sara to the hospital. I do hope everything's alright."

"What happened?!"

"I don't know, but they had Sara on a stretcher. They raced out of here not twenty minutes ago."

Before Mrs. Cohen could finish, Kyle was running back to his car and speeding off into the night.

\*\*\*

"Keeping breathing," the maternity doctor said, "you're doing fine. You're fully dilated, but you have to push."

Sara thrashed her head while the doctor crouched between her legs. Her pink eyes turned red as blood vessels popped. The doctor motioned for another nurse to make an incision, causing Sara to bleed on the table beneath. The top of the baby's head was starting to show. She pushed, then breathed, then pushed again.

"Alright, the head is almost out. Keep it up."

"Kyle," Sara gasped. Her parents looked at each other with guilt. Kyle was not yet there, but speeding down the last stretch of road to the hospital—now frantically watching the clock in his car and praying he wouldn't get pulled over.

"Kyle!" Sara called out again minutes later.

"We're here for you, honey." Sara's father walked closer to the bedside. "My little girl, you're doing great... don't worry, Mommy and Daddy are right here for you." Suddenly, he and the others in the room heard yelling outside the door.

"I'm the father! Let me in!"

"Kyle!!" Sara yelled.

Sara's mother looked at her husband. He then hurried out of the room where he found a security guard pushing Kyle down the corridor. The young man struggled and slipped on the floor, the security guard now trying to pick him up amidst his flailing arms and kicking legs.

"No, wait!" Sara's father shouted, "Let him go! He's the father."

The security guard loosened his grip on Kyle's shirt. Kyle ran back down the hall, and followed Sara's dad into the room.

"Kyle!"

Kyle hurried over to Sara.

"Stay..." Sara panted "with... me!"

"I will. I love you, Sara," Kyle's words were quick and desperate. He brushed her wet hair from her face. He then took from his pocket a diamond ring and held it up for her to see. "Sara, please marry me. I love you."

Sara's hair was saturated with sweat and clung to her neck. Her skin had turned a sick shade of pale. Catching her breath, Sara at last looked at the ring. She smiled, she sighed, and her squinting eyes widened for a moment, then rolled back.

"No Sara! Please don't!" Kyle cried out.

"Doctor, we're losing her!" yelled one of the nurses.

Kyle was moved aside, and drifted like a cold draft around the room with the ring in his hand as the doctor administered emergency measures. Sara's spent body lay limp on the table as the silent blue baby was pulled out and whisked away to another room for emergency measures of its own.

The world was vacuous; motion stopped and raced all at once. Kyle found himself out in a waiting room without knowing how he got there. Sara's parents were weeping next to him, but every sound was muted. A nurse approached and explained to them what was going on and Kyle lifted his head but heard nothing but the sound of Sara's voice. He heard Sara saying "Yes," when he asked her to dance at the Junior Prom. "Yes," when he asked her if he could kiss her for the first time. "Yes," when he timidly asked to make love the night she conceived. He then heard the nurse tell them that the doctors had done all that they could.

# ❄ Chapter 41 ❄

## A MELTING SNOWFLAKE

Awakened early by a knock on the front door, Nadine threw off the wool blanket, jumped out of bed, and started to dress. Who on earth?! What was wrong now? Instinctively she began to worry about her children, but then out of the corner of her eye she saw Eduard lying on the bed. She slowly approached his thin, pale body, and knelt beside the bed. He barely resembled the man she had met so long ago.

Her weeping, like the knocking at the door, grew louder until at last Anna rushed into the room to find out what was wrong. Julia soon followed, marionette still in hand, and the two knelt beside their mother, arms wrapped around each other.

"Honey," Nadine at last said to Julia, "please go see who is at the door."

"But mother."

"Please, Julia... go."

As Julia took her marionette and left for downstairs, Anna said, "Mommy, why did daddy die?"

Nadine pulled Anna closer. "I don't know, sweetie. Daddy was just sick and needed some rest. But... but, he's better now, and even though we'll miss him, we'll see him again."

"When?"

"Someday, sweetie."

"Mommy..."

"Yes, honey."

"I'm sorry."

Nadine hugged her daughter. "Thank you; I'll be alright... the three of us will be alright. Why don't we say a little prayer for daddy; does that sound good?"

Anna nodded 'yes' and the two bowed their heads.

By now the knocking on the front door had grown incessant. When Julia answered, she was greeted by two imposing police officers and an orderly. The officers held batons in their hands.

"Well, hello there," said one of the officers down to the confused girl "Is your father home?"

"He's upstairs, sir."

"We'd like to see him if that's alright. It's something very important. May we come in?"

Julia led the men up the stairs. She opened the door, but upon seeing the distraught woman mourning her dead, the men quietly shut the door again and Julia showed them back downstairs.

"Well, case cracked," Julia could hear one officer joke to the other after the front door closed. Julia was old enough to understand the insult, but too young to gracefully ignore it. She threw her marionette against the closed door, breaking off one of its legs, then ran upstairs.

"Who was that? Nadine said.

"Just a beggar, mother, I sent him away."

"Well, thank you Julia, Mommy really appreciates your help. Now listen to me, I need you two to go down the road to the Trommler's house, and tell Mr. or Mrs. Trommler to come here as soon as they can. Will you do that for me?"

The children nodded, dressed, and in ten minutes were gone, leaving Nadine alone in the room by the bed.

"I don't understand what happened," she whispered and stroked Eduard's cheek, "Why?"

She laid her head on Eduard's chest and took him by the hand. She took the scribbled note in it and straightened back up to read the shaky words: "good night nadine"

Holding the note to her chest she whispered, "Goodnight, honey," then leaned over to kiss his forehead. "You were a good man, a good father... I hope you know that now. Dream eternal... Greet our son... I'll meet you there." Nadine then noticed the snowflake pin in his other hand and pulled it from his clenched fingers. She held it tight along with the note.

The children later returned with Diederich Trommler, who helped Nadine make funeral arrangements with Father Kraus, and helped watch the children over the next few days while Nadine worked with Ludwig to wrap up loose ends at the office. Ludwig gave Nadine a sizable wad of money he had been saving for a trip to America someday.

"I was saving it for a honeymoon," Ludwig said, "but my recent prospect didn't work out. Getting too old to bother anymore. So here, it's the least I can do."

Eduard Strobl's body was laid to rest in the property outside of St Stephen's and a touching mass followed. Neither the hospital nor the Strobls ever knew for sure how Eduard made it home on his own, but next to his plot was lain another man who had also recently passed away, named Lukas Hein.

Nadine Strobl learned shortly after Eduard's death that she was pregnant, and not long afterwards she and her children relocated to Augustdorf, Germany, where her sister's family lived. There, she raised her two daughters and her newborn son. She named him Alexander after the name of the first son who had died at birth.

# ❊ Chapter 42 ❊

## HEIRLOOMS

"She has your eyes." Kyle's aunt said, hanging her head over the white crib. The baby was in perfect health. It was now July, and the weather was warm and the skies as blue as the baby's eyes.

"She's beautiful, isn't she, Mom?"

Kyle's aunt looked away from the crib and over to Kyle who was also hovering around the baby. Her face had a mixture of surprise and confusion.

"What?" Kyle said.

"Oh nothing, you just never called me that before, that's all."

"Do you mind it?"

"Absolutely not."

Kyle thought for a moment and carefully continued, "I don't want to hurt you or Uncle Pat, but I've been thinking lately that maybe I should start using my parent's last name again... you know, just because it seems like I've had to fill out a lot of forms lately, and well... mostly, I'd just like to remember them again... stop running away from stuff."

"Kyle," his aunt said, "I couldn't think of a nicer thing you could do. We all loved them very much. Your dad and I had so many wonderful times growing up, and your mother was like the sister I never had."

"Thanks. I guess the past year has gotten me thinking about a lot of things, especially since Sara passed."

Kyle's aunt returned her attention to the baby in the crib and said, "It's been over three months now, how are you holding up?"

"Well, I mean... it's been pretty hard," Kyle said, "but, I don't have much of a choice. I'm a father now, and little Anne here needs me. Can't wait to tell her someday about her mom. Sara's parents have been great too. It's funny how much things have changed between us. They treat me like a son too; it's a nice change, I have to admit. Heck, even her brother Scott called a few times and apologized for stuff. I guess I can see now why they were so protective of Sara. I don't think any guy will be good enough for Anne."

"Do you still have the ring with you?"

Kyle patted his shirt pocket, "Yeah, kept it with me since that day in the hospital. Going to hand it down to this little peanut someday."

"Well, I think she'll appreciate that. The box is still in the attic, and it'll be safe there if you want to store it. But, you can hold onto it too, if you want."

"Yeah, I should probably put it somewhere safe," answered Kyle. "Uncle Pat seems concerned. In fact, do you mind watching this cutie for a few minutes?"

"Mind? Look at that face, awww..."

Kyle laughed. "Alright then, I'll be back in a minute, just yell if you need me, okay?"

As his aunt occupied herself with funny noises and the tickling of toes, Kyle crept out of the living room and down the hallway, but only made it past the kitchen.

"Kyle, come in here for a second." Hearing Kyle coming down the hall, Kyle's Uncle Pat called from within his room where he was sitting on a chair shining a pair of black shoes.

"What's up, Pat?" said Kyle from the doorway. "Oh! Those are fancy! You got a hot date tonight?"

"I'm taking your aunt to dinner, but don't tell her, it's a surprise."

"My lips are sealed."

"Kyle," Pat continued, "I want you to know how proud your aunt and I are of you. You've gone through a lot, but I've noticed a big change in you."

"Well thanks, Pat. I know I've put you guys through a lot over the years, but—"

"But nothing, Kyle. You were a kid, and kids do a lot of crazy things. Heck! I know I did. The point is that you're a man now, and if you don't mind me saying so, I know your father would have been very proud of you."

"Thanks."

"And, you know that you always have a place to stay, a job at the garage, and two babysitters if you need them. I don't want you to ever worry about the future, how you're going to manage, money, or things like that."

"I appreciate that, Pat. I'm actually thinking about finishing the G.E.D. and maybe tech school after. Although I'm thinking maybe music school too."

"Well, we'll help you out, as long as you're serious about it."

"I may take you up on that."

"So, no more band, then? They're still not talking to you?"

"Well, I talked to the guys last week and we worked out some of our differences. I guess Mark's girlfriend had to apologize to the owner of the club after I bailed, but he was actually relieved. So was the other band because they got to go on earlier. But he said he'd give us another chance. Oh, and that guy from the label never even showed up anyway. Maybe next time... who knows?"

"Well hey, are you hungry? I was going to make myself a sandwich."

"Oh, I'm just gonna put some stuff away, and then I'm meeting up with Sara's friend Jen at the Athens Diner to show off Anne. After that we might stop at the high school to see the new '*Sara Riley Exhibit*' Mrs. Donahue put up in the library for next year."

"Jen? You mean the 'Jen' that called here that time screaming at you for an hour?"

"That's the one," Kyle laughed "but that was a few years ago, she's calmed down a little. Besides, I deserved it; I left her and Sara at a party with no ride home."

Pat shook his head, "Oh Kyle, what am I going to do with you?"

"Ha! Love you too, 'Dad.'"

Kyle left his uncle dumfounded, and continued down the hall to the attic. He pulled a short rope hanging from the ceiling and folded down the wooden stairs.

"Sorry, Eddie, you can't come up here." Kyle nudged Sara's cat away from the steps, climbed the stairs into the attic, and switched on a light. Ducking down so as not to hit his head on the exposed nails, he made his way to the back of the attic where a large box was filled with crumpled newspaper.

"Eddie, what did I tell you?" Kyle pet the cat purring and snuggling around his leg. "I'm not carrying you back down, buddy. You climbed up, you can climb down."

Kyle opened up the top of the box and sighed. The last time he and his aunt went through the box they left the small ring case at the bottom, and piled up the other contents around it. Now he carefully moved aside the old family heirlooms: a silver snowflake brooch, and two very old marionettes—one of which had a broken leg.

"Someday you'll make someone very happy," he said as he placed the ring back in its case. He then piled up the other contents and the newspaper around it, picked up the cat, and left back down the attic stairs to rejoin his aunt.

"Did you find the box alright?" his aunt whispered in between a lullaby when she heard Kyle return, "It's the one marked 'Strobl'."

Kyle came closer with the cat in hand to look with pride at his sleeping daughter. "Yeah, I found it, Mom. Thanks. Eddie here helped me."

# ❄ Epilogue ❄

"You look like a princess. Your mother's eyes sparkled just like yours. I just know somewhere 'up there' she's looking down and smiling right now."

"Oh Dad! Don't you dare make me cry tonight, the girls spent too much time doing my makeup."

Kyle Strobl spun his daughter Anne out with one arm, then pulled her back in and laughed. The lights around them caused the beaded wedding gown to glisten; the hurricane lamps on the surrounding tables embodied the warmth of the evening, the cheer in the wine, and the love of two families joined together.

"I've waited a long time for this," Kyle said. "I can't tell you how happy I am for you. It seems like only yesterday I was changing your diapers, fixing your bike, and helping you with your homework."

The father and daughter dance ended with a charming dip and applause. Anne's new husband, who had also been dancing with his mother, shook Kyle's hand while the photographer snapped a picture.

"Let's hear it for the parents of the bride and groom," the D.J. said over the speaker and the murmur of conversation.

Kyle hugged his daughter and the two took a comical bow together before returning to their seats.

"Folks, we got an exciting night ahead of us," the D.J. continued, "I hope you're ready to eat, drink, and dance 'til you drop. But right now I'd like to invite the best man, Bob Taylor to give a toast."

The guests applauded again while the best man unfolded his notes and took a deep breath.

"Thank you," the burly jock said. "Boy, is it nervous in here, or is it just me? Anyway, thank you all for coming out to celebrate the marriage of Paul and Anne— two very special people whom we love and care for deeply. But honestly, Anne, I can't believe you married this guy. Do you have any idea what his dorm room looked like? I hope you have some bug spray handy."

The groom laughed and booed. Anne nodded, knowing exactly how messy Paul's dorm room at college had been. "I bought a few cans, Bob," Anne joked in her chair, "don't you worry."

After a few more bad jokes, the best man's toast was through. Glasses were then tapped with silverware signaling the newlyweds to kiss.

The night went on with exuberance. Later that evening, the D.J. even played a few famous hit songs from Kyle's old band Sticky Wicket, which made him hide his head at the table when Paul's dad razzed him about one tune, *Never Grow Old*. It had been about ten years since he left the band to teach at a music college, and the irony of the song at his baby girl's wedding made him laugh and blush. When his red face cooled, he turned to the table behind him where his aunt and uncle sat, along with Sara's Riley's parents, and winked. He had indeed grown older, but not reluctantly.

Kyle's wife Jen took hold of Kyle's hand at the parents' table and squeezed tenderly. Upon her finger was the ring Kyle had given her twenty years earlier which had been in his family as long as anyone could remember. He and Jen had offered it to Paul when the young man asked permission to marry Anne, but Paul had already bought a ring that Anne had fallen in love with. So instead, Kyle gave Anne the silver snowflake brooch—which now graced her silk dress and flashed electrifying beams of light like the disco ball above the dance floor.

For more books by Erick Blore: